PRAISE FOR
THE FEVER CABINET

"Justin Joschko's *The Fever Cabinet* is historical horror at its most impressive and with so much to say about trauma, prejudice, and mental illness. Each exquisitely written page of this novel drips black with a darkness you don't find in many books. Highly recommend!" —Eric LaRocca, author of *Things Have Gotten Worse Since We Last Spoke and Other Misfortunes*

"[*The Fever Cabinet*] succeeds in turning an unusual historical artifact into a source of supernatural terror. Fans of historical horror should check this out." —*Publishers Weekly*

"A crowd-pleasing blend of historical, occult, and psychological horror" —*Booklist*

"*The Fever Cabinet* is a fever-dream of a novel, a juicy-pulp tale of gothic shadows and infernal affairs, yet it always zigs and zags in surprising directions. Like an appealing mix of King, Straub, and del Toro, Joschko's dark fantasy flirts with horror, history, and heartbreak, but it finds a moody path all its own. Told with authenticity and intelligence, there is real meat on *The Fever Cabinet's* bones...and inside, a delicate, bloody, beating heart." —Polly Schattel, author of *Shadowdays*

THE FEVER CABINET

JUSTIN JOSCHKO

JOURNALSTONE
YOUR LINK TO ARTIST TALENT

ISBN: 978-1-68510-021-6 (sc)
ISBN: 978-1-68510-022-3 (ebook)
Library of Congress Control Number: 2022931591

First printing edition: September 23, 2022
Printed by JournalStone Publishing in the United States of America.
Cover Design: Mikio Murakami
Edited by Sean Leonard
Proofreading and Cover/Interior Layout: Scarlett R. Algee

JournalStone Publishing
3205 Sassafras Trail
Carbondale, Illinois 62901

JournalStone books may be ordered through booksellers or by contacting:
JournalStone | www.journalstone.com

To Leo Joschko and Dennis Gienow
The two men I most wish could have read this book

THE FEVER CABINET

So it was that before there was a Christian hell in books and sermons—and perhaps afterwards too—there was a hell on earth that men saw and looked at and knew well indeed. For it is the nature of man that he can only write of the hell he has first created himself.

—Howard Fast

1

THE SWITCHING YARD stank of diesel. Roland had grown accustomed to the smell over the previous weeks, but each evening when he returned from the wharf the odor struck him anew. He exhaled through his nostrils, hoping to clear the worst of it, and crossed the dozen pairs of tracks to a clearing of boot-scarred earth, where men gathered about a steel drum. Smoke plumed from a flame in its belly. The men wore outsized clothes patched with whatever scraps of fabric they could find, their fingers stained a sooty black that no amount of scrubbing would ever dislodge. One of them looked up and waved at Roland.

"Ho, Jerry! Belly up, my boy. We're fixin' a Mulligan."

Roland approached the gathered men, greeting them with a smile that never fit right on his face. Where he came from, smiling was an intimate, spontaneous thing, a private moment between friends. Here, it seemed the baseline feature of a face, to be worn in all weather. A man who didn't smile was assumed rude, antagonistic, perhaps even dangerous.

John Doyle, the man who'd summoned him, clapped Roland on the shoulder. He was large-boned and slightly stooped, with the loose skin of a man once fat whose weight loss came through a reversal of fortune rather than a deliberate regime of diet and exercise. Bulges of red-veined flesh hung beneath his eyes, though his smile, despite the alarming gap imposed by a missing front tooth, always seemed sincere.

"How are yeh, Jerry, my son?"

Roland had told Doyle his name on more than one occasion, but the man treated each introduction with willful forgetfulness, nodding in response and then promptly calling him Jerry again within a couple of sentences. At first Roland assumed he suffered from some sort of memory trouble, but he struggled with no one else's name, and in his manner it seemed increasingly clear that the mistake was deliberate. Roland knew such a display should be insulting, but he couldn't help but feel a strange gratitude to the man all the same, since Jerry, though implicitly pejorative, was at least a real name. The other men treated Roland with hostility when they didn't ignore him outright, and a name as friendly as Jerry was unlikely ever to cross their lips; to them, he was simply The Hun. It was a term Roland despised, one that dredged up ugly memories of the Great War, but that no amount of pleading or arguing could dislodge. That was the thing with nicknames: seek them and they run like water through your fingers; try and shake them off, and they stick like molasses.

"I am well, John, I thank you," said Roland.

"Glad to hear it, my boy, glad to hear it. Warmed your knuckles down at the docks, have ye?"

"Yah. A big shipment went out today. Many boxes."

Doyle laughed. Roland rifled through his words, searching for the joke, and found nothing but a bland statement of fact.

"Krauts, I tell yeh, lads. No one like 'em for puttin' their shoulders to the wheel. Y'ask me, they're like as not to win it this time round. I reckon we'll all be spreckin' dee Doitch by 1950. You just remind them boys when they goosestep 'cross the Atlantic that the Emerald Isle never lifted a hand against 'em. We may talk Tommy, but there's nothin' like a dead Brit to put a smile on an Irishman's face."

A few of the men smiled at Doyle's little speech, but most ignored him. They huddled about the fire, sipping steam-fronded liquid from whatever container they could scrounge. Discarded cans were the most common, though two men used ladles with broken handles and one drank from the heel of a woman's shoe. The brine came from a stout iron pot balanced atop a steel grating, beneath which the fire crackled forth its smoke-gritty heat. Inside simmered a thin, yellow broth, its bubble-tossed waters flecked with table scraps: onion skins, potato peels, turnip leaves, the bones of an unidentified animal. Mulligan, they called it, gnawing the adjective clean from the noun, for affixing the name of stew to such watery leavings only heightened its mockery.

Doyle handed Roland a tin can with its lid removed. Remnants of reddish-black gunk clung to its corrugated sides. With a nod of thanks, he grabbed the can and dipped it toward the brine. A grey-haired stump of a man named Mullins blocked him with one bulb-knuckled hand. A scowl seamed his face in a dozen places, rumpling it into a mask of distrust and wizened leather.

"Lessen your haste, Hun. None sips the Mulligan 'cept he who shares. Toss your alms in the mix or begone with ye."

Roland reached into his jacket, where he'd sewn a strip of cloth to the lining to make a hidden pocket. From this cavity he pulled a thin parcel wrapped in butcher's paper and sealed with twine. He tugged at the bow and the twine unraveled, revealing a slab of raw chuck. A scraping from the outer shoulder, gristle-stiff and spongy with ligaments, but to the eyes of the men around him it was a cut of unsurpassable quality. The air grew slippery with the sound of tongues circling lips and lips smacking gums.

Having revealed the bounty, Roland questioned his decision to share at all. He'd better serve his belly by keeping the chuck to himself and leaving the others to their "stew." But he craved the company, sour as it was, and furthermore knew that a man never lasted long in the jungle by hoarding. If he didn't share what he had voluntarily, they'd simply take it. Not today, maybe, but next time, or while he slept. He ripped the chuck into strips and tossed them in the broth to cook.

The men watched in hungry stalemate as the lumps of meat drifted about the soup, pink flesh darkening to a brownish grey. Roland counted twenty-three seconds before the first man snatched a cup's worth, scalding his hand in search of the biggest chunk of half-cooked meat. He dipped his fingers in the cup, fished out the flesh, and popped it in his mouth. A gush of pink liquid dribbled down his chin and clotted in the matted hair of his beard. The others quickly followed, and soon the broth was as it was before Roland's contribution, apart from a few scraps and skein of fat rendered from the meat and stretched amoebic across the soup's surface.

Roland waited a few extra moments for the meat to cook, but fearing the encroachment of seconds he scooped his claim. He frowned down at the cup's contents. He'd had a long day at the wharf, shunting crates up a rattling gangplank and into the hold of a rust-flecked steamer, and spent all but a few pennies of his earnings on the hank of meat now partitioned among half a dozen people. Weighed against his labor, the cup of thin broth in his hand seemed a meager, insulting thing. He glanced at the other men's portions and found his to be the smallest. Sighing, he slurped it up and shifted closer to the fire.

The damp air coming off the lake left a rime on his bones, and even with the fire it was slow in thawing. His back creaked and groaned and he hunched towards the flames, rubbing his hands together for warmth. He held them over the coals, bringing them close as he could without burning them.

The other men chatted as they ate, their words swift and slippery to Roland's tired ears. He soon tuned them out and turned his attention to the gentle *rustle-hiss-pop* of the flames in the barrel. It had a comforting voice, fire—at least, when it spoke softly; in throes of anger, it was another matter. But in its placid semi-slumber, it was quite pleasant.

Roland watched the soft undulation of the flames, charted the whirligig ascent of ashes caught on updrafts of superheated air, studied the grey calligraphy of pluming smoke. As he stared, he began to notice peculiarities in the ashes. What had once seemed a flat bed of glowing embers took on a new dimension, telescoping into a flame-walled shaft of startling depth. Attached to the wall was a spiral staircase, and as he looked closer, he saw that the individual steps were built of bodies stacked like cordwood. They wriggled in a pile of heat-blistered flesh, seared and simmering without ever succumbing to the soot-black release of combustion.

Oh God, he thought. *It's happening again.* He tried to shut his eyes against the encroaching madness, but it was as if the smoke had paralyzed his eyelids, pried them open like cruel fingers and forced him to witness the impossible scene unfurling amidst the flames.

Atop the burning men trod grey-skinned figures bearing sacks on their shoulders, which they lugged endlessly upward and downward with some inscrutable purpose. Their heavy feet left gashes in the backs of the burning men, though the wounds soon blistered over and shriveled into scars. From the eye of the gyre, invisible with distance, called a voice.

"Komm runter, liebe Roland! Es ist warm und gemütlich. Du wirst es mögen."

Roland shook his head. *"Nein, nein!"* he said, whispering through clenched teeth. *"Ich will da nicht hineingehen!"*

The other men stopped their chatter and stared at Roland, their expressions ranging from concern to outright hostility.

"What's he on about?"

"Talk sense, Hun."

"We ain't in the Rhineland now. Speak proper or clam up."

Doyle grabbed his shoulder and gave it a shake. "Everything all right, Jerry? You're not goin' buggy on us, are yeh?"

Roland ignored him. His attention remained fixed on the nexus of the flaming tunnel, from which the voice continued to beckon.

"*Alle deinen Freunden sind hier! Vom Somme, von Ypern, alle die Felder haben nach uns geführt. Warum nicht deiner? Hier ruhen sie für immer in die Wärme aus. Und es ist immer zu kalt, dort hinauf, oder?*"

"*Hor auf, bitte,*" Roland pleaded.

"*Wie du willst,*" the voice replied. "*Zur Zeit. Träum süß, liebe Roland. Auf wiederhören.*"

The gyre closed, and the space beneath the fire flattened to a bed of ashes. Roland looked up from the flames, noticing for the first time the ring of eyes staring at him.

"*Es tut mir...*er, I am sorry. Bad dreams."

The men let it go at that, though Roland noticed in their eyes something new beneath the usual sheen of indifference flecked with the occasional flash of snickers or contempt. Something that came close to fear. He left the fire shortly afterward. As he did, a low muttering erupted among the other men. Most of what they said was spoken too softly to catch, though he managed to hear Mullins.

"They're all mad, them krauts. And that Hun there might be maddest of them all."

The name struck Roland like a dart in his back. *Roland*, he wanted to plead. *Please, my name is Roland!*

The loss of his name was neither sudden nor unexpected, but rather the culmination of a steady but irreversible slant into social and material poverty. His job went first, handed to a returning soldier wounded in Belgium, who glared at Roland as if he himself were responsible for the injury. Roland's colleagues, many of whom he'd counted as friends, had studied the floor and said nothing as he boxed up his few possessions and walked to the exit for the final time, a security guard at each elbow. His apartment went next, as the jobs he found after his firing were tenuous and brief and poorly paid. Along the way, friends paid fewer visits, letters and phone calls went unanswered, and those who had once stopped for friendly chats on street corners averted their eyes or mumbled half-hearted greetings without slowing their strides.

Unemployed, evicted, and ostracized, he drifted south from Toronto to Queenstown, seeking work in the booming shipping yards, which had swelled to accommodate the outflow of munitions and manpower to the conflict in Europe. Unfortunately, such a move was hardly unique, and men unfit or unwilling to serve crammed the wharfs from end to end, a surfeit that sloshed over every boarding house, hostel, and shelter, and devoured all but the meagerest scraps of employment.

It was thus that Roland found himself in a strange city, too broke to afford the train fare back to Toronto, where the few people who still knew his name resided. In the wake of these last few acquaintances drifted an inflow of belligerent strangers who spoke of him in spat-out syllables and eyed him with distrust, pity, or fear. He'd lost his job, his home, his friends, his name.

And now, it seemed he was to lose his mind too.

He thought back on the fire, of the hell-spawn creatures that had populated it, and shuddered. It hadn't been the first vision he'd encountered in recent days, but it was by far the strongest. They'd first occurred shortly after he arrived in Queenstown—brief flashes, impressionistic smears of emotion and color. He'd told himself they were merely another cruel side effect of stress and fear and hunger, misfirings of an overclocked mind, and that good food and steady work would sort them out in time. But food and work remained scarce, and the visions had sunk ever deeper into the permeable bedrock of his mind. And now, with the stairway in the fire, they'd moved from fleeting glances to a sustained, absorbing delirium. It had a sturdiness the other visions lacked, and a consistency beyond the scattershot logic of dreams. He'd known it for madness, and yet he'd been singularly unable to turn away. And the *voice*. It had spoken with him in a language he'd not conversed in for a decade, responded to his pleas, felt in every way like an outside entity. And yet surely the voice, like the vision, had come from somewhere inside his own head. But from where? And what was it trying to tell him?

Roland pulled back a tarp and crawled into a wedge of space between two disused shipping crates. He drew a dirty blanket from behind a slough of trash, shook out the worst of the dirt, and laid it on the ground. He lay on one half and folded the other over top of him, plumping his sack for a pillow. A slash of night sky showed between the slatted boards that lay across the crates as a makeshift roof, its black belly pimpled with stars.

***

"Hey, Hellmich! Step to it, man."

The voice bellowed from the deck of a large grey steamer. Roland peered up and spotted a matchstick figure in a blue suit shaking a fist. The distance was too great to make out the man's features, but the voice marked him as Horace Green, the dock foreman. With a final punctuating gesture, he disappeared from the railing into the belly of the ship. Roland knew he would see the man again shortly, this time in much closer proximity.

Sighing in anticipation of the lecture to come, Roland finished shifting the topmost box onto his dolly, tossed the securing belt over the stack, buckled it to its mate snaking up from below, and cinched it tight, pulling from the shoulder to ensure a secure hold. He did the same with the lateral band and was just about ready to set the dolly on its wheels when Green stomped down the gangplank and thrust a finger in his face.

"I've had it up to my neck with your lollygagging, Hell Mitch," he said, breaking Roland's surname in half and spitting out its remains as two unrelated syllables. "This rig sets sail by noon today. It's nearly ten forty-five and you're out here fumblin' around with a load should already be below deck."

"I have only to fasten the security belts, sir. The crates will topple if I do not do this."

"I don't give a damn about your excuses. Cram 'em back down your throat and get that barge loaded. We've got a war to win. Or is that what's slowin' your hand up?"

"Yes, sir. I will, sir."

Satisfied, Green gave a curt nod and stomped back up the gangplank, returning to whatever task he'd deemed unimportant enough to interrupt with a pointless venting of bile. The dolly Roland had just packed contained his forty-eighth load for the day; none of the men around him had yet finished their fortieth. Several had barely passed thirty. They knew this as well as he did, which may have explained the gleeful snickering he'd heard from some of them during his upbraiding. Even those who didn't laugh merely averted their gaze and continued working.

Pointing out these facts to Green would get him nowhere—except, perhaps, out of a job. There were always more young bodies willing to haul freight for bread and a bit of beer, and Roland didn't delude himself that his efficiency would earn him any respite, even if it had been noticed. After all, his behavior on the job had never really been the problem. It wasn't what he did or didn't do, but who he was: the Hun, Herr Hitler's sneering mongrel boogeyman. That he'd voted

Social Democrat before emigrating and arrived in Canada while the mustachioed little upstart was rotting in a Weimar prison mattered little.

Roland wrapped his hands around the dolly's handles, squared his shoulders, and pulled back, bracing the bottommost bow with the tip of one foot. The weight of the boxes twanged the small of his back before reaching equilibrium across the dolly's inflated rubber wheels. He muscled the dolly along the pier to the loading platform, a metal grid affixed to a crane by a harness of inch-thick chains, and set the crates down next to a stack of identical height. A single deft sweep of his arm unfastened both belts. He shimmied the dolly's ledge out from under the crates and returned to collect the next payload.

The work continued until shortly after noon, when the last load of boxes swung onto the deck and a steam whistle called the stevedores to lunch. Roland found an unused bollard along the edge of the quay and took a seat on its ridge. The cold metal felt soothing against his back. He reached into his pocket and took out a wad of old newspaper, inside of which he'd wrapped a heel of day-old pumpernickel and a bruised plum.

He spread the paper across his lap and placed his meager rations in the center. His belly sizzled like a kettle boiled dry, all blackened metal and arid space aching to be filled. The bread and plum vanished in a few bites, burned to cinders by the relentless heat of his work-stoked innards. He sighed and drank deeply from a public fountain until the worst of his hunger pangs subsided.

Surplus water sloshed in his belly as he waddled back to Pier 6, where he joined the growing crescent of men gathered around Horace Green. Green stood on a small platform near the edge of the dock, his back to the lake. An unbroken dome of grey clouds bled over the horizon, smudging the border between water and sky. A landward wind riffled the hem of his blue quarter coat, and threatened with every gust to snatch the cap from his bald head. He held it by the brim with one hand as he spoke.

"All right, listen up, the lot of you, I only wanna have to say this once. Turns out we got a piece of bad news over the wireless. The Proudholme was supposed to dock here from Bermuda for unloading this afternoon, but she hit some bad weather off Virginia and she's been delayed a couple of days at least."

A chorus of muttering burbled through the crowd. Green soothed it with a patting motion of his hand.

"I ain't sayin' I'm happy about it, I'm just sayin' it is what it is. Now, Letourneau over at Pier 4 is short a few hands, so if you're real hungry for work come see me and I'll give you a docket you can bring to him. I ain't got enough for all a' you though, so don't go mobbin' me about it. This ain't a first come first serve business."

Green stepped down from the platform. The crowd swarmed him, hands outstretched, burbling requests. He waved them back and trudged over to the sheet metal trailer that held his office, where he got a short stack of dockets and began handing them out to whoever caught his eye. Roland shouldered his way through the crowd and wound up in front of Green as the stack of dockets dwindled to the last few. Green signed his name along the bottom line, started handing it to Roland, and yanked it back as he noticed who was standing in front of him.

"No chance, Hellmich."

"Please, Mr. Green. I am in much need."

"Your need don't make no difference, pal. Letourneau finds out I sent him a kraut, he'll crush my nuts in a vice next time I see him. His boy fought over there at Dunkirk. Lost a leg."

"I am sorry to hear that."

"Yeah, you're sorry. You damn krauts are always sorry when us decent folk are finished handin' you your asses. You're just lucky there's a few men like me broadminded enough to give a Jerry a shake. Now get outta my face. The Proudholme'll get here in a day or two, you can sign on then."

Roland walked inland across the quay to a stout brick building that served as the dockyard's main administrative center. Inside, a tiled hall ran past an infirmary and a change room that reeked of sweat and ammonia, and spilled into a carpeted annex with molded chairs bolted to the floor. A few men sat at tables, chewing on sandwiches and flipping through newspapers spread out in front of them.

A punch clock hung on the wall beside a metal rack containing hundreds of slotted inlets, each one bulging with timecards. Roland found his card and slipped it in the slot at the top of the punch clock, where its innards stamped the time with a *ka-chunk* in the appropriate box. He brought the card to a counter separated from the lobby by clear Lucite, behind which sat an old man in overalls and a checked shirt. Wisps of thin grey hair floated fog-like atop his bald pate, and gold-rimmed glasses balanced on the bulbous outcrop of his nose.

Roland slid his punch card through a narrow concavity in the Lucite barrier. The old man initialed the card, scrawled something on a piece of yellow paper and ripped it from a booklet along its perforated edge. He handed it back through the slot.

"What is this?" Roland asked. "This is not a cheque."

"No, it's your chit."

"I cannot feed myself with chits," said Roland. "I have done my work, I would like my pay."

"Sorry, mac. We pay on full days only here. You'll get the balance added when the next boat comes in."

Roland opened his mouth to argue further but thought better of it. The old man had a sleepy, disinterested look that further discussion was unlikely to sway. Besides, the only thing that raised eyebrows quicker than a German these days was an angry German. He left, folding his chit carefully and tucking it in his breast pocket.

The day was warm for mid-October, but the damp lake air had chilled him as it always did, and he found himself shivering despite the sunshine. He looked with wonder and envy at the men and women pacing the streets around him, their jackets unbuttoned, their heads raised, their strides sleek and confident. It was as if a private specter clung to his waist and followed him wherever he went, its cold caress leeching the sun's warmth from him before it could sink through his skin. And yet the kettle in his belly burned on, warping from the heat of its hunger yet sharing none of it with his frozen extremities. He thrust his hands in his pockets and walked with his body bent forward, shifting his weight until the pressure he put on his insides subdued the cramping.

Queenstown changed quickly as you walked inland. Its industrial lakeshore, clad in grey concrete and horned with smokestacks from the city's bustling factories, morphed after a few short blocks to cobbled streets lined with row houses of stately red brick. Goods glistened behind shop windows, as citizens bolstered by the war's boom in production spent their paychecks on gadgets and baubles for their families, startled by their sudden tumble into affluence. The women wore fur stoles and silk blouses, the men suits, both aping a glamour they'd seen in films and wanted for themselves. Roland eyed their largesse with longing. For all of Green's faults, the man was right about one thing: there really weren't a lot of folks willing to hire a German these days. Not one with an accent as thick as his, anyway. Why risk employing a saboteur when there were plenty of good, honest Canadian boys around?

The switching yards stood at the west end of St. Paul Street, a broad four-lane road that began at the shoreline and ran arrow-straight through the city's middle, losing opulence with every mile until it sputtered into a dirt path at the edge of town. Roland didn't need to walk to quite that point, but by the time he reached the rust-flecked strip of cyclone fencing that marked his ersatz home in the switching yard, its bottom bent upward in spots to accommodate entry, he would've come pretty close. He trudged uphill, watching as the buildings grew dingier and the sidewalks dirtier, suits and shawls replaced by grease-spotted dungarees and homespun dresses. Streetcars clattered by, sparks spraying from their pantographs, bleeting their horns at the automobiles that muscled into their right of way.

A brownstone apartment rose up on Roland's right. Eight stories of weathered brick spanning most of the block, it squatted like an enormous toad amidst the smaller buildings. A tattered awning jutted from poles affixed over its entrance, patch-studded canvas lapping at the street. He glanced at the doorway as he passed.

Oh no, he thought. *Here comes another one.*

The lobby pulsed with pink, membranous tissue. A tongue wriggled where the carpet should have been. Liquid dripped from nodules in the ceiling. The room extended twenty feet or so, where it tapered to a snug orifice that clenched and unclenched in a slow, steady rhythm. Burps of hot, sour air gusted from its aperture, each one slathering a fresh sheen of oil on Roland's cheeks. He watched, dumbfounded, as a young couple opened the door and stepped into the noxious cavity. The tongue curled upward, lay itself across their shoulders like a vast satin cape, and led them to the rear orifice, which stretched wide enough to admit them and closed with a wet slap.

Roland backed away from the building. Sweat prickled his hairline, forming beads that broke and ran in rivulets down the sides of his face. Admonitions to his lower mind that this was a delusion, a fantasy, that nothing he saw or heard could possibly hurt him if he simply closed his eyes and waited for it to pass, they did nothing to ease the fear welling in him. He was ensnared, a fly in a pitcher plant, trapped limbs scurrying pointlessly as they oozed ever deeper into their captor's belly.

He took two trembling steps and faltered. Invisible nails pounded through his feet into the pavement below, holding him in place as the doorway grinned outward, splitting first the street-facing facade and then the side walls until a great cleft hewed clean to its back. It toppled across its remaining fixture, spreading out wingwise until its unfurled skin blanketed a city block. Pink flesh thickened into a grey-brown landscape of craters and mud. Soldiers rose from the earth, shook graveyard soil from their shoulders, and charged. Bullets buzzed, heavy as corpseflies. An *Oberleutnant* waved his platoon forward, his voice half-buried by gunfire.

"*Jetzt, Männer! Töte die Schweinehunde!*"

Roland's head shook in palsied negation. His fingers trembled, tremors travelling upward from wrist to shoulder. "*Nein, hör auf! Es ist eine Falle! Sie wissen, dass wir kommen!*"

The nails in Roland's feet pulled free. He staggered backward, hands raised in a warding-off gesture. The dirt and blood of the battlefield seeped outward in an endless, gurgling flow, rising from foot to ankle to knee. He turned to run, legs mired in goop, as a mortar arced through the air toward him. It struck his shoulder in a starburst of light and sound and pain, knocking him sideways into the muck. The roiling sludge swallowed him, and all was darkness.

***

The courtroom was bright and hard and loud, all wooden benches and polished brass. Words spoken in its confines seemed not to vanish, but instead to rebound from wall to wall, absorbing improbable strength with each echo, until the voices thickened into a dense, throbbing fog of noise. Roland sat on the bench, his hands bound with steel shackles. An ache burrowed into the fleshy hollow beneath his left shoulder blade. He tried to massage it, but the shackles made it impossible to reach, and he had to content himself with pressing the hurt into the bench's backrest.

To his left sat a small sweaty man who wept constantly in a steady sniffling drizzle that never quite broke into a sob. To his right was a mute, solemn tuber of a man, his head sunken into his shoulders, his arms crossed so tight across his ample chest that they seemed merely the illusion of limbs, the way a talented carver can suggest motility through a single block of deftly hewn wood. More figures stretched to either side, their faces rendered smudgy and anonymous with distance, all of them wedged tight into the bench until their bodies enmeshed, a slurry of human *Wurst*.

At the front of the room ran an elevated structure resembling a cross between a table and a podium, behind which sat a man in black robes with a scowling face. He loomed over the quivering men of the lower benches like a vast wave frozen mid-crest, awaiting the instant where it will sweep a small and impoverished island out to sea. Occasionally he would excrete another word into the gathering din of sound. The chain of flesh, of which Roland formed a single link, would shift leftward, as a glob of humanity squelched into the hall and a fresh slab was crammed in from the right. The process moved with the precision of a slow but thorough machine, an engine that processed delinquency into some nominally more useful form.

By the time Roland's turn came, the fog of noise hung so thick in the air he could almost see it, a thicket of scribbles defacing his vision. A bailiff grabbed him under the armpit and dragged him to a small, flimsy table positioned beneath the panel. Roland felt a smear of eyes on the back of his head, their gaze oily and unfocused. The eyes that met his, by contrast, were hard as ball bearings and cold, cold, cold.

The judge scratched the skin beneath his left nostril. "State the next case, please."

Paper rustled to Roland's right. He looked over and noticed a man in a grey suit, his lips mere suggestions behind the fronds of his moustache. The man ran his finger along a piece of paper and read out a string of crisp, angular syllables that Roland eventually identified as English. "Derelict, possible drunkard. Found on St. Paul Street in a state of incoherence. Lunged into the path of a street car, causing an interruption of traffic alongside general disorder and concern. Unresponsive when approached by local authorities. Rambled in an unconfirmed language, possibly German. May or may not be fluent in English."

The judge absorbed this description with furrowed brow. He turned his head to face Roland. "Do you speak English, sir?"

Roland nodded. "Yes, sir, I do."

"What is your name?"

"Roland Hellmich."

"A German, eh?"

"I am a Prussian by birth, sir, but I am now a legal resident of Canada."

The judge's scowl deepened. "Do you contest the facts presented before the court?"

The rattle of words grew still louder, the ache in Roland's shoulder worse. "*Ich habe Sie nicht ver*—Er, I am sorry, I mean, I am not understanding you."

The judge closed his eyes, pinched the bridge of his nose between thumb and forefinger. "Did you in fact stumble illegally into the road, causing a disturbance to traffic and imperilling safety?"

"I do not remember doing this, but I am guessing that I did."

"Can you tell the court what exactly you *do* remember about the incident in question?"

Roland's mind turned to the moments before he lost consciousness, the vast and dreadful unfurling of the building to reveal the long-dead war raging within. The smell of the battlefield returned to him—mud and sour puddle water, blood and smoke, necrosis and cordite—and for an instant he feared that this building too would melt into trenches and cratered dirt. That the farthest corners of the Earth would prove some treacherous sinkhole, crumbling beneath his feet and spilling him back into that rumbling abyss.

"I had... There was a vision. A memory. I saw it, and my mind... In any case, it is gone now. I am sorry for the trouble I caused. It will not happen again."

The judge gave a sour smirk that Roland found, if anything, more unpleasant than his scowl. "I very much doubt you're in any position to make such a promise. Are you employed?"

"Yes, sir. I am a dockworker."

"The court recognizes this claim and will seek to verify it. However, regardless of your employment status, your behavior is disconcerting and could conceivably prove a risk to public safety. As such, I am sending you to Walpole as a ward of the state, for an assessment of mental hygiene."

The judge banged his gavel. Rough hands scooped Roland up by the armpits and led him away. He went with them at first without a struggle, though a single word the judge spoke had sliced through the thicket and lodged itself in his chest: *Walpole.* Stories of the asylum drifted through the train yards in nervous whispers, tales of cackling lunatics who wrote screeds in their own excrement and clawed the eyes from their heads, of cruel doctors who jolted you with electricity or cut away bits of your brain until you were docile as a cow, of chains and straps and doors that closed and never opened again.

Roland hooked his ankle around the leg of a bench and used the leverage to buck free of his handlers' grasp. He approached the judge, hands clasped before him, chains jangling with the force of his plea.

"Your honor, please, I am not a madman. If I do not return to the docks, I shall lose my job."

The judge regarded him as one might a beetle being washed down the drain, its frantic legs and clicking mandibles a source of revolting fascination. He said nothing, merely watched as the handlers once again took hold of Roland and dragged him, wriggling but trapped, from the chamber.

2

THE FIRST THING Martha noticed about the room was its brightness. Though illuminated only by a lone window—albeit a large one; downtown Queenstown was a panorama of red brick behind its glass—and a pair of incandescent bulbs, it seemed to radiate light from every surface, as if infused with some otherworldly material. Ceramic tiles flashed across the floor, brass fixtures smoldered with an amber glow, marble columns set in the far wall blazed like pillars of flame. Even the uniform of the woman sitting opposite her was impossibly white, a jibbing sail of pressed cotton, taut and pale as an unblemished canvas. How on Earth could a working nurse keep a uniform that clean? Looking down at the brown threadbare drabness of her dress, Martha felt like a blotch of mustard on an otherwise pristine tablecloth. She tugged at the hem of her skirt, smoothed her thumb over a wrinkle that forty-five minutes of meticulous ironing had somehow missed.

The woman behind the desk held up a manila folder, tapped it primly on the desktop to align its pages, and spread it open. Her index finger—its nail emeried to a perfect white parabola protruding just past the fingertip—skimmed the top line of text before dropping down and slashing across key items here and there. A pair of spectacles perched on her thin nose.

"So, Mrs. Donnelly—Miss or Missus?" The woman's eyes snapped up from the paper as she asked the question. Martha nearly jumped at the sudden intensity of their focus.

"Miss, I suppose, ma'am. Though it's all the same to me what you call me."

"Mmm." The woman's eyes returned to the paper. "From Ireland, I see. County Cork. That's in the south, is it?"

"South as she goes, ma'am."

"And it was there where you received your schooling?" The woman consulted the paper. "Our Lady of Mercy, was it?"

"Aye, ma'am."

"That is a collegiate?"

Martha tugged at her shirtsleeves. "No, ma'am, t'was a primary."

"I see. So, you have no formal training?"

"Formal, no. But I was a nurse for near on five years before I left. The sisters took me on. I can change a dressing and give a needle quick as anybody, and I've no fear of blood or the like. I had Sister Magdalene—she was the Mother Superior, you know—write a letter on my behalf. You'll see it in there."

"Yes, yes. I reviewed it earlier." The woman removed her glasses and rubbed the lenses on the cuff of her blouse. "You are a Christian, I take it, Miss Donnelly?"

"Aye, ma'am. Born and raised."

"What denomination?"

Martha shifted in her seat. "'Tis all the same to me, ma'am. I was taught growing up that a true-felt love of the Lord is all that matters."

"Quite, but that doesn't change the fact that there are certain...cultural differences that can complicate matters. You are aware, of course, that Prince George Hospital is a Protestant institution?"

"What a patient believes matters little to me, ma'am."

"Perhaps. But as director of nursing for the hospital, I must consider many facets of the applicants who walk through my door. Experience and disposition are well and good, but there are other factors that determine a candidate's overall merit. Qualifications. Family. Breeding. On the whole, I'm afraid that you are simply not suited for the role."

"I understand, ma'am. Thank you for your time." Martha braced her palms against the chair's armrests and hoisted herself upright. Her mind turned to the cupboard in the one-bedroom apartment she shared with her family, how empty it had been when she'd left that morning, how much emptier it would be now, after she'd walked the four miles home.

"Now, now," said the woman. "There's no need to go off in a huff. I can see you're an eager girl, and this Sister of yours goes on at some length about your skills. Ours may be the most prestigious hospital in

Queenstown, but we are not the only one. As a matter of fact, there is an institution in our city that is currently understaffed. I have it on good authority that they are eagerly seeking young women of your experience. Should you apply, I am quite confident you will be accepted. Here, allow me to get you the details."

Martha sat back in her chair. The motion was only partly voluntary—relief seemed to have drawn much of the strength from her legs. She pinched her hands beneath her knees to calm their shaking.

"Oh, that would be lovely, ma'am. Thank you."

"Not at all, not at all."

Setting her glasses back on her nose, the woman opened a drawer and removed a small box containing hundreds of index cards. She riffled through them, fingers scissoring with the dexterity of long practice, and seized on one in particular, which she removed from the stack and placed in front of her. Dabbing her pen in the inkwell, she jotted down the details on a blank index card. When she finished, she slid the card across the desk. Martha scanned the woman's stiffly elegant script, which read: *Erasmus Walpole Institution for Mental Hygiene. Contact Mr. A. Verloc re Pub Ward Position.* An address followed.

"This...this is an asylum, ma'am."

"Their preferred term is 'psychiatric institution,' but yes, you are essentially correct. Is this a problem?"

"No, ma'am, it's just... I've never cared for such patients before."

The woman returned the original index card to its place in the box, closed the lid, and stored the box in her desk. "One patient is very much like another, Miss Donnelly. The stories you have heard about such institutions are grossly outdated where they are not simply wrong. I assure you, Walpole is a humane and modern facility. I suspect you will feel quite at home there."

Having stored the last of her things, the woman folded her hands in front of her and gazed at Martha with a look that clearly announced their meeting was over. Martha collected her folder. The papers held within, so neatly collated by the woman's precise taps, grew a ragged border of misaligned pages under Martha's grip. She clutched the folder to her chest to keep its contents from spilling and stood.

"Thank you again, ma'am."

The woman responded with a curt nod. Martha took the hint and left.

Outside, the brightness dispersed despite the noonday sun. She walked amongst the shadows and soot to the nearest post office, where she consulted a city map. After a few minutes' search, she found the asylum's address block on a windy road at the outskirts of the city. It was about two hours away on foot. The tram could get her most of the way, but trams cost money. *If I get the job, I'll take one home.*

The thought gave her a momentary thrill, but it soon abated, leaving a pang of anxiety in its wake. Could she really work in an asylum? Diseases and wounds of the body had never bothered her much—it was all simply tissue, after all, bits of flesh and bone in need of mending—and her years at St. Agatha's had scoured away what little hemophobia she might have had. But the mind was a different thing, a mysterious and impenetrable space behind the brain's rumpled grey curtain, and the wounds that cut beyond its frontier could not be so easily salved or stitched. Who could say where such afflictions began, or how—or even if—they could be mended? And a patient with neuroses wasn't like one with a broken leg or diphtheria. Those patients knew they were ill, and shared with her the common goal of retaining their wellness. A lunatic was likely as not to have no idea where they were, and might see her as an angel or a devil or anything in between.

Martha knew that mad people deserved care just like everyone else, but was she really the right woman to provide it?

She thought of the cupboard in her kitchen, and decided that she probably was.

***

Martha's first glimpse of the Erasmus Walpole Institution for Mental Hygiene didn't fill her with confidence. She hadn't even reached the building yet, but the grounds alone were intimidating. Iron gates snarled between stone walls ten feet high, their upper edges crenellated like the fortifications of a medieval castle. She knew full well that an asylum was not a regular hospital, and security was necessary to protect the patients, many of whom would simply wander off if their movement were unrestricted. But even the stories she'd heard as a young ward at St. Agatha's—whispered tales of the shrieking, shit-smeared halls of Bedlam—didn't prepare her for the edifice of entrenched, looming stone that confronted her. She felt like she'd been sent to storm a fortress single-handed.

A wooden booth with a steeply gabled roof stood just beyond the gate. Inside leaned a man in a uniform of starched grey-white linen—an orderly's outfit, albeit one belied by the stout oak club dangling from a lanyard at its belt. A short-billed cap resting on his head furthered the look of marshal authority. He spotted Martha and emerged from his booth, walking with wide strides to the gate.

"Purpose of your visit?"

"I...I'm here about a job. The woman at Prince George said I should apply. She told me to speak with a Dr., um..." She fumbled in her bag for the piece of paper the woman had given her. Seconds oozed past, her sweaty fingers grubbing blindly in the bag's recesses. *You should have had this ready, you daft ninny!* The guard watched her struggle, impassive.

After an endless search, she found the paper and pulled it triumphantly from the bag. "Aye! Here it is! A Dr. Verloc." She smoothed the paper's crumpled edges and handed it through the bars to the guard, who inspected it for half a second and handed it back.

"Move back, please. I'll open the gate."

The guard took a ring of keys from his belt and unlocked the gate. The tumblers rattled with a great hollow *clickitaclack* and the gate swung outward. Martha walked a winding stone path to the building's front door. Steel bars as thick as her thumb crisscrossed windows set deep in concrete sills. Vines shed of their summer foliage crept along the southern wall. She tried the front entrance—a set of oak double doors with contoured brass handles—and was surprised to find it unlocked. With a final glance back at the guard to ensure she wasn't acting out of bounds, she pulled the door open and stepped inside.

Martha's hopes began to rise as she entered the lobby. It was large and well-lit and tidy, a sweep of white tile floors and plaster walls rising forty feet to a domed ceiling. Twin staircases rose in mirrored arcs to a balcony fifteen feet aloft. People came and went through the room's many doors, all of them dressed in attire made from the same grey-white cotton: the men in slacks and buttoned, collarless shirts, the women in plain long-sleeved dresses that hung shapelessly from shoulder to ankle. Their stride was uniformly brisk.

One figure alone remained stationary. She sat behind a large oak desk that would not have been out of place in the office of a media baron, but which for all its grandeur felt diminished and out of sorts in its current location. It lay to the left of the entrance, its exact position unmoored from any architectural foothold, giving it the listless look of flotsam in a bestilled sea. Potted Ficus plants stood to its either side like buoys anchoring it against the room's current.

The desk, dwarfed by its surroundings, responded in turn by dwarfing its occupant. She was a small woman—not short, but small, her every feature scaled down to elfin stature. If not for her dress and her hair—curled into a tight bun on the back of her head—Martha could have mistaken her for a ten-year-old boy.

"Excuse me," Martha said. The woman jumped, blue eyes widening until they spilled from their sockets and splashed pale across her face. Martha tensed, stung with the unexpected reverb of so benign a statement. They stared at one another in sympathetic awkwardness. The woman gave a small giggle with which to wash away her initial reaction.

"Sorry," she said. "I can be jumpy sometimes. How can I help you?"

"I'm here to speak with Dr. Verloc about a job."

"Okay, sure, I'll bring you to his office! Please follow me." The woman sprang from her desk and rushed off, leaving Martha to catch up. She managed to reach her near the top of the stairs, where the small woman's pace relaxed into something more closely resembling walking speed.

"So," Martha said, searching for words to fill the silence spreading between them. "How long have you worked here?"

"Me?" She giggled again, a nervous sound that seemed to punctuate most of her statements. "Oh, well, I don't really work here, actually. I'm a patient."

"Oh, I'm sorry, I wouldn't have guessed..."

"It's fine, it's fine! I'm not one of the really bad ones. It's just nerves, you know. Just nerves." More giggles. "Dr. Verloc has a lot of us do little jobs around the hospital. Reception, cleaning, gardening. Occupational therapy, you know. Good for the mind."

They passed a number of people on their way down the hall, all of them dressed in the same off-white cotton. Martha realized that they were probably patients too, and that the bustle in the lobby she'd taken for employees was just patients going about their business. Apart from the guard at the front gate, she wasn't sure she'd seen an actual employee yet at all. Her shoulders tensed at the sudden knowledge that she was surrounded by lunatics, that the wretched snarls of misery and sinew she'd always pictured were all around her, uncaged and unshackled. That they could, if so directed by the capricious winds of their madness, fall on her in a pack and tear her to pieces.

These thoughts crashed over her in a wave of fear, but soon ebbed, leaving in their passing a damp stretch of shame. Whatever she'd been told about mental patients, whether true or not, was obviously not the case here. "It's just nerves," the small woman had said, and Martha had no reason to think otherwise. Nerves weren't so bad. She could deal with patients whose only affliction was an attack of nerves.

The small woman made an abrupt turn and passed through a door with a frosted glass panel. Beyond was a modestly furnished office backed by a plate glass window. A pudgy man sat at a desk, head down, scribbling notes in a leather-bound ledger. Tufts of grey hair ran in a horseshoe along the back of his head. Bookshelves lined the wall to his left, while two chairs and a small table ran the length of his right, atop which hung several degrees in ornate frames.

"Someone to see you, Dr. Verloc," the small woman said.

The man looked up from his writing. Glasses in wire frames sat low on his nose, and he pushed them back into position with his index finger. "Does she have an appointment?"

The woman bit her lower lip. "Er, I guess not."

"Does she have a name, at least?"

Her teeth sank deeper into the flesh of her lip. Sighing, Verloc gave a dismissive wave of his hand. "No matter, Emily. Thank you. You may go back to your desk now."

Emily needed no further prompting. She disappeared without a word, leaving Martha alone with Verloc.

Verloc pushed his glasses onto his forehead and rubbed his face with one meaty palm. "I apologize for the disarray. Emily means well, but she is new to her duties and still struggling with the manifestation of her particular nervous disorder." He settled his glasses back on the bridge of his nose, folded his hands in front of him, and met Martha's eyes with a steady gaze. "Now, how may I be of service?"

"Well, Doctor, I'd heard from a lady at Prince George that you may have need for more nurses here. I've some experience nursing, though it was for patients who were... I mean, for polio and broken bones and such."

She handed over her paperwork. Verloc took it and flipped through the pages, barely bothering to turn them over all the way. He stared for a few moments at the letter from Sister Magdalene, tapped the papers back into shape on his desk, and returned them to Martha.

"Welcome aboard, Miss Donnelly. I'll show you to the ward nurse. She'll set you up with an outfit."

Martha blinked. "You've no questions for me or anything?"

Verloc shrugged. "We don't have much time here for such pleasantries, I'm afraid. Besides, the job will sort out your capabilities, one way or the other."

"Meaning no disrespect, and I'm grateful as all for the job, but I'm surprised to hear you say that. Things seemed to be running pretty smoothly, from what I saw."

"Ah yes." Leaning back in his chair, Verloc made a steeple of his fingers. "That would be the private ward. The guests you encountered out front have mostly enrolled voluntarily, and are financially supported by their families. Most suffer from minor neuroses, though there are some who have more severe symptoms and generally stick to their rooms or the lounge. The public ward is located farther in the building. We find this presents a more...amenable image to visitors, and the general public. Anyhow, it is in the public ward where your skills are needed."

Martha swallowed. "Aye, and this public ward, what manner of patients should I be expecting there?"

"There are many types. But come, it's perhaps easiest if I show you." Verloc grimaced as he hoisted his bulk from the chair, the wooden legs of which groaned from the sudden decrease in pressure. "Then you can tell me if, in regards to the position, you remain as grateful as you say."

***

Martha heard the public ward before she saw it. The sound of it echoed down a narrow, low-ceilinged hall that separated public and private, both ends capped with stout steel doors that gave it the sensation of an airlock, a hermetic place of transition between two incompatible environments. It was a fusion of moans and giggles and mumbly incantations, brambled with the occasional shriek, and it took its place in Martha's head like a haunting, a stubborn ghost not easily exorcised. Such was its power that when Dr. Verloc opened the door, her mind superimposed a bedlam of tortured, writhing souls atop the room's drab but benign reality.

The vision faded, revealing a stretch of dull grey tile occupied by thirty patients in identical khaki uniforms. They sat at round metal tables bolted to the floor or on benches fastened to the walls, gazing forward into some unknown distance. Some wore straitjackets or canvas straps binding them to iron fasteners, but most were unrestrained. Even the noise was more bearable without the echo of the hallway and the closed door to lend it a dread obscurity. They were still unpleasant sounds, but they were of human source and unremarkable: the groans of a woman with frizzled grey hair slumped forward on her table, drool puddling in the gap between her arms; the rustle of starch-stiff khaki; the yips of a girl not much older than Martha, arms flapping against the canvas leash binding them to the armrest of her bench; the mushy litany of disjointed phrases from patients old and young.

"We come first to Wing B, which houses our acute cases. This is the recreation room," said Dr. Verloc, apparently without irony. "Patients whose capabilities allow a certain degree of socialization are welcome here during daytime hours, outside meals and therapeutic activities."

Martha looked at the patients sprawled about the room. Many spoke, but almost none of them spoke with one another. Most posed questions or told stories only to themselves. The patient nearest her, an old man with wisps of hair clinging to an otherwise bald skull and an alarming growth on one cheek, looked skyward at a flickering light in a wire fixture and recited a meal plan, whether future or past, real or imaginary, Martha couldn't say. "It's rice and beans at noon, rice and beans sure as anything. Too much spice in the beans, though the rice is mighty nice. A blue pill with supper, beef with gravy at five o'clock, burn the beef but the gravy keeps her soft. Eggs come breakfast at seven AM, poached and runny, oh yes oh yes, and toast crisp as anything..."

"They don't seem very up to socializing to me, Dr. Verloc."

"It's a relative term here, Miss Donnelly. You must remember that these are often individuals suffering a profound degree of psychosis. The recreation room offers a critical form of stimulation. Simply being in one another's company has a therapeutic effect, subtle as it might seem."

Martha thought such therapy must be subtle indeed, given the vacant gazes that crept about the room's bare walls, but said nothing.

Verloc led Martha through the recreation room to another hallway, this one lined with doors. Most stood open, revealing dormitories with beds running in two rows from wall to wall, the space between them barely wide enough to walk through. Patients lay atop their covers, bodies rigid with catatonia, or rocked back and forth with knees tucked to chest. A smell of must pervaded the entire hall, growing worse as they passed each doorway before receding for a merciful moment in the spaces between them.

"These are the shared rooms. The more docile of our patients find the comradery of shared living quarters beneficial. The set-up has the added benefit of allowing patients to observe one another's behavior and report issues to staff before they arise. This, in turn, allows our monitoring to be less draconian."

In one room they passed, a young nurse struggled to contain a middle-aged man undergoing some kind of fit. She held a hypodermic needle in one hand, its tip pointed out and away to avoid accidentally jabbing herself, while the rest of her body lay atop him, leveraging its meager weight in an effort to keep him contained. The man reared back and slapped her across the face. The blow made a damp meaty sound atop his grunting. The nurse's head snapped back, but rather than reeling, she seized the man's outstretched arm and took the opportunity to jab the needle into his bicep. The man gave a final convulsion and lay still, allowing the nurse to climb down from his prostrate body and take half a second to smooth her dress before racing off, past Verloc and Martha, and away. Martha absorbed the scene in stunned silence, while Verloc seemed to barely notice at all. He went on with his narration as if nothing had happened.

"We come now to a junction. Ward C, to our right, follows a similar pattern to Ward B, though it caters exclusively to our more elderly patients. Wing A, however, is a bit different, as you shall see. It houses patients whose condition does not make them amenable to group residence."

They turned left and entered a hallway of metal doors with Lucite portholes, through which Martha observed patients engaging in various forms of behavior that she would, if pressed for diplomacy, have called erratic. A woman with alarming bald patches, her arms bound in a straitjacket, beat her head against a padded wall. A man with sagging jowls and a prominent belly berated an invisible entity. Another man, this one thin to the point of emaciation, huddled in the corner of his room, knees drawn to his chest, and somberly intoned Psalm 23.

While most of the doors in Ward A were closed, Dr. Verloc and Martha passed by one that was open. Inside, two orderlies held down an elderly female patient by the arms, while a third repeatedly punched her in the face. The bedsprings squeaked with each blow. The old woman shook violently, head whipping from side to side, blood-flecked foam pouring from her mouth. An ammonia stink rose from a puddle on the bedsheets where she had wet herself.

The third orderly readied another blow, elbow cocked back, fist clenched, but spotted Verloc from the corner of his eye and let the punch drop. He straightened, turned his body to display his left cheek, and pointed to a scratch running from beneath his eyelid to the corner of his lip. He was tall and leanly muscled, with a cleft chin and a strong jaw. Martha would nearly have called him handsome, if not for his eyes, which were too small and close-set for his face.

"Sorry for the dust-up, Doc," he said. Martha waited for his eyes to drop to the floor—if not from shame at his actions, then at least from being caught—but he held Dr. Verloc's gaze without flinching, the corners of his mouth turning up in an almost imperceptible smile.

Verloc looked sideways at Martha before turning his gaze back to the orderly. His mouth shrank to a thin line.

"Fox. Please explain yourself."

The orderly's smile vanished, though he continued to stare at Verloc with unchecked confidence. "The patient got violent on me. You know how she is. She needed to be restrained."

"And was this degree of force really necessary?"

Fox looked at his right hand. Splotches of blood reddened the skin between his knuckles. He wiped them on the seat of his pants. Verloc looked from him to the other two orderlies, whose downcast eyes betrayed the sheepishness Martha expected of Fox, who merely shrugged.

"Pluck, MacCruiskeen," said Verloc. "Release the patient, please."

The two other orderlies did as told. The patient stayed where she was, staring upward with a glazed left eye—the right was fast swelling shut.

"Restraint is all well and good when necessary," Verloc added. "But in the future, I recommend that you consider exercising some yourself. Is that clear?"

"Yes, sir," said Fox. Pluck and MacCruiskeen mouthed words of similar assent. Verloc nodded.

"Good. Get her cleaned up. If the bleeding continues, get her to the infirmary."

This pronouncement made, Verloc carried on down the hall, leaving Martha alone in the doorway. Fox looked her up and down, his small smile returning. She fled after Verloc, who once again resumed his tour.

"The rooms continue on this way, but it's really more of the same. Instead, I'll show you the therapy rooms, where patients can undergo the latest medical interventions and—"

"Doctor," Martha interrupted. "Begging your pardon and all, but that man, what he did to that patient... It just doesn't seem right."

Verloc stopped walking for a moment and faced Martha. His thumb worked circles over the topmost button of his jacket. "You must understand, Miss Donnelly, that appearances among these types of patients can be deceiving. The psychotic is generally a timid beast, but ferocity can spring from the most unexpected places, and with a strength that belies the frame. I have seen an elderly woman all of 86 pounds tackle a man twice her weight to the ground and choke him nearly to unconsciousness. What may appear as excess, or even cruelty, is in many cases entirely justified by the exigencies of the moment."

"And what that man Mr. Fox did, that was justified?"

"Naturally I don't know the whole story, having witnessed only part of the event, but I will expect a full report on the incident by the end of the day, which will undergo the most thorough possible review. We take patient safety very seriously here, Miss Donnelly, of that I can assure you."

Turning on his heel, Verloc continued down the corridor toward the therapy rooms. Martha followed him, though her gaze lingered on the doorway over her shoulder, beyond which the three orderlies remained with the injured woman, their actions unseen. As she watched, a hand reached out, wrapped its fingers around the wood, and pulled the door shut.

3

ROLAND APPROACHED THE Erasmus Walpole Institution for Mental Hygiene at the head of a phalanx of half a dozen uniformed men. Most were police officers, though among them was an orderly sent to direct the group. He stood to Roland's right, separated by the burly frame of a mustachioed sergeant with a potbelly protruding over his belt. Given Roland's behavior at the courthouse, the officers apparently expected him to be trouble and had decided this retinue was necessary to ensure he didn't make another dash and run amok.

They needn't have bothered. What little fight he'd held was gone, snuffed out by the cold iron shackles around his wrists and the still colder dispassion of the judge's gaze as he'd been carted away. He was trapped, and his only escape would be from the system itself, which would surely acknowledge its error at some point. After all, he was not insane—of that he was certain—and it was only a matter of time before the professionals noticed as much. Further outbursts would only muddy the waters of his sanity, making its contours harder to spot. He resolved to act with dignity and politeness until the matter was resolved. This was still a free country, after all, and he firmly believed that the prejudices of its citizens could not tarnish the edifice of its laws.

It was such a belief that brought him onto that steamer in the first place, with its rats and dripping portholes and usurious fare. He'd lingered on the deck and watched as Hamburg receded into the distance, savoring the salt-sour tang of the sea air before the stern-faced deckhands muscled him into the ship's hold, where they would remain for the rest of the crossing, and saw in its shrinking visage the bent and scrawny legs of the Weimar Republic, trembling to hold up a burden they were never strong enough to bear. The image lingered as he trudged into the hold where he and six hundred others would share a space barely large enough for half their number, bodies strewn atop strips of moldy canvas draped over fishing nets fashioned into hammocks, tobacco smoke pluming from pipes and hand-rolled cigarettes, dingy walls roiling with the constant din of snores and creaks and the jiggle-squeak of clandestine masturbation. His old country was a bruised, battered wreck, disfigured by petty politics and war, and even if it survived its trauma, whatever creature stitched together from its remnants would be ugly and grizzled and mean. Better to endure a few weeks of reek and jostling in a grubby ship's hull and emerge, impoverished but whole, in a land where the bedrock of society held firm. Even if the transatlantic jump left him dangling from the lowest rung, at least the ladder from which he hung was bolted to something sturdy.

The officers removed Roland's chains and handed him off to the orderlies, who led him to a small windowless room with concrete walls painted a depressing shade of pea soup green. The only furniture inside was a pair of metal chairs with their legs bolted to the floor. The attendants sat Roland in the less comfortable-looking of the two, and waited in grim silence for the arrival of a harried heavyset man with a clipboard. He wore a white jacket seemingly tailored for the express purpose of conveying medical authority, its lapels embroidered with arcane insignia and its tails whipping with the force of his stride. He wiped a sleeve across the top of his head, which was bald apart from a horseshoe fringe of wispy grey-blonde, set a pair of gold-rimmed glasses on the bridge of his nose, and slammed his haunches onto the chair opposite Roland.

"Doctor," Roland said. "I am very grateful to see you. It seems there has been some sort of misunderstanding. I am not in any way mentally ill."

The doctor gave no indication that he had even heard Roland speak. He continued scanning the document. "Hmm. Dissociative episode, disruption of public thoroughfare, recalcitrant demeanor. It says here employment was confirmed. What is his occupation?"

Roland opened his mouth to answer, but the orderly who had accompanied him from the courthouse responded for him.

"A dockworker, sir. Part time only, though."

The doctor made a small tick on his clipboard. "Any progress on the citizenship question?"

Again Roland intended to speak, but was afforded no opportunity to do so.

"German. Recent immigrant. Poorly assimilated, judging by language skill."

"I have been here for over ten years," Roland argued. "I would not say I am recent."

The doctor nodded and went on as if Roland hadn't spoken. "Right. A clear case of neurosyphilis. All too common among this breed, I'm afraid. Send him for shower and delousing and get him a spot in Wing B. Treatment to begin at earliest availability." He slapped his hands against his thighs, hoisted himself from the chair with a grunt, and left the room with the same authoritative stride he'd used to enter it.

Roland watched the doctor's exit, stunned, half expecting him to return with an absent-minded smack of the head to pose some key forgotten question. But the door merely swung shut behind him, leaving Roland alone with the attendants who, having received their orders, took him to a communal shower room with tiles the color of a smoker's teeth. Water dripped from a loose gasket somewhere in the room's bowels, plinking a steady mournful note that spread through the echoey silence. The heady stink of ammonia lay over the duller smells of mold and rust like a blanket draped hastily over an untidy floor.

"Strip," the first orderly said.

Roland took off his shoes first. The floor was damp and his socks sopped up water greedily. He peeled them from his feet and stuffed them inside his shoes. He removed the rest of his clothes, folding each item and setting it in a prim pile on the driest piece of floor he could find. He thought it likely that he would never see these clothes again, but felt an obligation to keep them as pristine as possible anyway. His underwear came off last, leaving his slouched and hairy form revealed to the three attendants.

One of the orderlies turned on the nearest faucet. Harsh jets of water barked out the showerhead, interspersed with clanging air pockets before the flow smoothed out into a steady punishing stream. The orderly motioned to the running shower with one finger.

"Go."

The water was cold and it pierced him like an icy needle. He gritted his teeth and balled his hands into fists, forcing himself to keep from crying out. The orderly handed him a bar of soap and mimed scrubbing. Roland set to work, working a brisk lather over his upper half and mussing it through his hair. Once the job was done, the attendants snatched the soap back and handed him a starch-stiff towel.

They led him, still nude, from the showers and down a hall, where half a dozen patients milled about, men and women alike. He cupped his genitals and blushed, though the patients made no indication that they even noticed him. Most mumbled to themselves or engaged in fierce arguments with thin air, though the few that seemed outwardly lucid paid him no more interest than the obviously mad. Likely they'd undergone similar treatment themselves, and feigned ignorance out of courtesy for a fellow patient. Whatever the reason for their averted gazes, Roland was grateful.

The procession led him to another room much like the showers, except smaller. There they fogged him with a cloud of antiseptic powder and handed him a pair of pants and a shirt sewn from drab beige cotton. He dressed and went on to the next room, where a skeletal woman in hospital garb sheared off his hair with clippers and shaved the stubble from his chin. He accepted this treatment with dull passivity, arms at his sides, eyes fixed forward. Clothed and shorn, he trudged to the end of the hall and emerged in a large low-ceilinged room.

A dozen tables and perhaps fifty chairs stood scattered about the room, their position showing no clear pattern or purpose. Two tables sat so close together their ledges overlapped, while another lay marooned in a far corner, bereft of chairs, floating in naked space. Chairs faced walls or doors or nothing at all, bearing slumped figures that appeared likewise disassociated from their surroundings. Many stared forward, slack silent lips emitting strings of drool or mouthing strange catechisms that no one could hear. Others mumbled to themselves, their voices more audible if not more comprehensible, arms wrapped tight around their chests or contorted at odd angles. Some rocked back and forth, or performed sharp, palsied rituals with their hands and feet. The most active among them wandered from place to place, ranting at unseen entities. Almost none spoke with one another, or even seemed to acknowledge the existence of other patients. They were each of them frozen in a resin of private misery, their borders colliding with sticky friction but impenetrable to sight or sound. Roland wondered how even a sane man could remain so in such a place, if the ooze that ensnared them would collect on him as well.

After a few forlorn minutes of wandering this ghost town of derelict faces, Roland found a man whose eyes met his. A smile of recognition played on the man's lips. He was a small man made to look still smaller from his confinement to a rusting wheelchair, his spindly legs folded at the ankle. Sprigs of curled white hair burst from his head in patches, congregating at the temples and the knot at the base of his skull. He had russet skin mottled with liver spots and creased with wrinkles, but his eyes were clear and sharp, marred only by a faint yellowing of the whites. Roland found an empty chair nearby, pulled it over to the man, and motioned to it with a free hand.

"May I sit?"

"Help yourself, stranger. Good to see someone with a little light behind the eyes. Name's Harvey Freeman." The man extended a hand. Roland shook it and sat down.

"Very nice to meet you, Mr. Freeman. My name is Roland Hellmich."

"You can hold off on that 'mister' shit here, friend. Ain't no one here but us chickens, as my grandma used to say. Harvey's fine. Now, what got your poor hefty carcass dragged in here today? Caught you squattin' in the wrong alley?"

"No, sir, Mr. Harvey. It is a simple mix up."

Harvey laughed. "The Institute don't do mix ups. Least, not so's they'll ever admit it. You saw a head shrinker, didn't you?"

Roland's brow furrowed at the term. "A which?"

"A shrink. A doctor. Fat guy in a white coat. He sit down with you?"

"Yes, but—"

"And he rattled off some mumbo jumbo, told the orderlies to get you suited up and shuffled in?"

Roland nodded.

Harvey threw up his hands in mock triumph. "And there you are. Diagnosis made. Welcome to the funny farm."

"But look around," Roland said, raising his arms and motioning at the surrounding chairs. "I am not like any of these people, am I? Surely I do not belong."

Harvey cocked an eyebrow. "You sayin' I do?"

Roland looked down, red-faced. He drummed his fingers on his thighs. "This is not what I meant, of course."

Harvey laughed and waved the statement away. "It's okay, it's okay, I'm just teasin'. I get your meaning. And you'll see soon enough it ain't all droolers and ravers 'round here. Most of them who've a marble or two left in their heads are out on occupational, pickin' apples and sewin' wallets. Won't be too long before a work detail picks you up too, strappin' young fellow that you are."

"And those who cannot work, they just...sit here?"

Harvey grinned. "It's therapeutic, you see. That's what they're always tellin' me, anyhow. 'Medical reduction of stimulus,' they call it. Course, it's pretty damn convenient for them too, not havin' to waste their precious time and dollars keepin' us entertained. But that's just a coincidence, no doubt."

"I care not what they wish to call it, it isn't for me. Surely, in time, the attendants will realize that I do not belong here."

Harvey's smile softened, took on a conciliatory tone. "I'm afraid it doesn't work that way, friend. The folks in Toronto and Ottawa, they already paid their money to get you your three hots and a cot. Ol' Verloc ain't about to give it back. You're here for the long haul."

"But his diagnosis—"

"You think he's gonna go on record saying he got it *wrong?* He does that, some nosey lawyer might start pryin' into other cases, carve himself out a slab of that juicy malpractice meat. Nope, sorry, you got what he says you got. Which was what exactly, you don't mind me askin'?"

Roland flushed an even deeper shade of red than he had at his faux pas. Harvey patted him on the arm.

"You don't gotta answer if you don't wanna, but it's a question you're gonna get a lot. We're not much for bashfulness 'round these parts. Everyone's got some bats in the belfry, just the breed that changes is all."

"Neurosyphilis," Roland mumbled.

Harvey whistled. "Hoo boy, my condolences, friend. That's a nasty one."

"So you think I really have it too?"

"I don't got the first damned clue one way or the other," said Harvey, shrugging. "That ain't the point. Verloc says you do, and that's all that matters."

Roland frowned. "Verloc cannot make me sick if I am well."

"S'pose not, but I wasn't whistlin' at the sickness. I was whistlin' at the cure. And that is somethin' that comes under Verloc's say-so."

"There is a cure?"

"Yuh huh. And unless Verloc says you're too far gone—which I doubt, since we're here speakin' to one another—I reckon you're gonna get a taste of it."

"Of what?" Roland asked, not sure whether he wanted Harvey to answer.

"Of what else, friend? The fever cabinet."

***

Roland spent the next several hours far from the Erasmus Walpole Institution for Mental Hygiene. His body remained in place, slumped in a chair and indistinguishable in many ways from the vegetated souls around him, but his mind catapulted across an ocean and a score-plus years to a French mill town ten miles from the Front, where he had frittered away the scant hours of leave afforded him in the final months of the war.

It was his diagnosis that compelled him back to this place, a shadowy bivouac in the outer frontiers of his memory. Roland was no medical man, but he knew the word "syphilis" well enough. In German it was *die Lues,* but the symptoms were the same everywhere. He'd been a soldier and a working man for all his adult life, and there wasn't a soul from either group who was unacquainted with its vengeful presence and the caved-in, noseless faces and pockmarked minds it left in its wake. He knew the madness it instilled was unique, arising not from the Freudian sludge of subconscious memory, but from a germ as real as any flu or pox. But unlike the flu, which dwelled in sneeze or cough or unwashed hand, *die Lues* had only one vehicle at its disposal. And Roland's dalliances had been infrequent enough that he could safely guess when the disease—assuming he did, in fact, have it—had arrived.

The town had a name, of course, but Roland couldn't remember it. In those days one place was very much like another, and while the Front moved little in the waning years of the war, the towns chosen for leave always varied—this kept the soldier from forming attachments to the French locals. Better that the places be seen as waystations of brief repose, featureless dispensaries of pleasure.

But while the town's name escaped him, its face rose to his mind with indelible clarity. He could picture precisely the cobbled, down-sloping streets, narrow channels strafed by half-timber houses with plywood-blind windows; hear the rumble of wagon wheels as horse-drawn carts from the countryside dragged the dwindling yield of produce scrabbled from the war-parched soil; smell the sour-piss reek of dirt and horseshit grouting the gaps between the cobblestones, ossified odors dislodged by the rain. He and the other men moved by instinct to a plaza at the city's valley-slumped center, where a fountain capped with a statue broken off at the knees vomited yellow water into a grime-slick basin. The buildings bore a look of homogenous disrepair, punctuated with gaps of rubble-jagged destruction where a miscalibrated mortar shell, guided by a confluence of strong winds and bad luck, overshot the front line and crashed down into the otherwise battle-spared town.

The men walked with hands stuffed into the pockets of their field jackets, joking and razzing one another to hide their nervousness. Roland was mostly silent, absorbing any japes lobbed his way with a good-natured smile. The men in his *Zug* called him *der Mönch* after this beatific response, but beneath his calm shell his nerves jangled like frayed wires hauling excess voltage, thickets of naked metal shorting at the slightest touch.

The sun set at their backs, casting its final flickers of reddish light over the strip of corpse-strewn, cratered earth twenty miles to the west that they had, for a blessed two-day furlough, left behind them. Dusk settled pungent and sooty over the streets, crouching in alleys and lurking in the doorways of derelict shops. A lamplighter trudged past them uphill, touching flame to a procession of iron lanterns that cast their tepid orange glow across the cobbled darkness.

The lights grew brighter once they reached the town's main plaza, paltry globes coalescing into a sultry orange sheen. Men played at dice or hawked liquor and chewing tobacco from makeshift carts, while young children darted barefoot to and fro, inventing games with bits of wood and stones. The only women to be seen were the ones in doorways, gartered legs cocked sumptuously at the passing soldiers. Roland and company eyed them with interest, but passed by in favor of the establishment on the plaza's far corner called *Le Chat Noir*. Unlike the surrounding buildings, the paint on its façade shimmered with fresh luster. Curtains bearing arabesque patterns hung from the windows of the building's upper stories. Twin lanterns sheathed in red glass glowed on either side of the doorway.

Inside spread a long low-ceilinged room lit by dozens of candles. A bar ran the length of its right side, behind which a man with a disfigured hand rinsed glasses in a basin of greyish water. Women in corsets and lingerie sat at every table, some alone, others with one or more men opposite them. The chatter was mostly hushed and intimate, a soft murmur that erupted with occasional barks of ribald laughter.

One of the men with Roland pointed to a table occupied by a thin redhead in a white silk camisole. A smattering of freckles dotted her pale shoulders and the smooth roundness of her breasts—fuller than one would expect from her frame. She caught the man's gesture and cocked a finger at him, her red lips curling upwards.

"Guten Abend, mein Herr," the woman said. Her voice stumbled over the unfamiliar German, and her next words slinked into their native tongue. *"Venez ici. Cherchez-vous une* Frau *pour la nuit?"*

The man spoke no French beyond *bonjour,* but the woman's tone told him everything he needed to know. He approached and sat down. The others hovered nearby, watching with obvious jealousy.

"Une boisson pour moi, s'il vous plait. Le vin rouge. Merlot, Cabernet, ça ne fait rien." She held up an imaginary glass to illustrate her meaning. The man nodded and flagged over a waiter with an impatient flap of the hand and pointed at the women to indicate he should take her order.

"Und ich hätte gern ein Bier, bitte."

The waiter returned with the drinks and the man paid him. The woman smiled over the rim of her glass, her lips blending with the rich crimson of the wine. Her gaze skimmed across the row of soldiers lurking over the man sat opposite her. A jolt passed through Roland's belly at the instant her eyes met his. He cast his gaze downward and restrained his reaction as best he could.

"Vos amis, ils peuvent s'asseoir, s'ils veulent. Il y a beaucoup de place."

Roland, who recalled a bit of French from his schoolboy days, understood *asseoir* and took the invitation. The others followed suit, and soon half a dozen men formed a crowded crescent around one half of the table. The woman laughed, throwing her arms back.

"Tous ensemble! C'est une fête! Jocelyn, Amelia, venez! Les hommes-ci sont solitaire."

Women trickled in from the other tables until the table reached equilibrium. The two groups chatted together in pidgin, fusing the German and French words they both understood. Gradually, with little overt discussion, the table's topography shifted as men and women paired off—first in conversation over drinks, followed by a mutual rise and disappearance through the curtain at the back of the room. Of the men soon only Roland remained, a half-empty glass of beer clutched to his chest, his gaze drifting over the disintegrating islet of foam on the liquid's amber surface. The woman seated across from him reached out and, touching her index finger to his chin, gently raised his head until his eyes met hers.

She was older than the others, mid-thirties by the look of her, with thin arms and a flat chest. Faint lines traced the sides of her mouth, their creases softened with powder. Her eyes, though, were gorgeous, the blue-grey of a still sea beneath an overcast sky. Roland thought that the men who came here probably passed her over in favor of her younger, curvier colleagues, and that those men were fools. He took her hand in his and kissed the tips of her fingers, a move that felt strange but that he'd heard spoken of as romantic. The woman smiled and, adjusting her grip, led him by the hand to the curtained doorway.

The sheets parted, revealing a long and dimly lit corridor lined on both sides by doors. Most were closed, though through the few open ones Roland saw tiny chambers like scaled-down bedrooms: bed, nightstand, bureau, chiffonier, all slender and finely wrought to take up minimal space without making the room seemed cramped. The woman led him to an open chamber and brought him inside. A few personal items on the nightstand suggested her tenancy—a comb, hairpins, a couple of loose papers. Otherwise, it was as anonymous as a hotel room.

She pulled the covers back from the bed and slinked inside, her body moving with an easy dexterity that was both sensual and intimidating. Roland wasn't naïve enough to think she hadn't done this many times before, but her effortless confidence made his own experience—mostly necking with girls in the momentary privacy afforded by long walks through parks or back streets—seem hopelessly inadequate. Sensing his concern, the woman curled into a sitting position, legs bent to one side, and patted the edge of the mattress. Roland sat down. The mattress squeaked beneath his weight. He jumped at the sound, laughing at his nervousness as if to spite it. The woman touched his shoulder with her fingers, a gesture more sympathetic than sensual.

"*C'est ta première fois, n'est-ce pas?*"

Roland nodded. Her hand drifted up his neck, settled in the short hairs at the base of his skull.

"*C'est correct,*" she said. "*On va doucement.*"

An orderly snapped his fingers an inch from Roland's face. "Hey, Adolf."

Roland looked up at the man who'd disturbed him. Mid-twenties, leanly muscular, he fixed Roland with a squint-eyed, mocking look, reinforced by the muted chuckling of his two companions. The orderly's smile bore teeth as he noticed he'd gained Roland's attention.

"Bit jumpy, huh? Got orders from Doc Verloc that your treatment starts today, so up on your feet and let's get to it."

Roland stood up and followed the orderlies. The one who'd spoken led the way, while the other two dropped back and followed a half-step behind on his either side, just beyond the edges of his peripheral vision. The grouping made him feel like an escorted prisoner, which he guessed might have been the point. He wanted to tell the men that he had no intention of trying to escape, but the words wouldn't come. Roland's English often failed him when he got frustrated or scared, the fragile bonds of its syntax breaking down under pressure. His German was far sturdier, of course, but what good did that do him here? He stayed quiet, hoping to pass into more pleasant hands soon, but the orderly decided to engage him in a little more conversation.

"So, crotch rot, huh? That's a bum diagnosis, friend. You've gotta mind where you stick your member these days. Me, I've had my fair share of innings with the ladies, no doubt, but I've got my standards. A whole face, for a start. Nose and all."

"Geez, Fox," said a thin orderly with a dusting of black hair across his upper lip. "You're so particular." The third man, big and wide-shouldered, brown hair shorn down to bristles, chuckled to himself.

"MacCruiskeen here, he's more your speed. He'd stick his momma's corpse if he could get away with it."

"Hey, my mom's not dead!" objected MacCruiskeen, mock-offended.

"She would be, you flashed your gherkin at her."

Roland tuned out their back-and-forth as best he could. The lead orderly, realizing he was being ignored, dug an elbow into Roland's ribs.

"What's a matter, Kaiser? We offending your sensibilities or something? They say the krauts got no sense of humor, guess there's some truth to it."

"Hey, leave him alone," said MacCruiskeen, grinning. "Guy's got enough to worry about. Them krauts love their bratwurst, and his about to fall off and all."

Mercifully, they reached the treatment room a few minutes later, and there the orderlies' escorting duties appeared to end.

"Okay, Kaiser," said the head orderly. "Here we are. Just through those doors there. Have fun." He leaned in, smile widening, and raised a cupped hand to his mouth to signal a theatrical whisper. "And word to the wise, whatever you're still packing in your trousers there, best keep it zipped up tight. The head nurse, she's a frigid little bitch. Plus, I hear she bites."

And with that and a jocular slap on the back, they were gone, a receding chorus of jibes and cackles that trailed echoes long after the figures producing them had vanished around a corner. Roland allowed himself a few slow breaths during which he savored their absence, and turned his attention to the door. Windowless and blandly clinical, it presented a drab grey slab of metal onto which had been stenciled two words: Fever Treatment.

Fever? He didn't have a fever. Wasn't even the least bit sick, as far as he could tell. He pressed the back of his hand to his forehead. If anything, his skin seemed too cold. Had the orderlies played a joke on him? He didn't think for a second that they were above such antics, but if it were a joke, he had to admit he didn't get it. Scratching his head, Roland pushed open the door and stepped inside.

4

"**N**ON, *C'EST CORRECT, ma chère,* it's fine." The voice was calm, gentle, spoken with a delicate cadence. Martha felt comforted by its tone, even as her hands trembled at the task before her.

The dressing had once been white, though age and fluids had rendered it a stiff yellow flecked with red in spots, its differing shades providing a grim catalog of use and reuse. Martha worked her fingernails under the adhesive strips holding it in place, wincing with every tug as if the skin underneath belonged to her. Its actual owner, by contrast, seemed oblivious to the procedure. Bedbound, she gazed at the ceiling through cataracts that turned her cerulean eyes the pale blue-white of river ice. Her lips worked in a continuous puckering the way a newborn baby quests for milk. Otherwise, she was inert. White hairs sprung bristle-stiff from her head, thin enough to reveal the spotted topography of her scalp. Wooden wedges, upholstered with vinyl to make them waterproof, forced her into a position somewhere between on her back and her side, revealing the bandaged bed sore on her left buttock.

Martha sank her fingers far enough to gain purchase and pulled. The dressing came free with a wet tearing sound, revealing a vast carbuncle. Yellow-red fluid beaded atop tiny fissures in its crust. Martha pared the dead skin back with a lancet, revealing a circle of raw red flesh.

She dabbed with a cloth until the surface was dry and dusted it with antiseptic powder. A bit of rogue dust reached her fingers and set her cuticles screeching, but the woman, despite receiving a dose orders of magnitude larger, paid it no mind. Martha supposed this was a small blessing. If one must lose one's senses of sight, of hearing, of reality even, then losing one's sense of pain along with it was the least you could ask.

The nurse watched over Martha's shoulder, marking the action with the occasional approving nod. Martha wished there was more light in the room to work by. She had dressed more than her share of wounds in her time, but even the austere wards of St. Agatha's offered adequate lighting. The room in which she worked now felt like a cellar. Two of the three fluorescents overhead had burnt out, and no one had yet come around to change them. She'd asked how long until they'd be fixed, and the nurse merely shrugged, saying she didn't recall them ever working. Meanwhile, shadows nested in the folds of the woman's deflated skin, pockets where the seeds of new bedsores might lie in fetid germination, and Martha struggled to tell good flesh from bad.

The nurse's name was Eloise Tremblay. Tall, mid-forties, with black hair pulled into a severe bun and thin lines bracketing her mouth, she was a Francophone whose family traced its roots back to the *voyageurs*. In title, she was manager of Ward C—the geriatric ward—but chronic understaffing had made her the de facto head nurse for the entire institution, and in some ways second only to Dr. Verloc in rank. There were other clinicians who held higher official authority—internal doctors and psychiatrists whose degrees afforded them unimpeachable status—but they were desultory figures with their own private practices to tend to, and rarely seen. They drifted about the asylum long enough to collect their salaries as resident physicians, but saw few patients. Eloise made the operational decisions, and none of them had the least interest in opposing her. Despite hefting such an intimidating mandate, she appeared to be likewise responsible for training new nurses. Verloc had placed Martha in her care, and Martha had taken to her immediately. There was a matronly calm about the older woman that she found immensely comforting, all the more because she sensed beneath it a core of rigid steel.

Martha placed the dressing in a nearby hamper, alarmed by the sodden weight of it, and peeled a "fresh" sheet from the roll—fresh being a relative term, as the faded yellow stains could attest. She could only hope that the bleach had done a more thorough job on the microbes than it had on the stains. Squinting against the dim light, she set the dressing over the wound and affixed it with adhesive tape. She smoothed the tape with her thumb to ensure a good hold, and she and Eloise worked together to extract the wedges and lay the patient down gently on the bed.

"Very good," said Eloise. "But does all go well with you, *ma choupette*? You are looking pale."

Martha grew aware of her posture, shoulders tucked forward, head sunk into her collarbone. She forced her body back into proper position. "Aye, of course, Mrs. Tremblay. I'm fine."

"I know this work, it is not always easy."

"It's not the task itself that bothers me. It's the way she just lies there while I do it."

Eloise raised an eyebrow. "Would you rather she cried out?"

"No, no, of course not. It's just... Sometimes it almost feels as if I'm not treating a human being..."

Martha shrank into herself at this confession, sure she would receive a scolding at her callous attitude. Instead Eloise flashed a sympathetic smile and took her hand. "Ah, but we all think this way from time to time. It is an awful thing, to see the mind fade before the body. But the soul, it is there, and it does not weaken from age or disease. It is for the soul that we tend these minds and bodies, however much they crumble."

Martha smiled, grateful for Eloise's words even if she questioned them. It wasn't that she no longer believed, just that God's presence seemed unusually distant behind these walls. She knew these were sacrilegious thoughts, but she found them difficult to shake.

"Come," said Eloise. "There is still much to be done. I need one of my girls for mail duty today. You've a good touch with the older folks, why don't you do it?"

"Aye, of course, ma'am. I'll be right on it."

Martha's enthusiasm was genuine, as distributing meals or mail to the residents on the geriatric ward was among her favorite duties. The other nurses often complained, seeing prosaic duties like handing out trays and wiping chins as beneath the calling of medicine. "If I wanted to fling hash, I coulda done that right outta grade school," opined one nurse on Martha's first day, to the somber nod of all in company. Martha didn't see the problem. It wasn't as if the other day-to-day work of nursing was particularly glamorous, and the same women who'd grumbled about spooning out tapioca changed dressings and emptied bedpans without complaint. Compared to those duties, a bit of light waitressing was a welcome change of pace.

Martha walked to the drab, windowless room that served as administrative center, storage closet, and mail room for the public ward. The air inside was dry and acrid, a mixture of dust and toner and the strangely intoxicating stink of mimeograph paper. A pile of letters spilled across a metal inbox marked "Patient Mail." She gathered them up and made a workspace for herself by elbowing a slough of loose papers to one side of the room's communal desk. Putting the envelopes to one side, she searched the file cabinets until she found the patient roster, a musty tome that consisted of loose-leaf paper clipped into a three-ring binder.

The public ward had no clerical staff, and the duty for entering new patients and updating the status of old ones fell to whatever nurse happened to be on duty at the time. As a result, entries varied in structure from page to page, their legibility dictated by the entering nurse's handwriting and their comprehensibility by her interest, competence, and effort. Some entries spilled across multiple lines, offering copious detail on the patient's condition, demeanor, even family history. Others were terse statements of name, age, condition, room number. Luckily, these tidbits of information were almost always present, and all she needed to sort the mail into wings A, B, and C: chronic, acute, and geriatric, respectively. Each group was housed in a different wing and adhered to different schedules, so sorting this way would save her from running back and forth through the building a dozen times.

Martha checked the name on each envelope against the patient roster and sorted the mail into three alphabetical piles. She had worked here only a few weeks, and most of the names meant nothing to her yet. However, there were a few she recognized, and these brought a smile of recognition to her face. She was especially happy to see Evelyn Chauncey's name on the addressee line, and doubly so when the postmark came from Europe.

Mrs. Chauncey was a patient in the geriatric ward with Alzheimer's disease. Her condition was tragic, but her sweet-tempered disposition and quickness to smile made it hard to pity her. She seemed to accept her dwindling faculties with a grace Martha couldn't help but admire, and Martha often lingered during the breakfast rounds to chat with her. Mostly she spoke of her childhood spent on a nearby peach orchard, though the conversation sometimes steered into more recent topics, usually involving her grandson Tobey, a pilot who had volunteered with the Royal Air Force at the outbreak of war between the United Kingdom and Germany. The boy was her only living relative (or at least the only one she ever spoke about), and any mention of him set off momentary flares of light in the gathering fog behind her eyes. A letter from the boy himself would obviously mean the world to her, and Martha relished the thought of witnessing her joy firsthand.

Patients in the public ward didn't get a lot of mail, so even with the cross-referencing added in the job didn't take long. Once sorted, she combined them into a single stack about half an inch high. Martha took them in hand and began her rounds. Her newness made it difficult to put faces to names, and often she needed to ask the attendants in the common areas for help.

Those patients who could read accepted the letters with thanks. For those who couldn't, she would read the contents to them. Most seemed grateful. Even the most catatonic patients betrayed some slight shift after hearing news from home—though Martha knew some of this might be her imagination. She only received one outright refusal, from a balding man in his fifties who insisted that the envelope she offered him contained poison dust. This letter she retained, and would return to the mail room; perhaps he'd be more receptive on a different day.

Mrs. Chauncey sat at a table in the geriatric wing, where she chatted lightly with a few fellow patients. The others suffered from dementia too, and each was farther gone than she was. A reed-thin woman named Betty nodded on occasion and spouted non-sequiturs about how lovely the food was, while the two men simply slumped in their chairs, mouths agape, and cast rambling gazes about the room in silent wonder. The interplay between the two women was less a conversation than a pair of occasionally intertwining monologues, but all the same Martha waited for a pause before intruding.

"Good morning, Mrs. Chauncey," she said. "It's Martha, one of the nurses here."

Mrs. Chauncey's gaze found Martha's for a moment, then drifted off to a space somewhere to the left of her head. It wandered out that way as she spoke, sometimes flitting back to Martha's face, sometimes not.

"Do I hear a bit of the old Irish brogue on your voice, dear?" She'd asked Martha this same question every time they'd spoken, without fail. After the first few encounters, Martha felt self-conscious about it, but now she appreciated the ritual.

"Right as rain," she replied. Experimentation had shown this to please the older woman most, so Martha led with it on most occasions. "And how are you doing this fine morning?"

"Oh, these old bones have some life in 'em yet." Another favorite reply of hers.

"I have a letter for you here, Mrs. Chauncey. I believe it's from your grandson."

Mrs. Chauncey's eyes snapped to Martha's. The vacant haze that clouded them cleared in an instant, as if blown aside by a strong and sudden breeze.

"Tobey? My Tobey's written me?"

She took the envelope and held it in trembling hands. Her fingers slid across the address and traced the ridges of the stamp, as if assessing that it was indeed real.

"Could you read it for me, Mary? My eyes are troubling me lately, and his writing was never the neatest, bless him."

"Of course, I'd be glad to."

Martha worked a fingernail under the flap and slid it across the opening, taking care to rip it as little as possible. She unfolded the letter and was surprised to find it typed on blank loose-leaf paper, rather than handwritten on stationary or a page from a notebook. Her eyes rested on the insignia of the Royal Canadian Air Force, and dropped down to skim the typewritten text.

Dear Mrs. Evelyn Chauncey,

On behalf of the Royal Canadian Air Force, it is my sad duty to inform you that your grandson, Lieutenant Tobias Reginald Chauncey, was killed in action over the English Channel on the 26th of September. I extend to you my sincere sympathy on your great loss, and hope you can take some solace in knowing your grandson died while in service to his country.

If I can be of any assistance to you in this difficult time, please write or telegraph me at the address listed below, or contact my office by telephone. Again, on behalf of the Air Force, please be assured of my sincere sympathy on your tragic loss.

Sincerely,

Lieutenant-General Philippe Lamoureux, Chief of Personnel

A lead sinker plunged down Martha's gullet and landed with a thud in her belly. She clutched the paper hard enough to press creases where her thumbs met her fingers. Her first feeling was one of all-consuming rage—at the enemy pilots or gunners who had killed Tobey, at the lieutenant-general and his empty condolences, at the war spreading like a vast chancre across Europe to the gates of her homeland. And at herself, for her ignorant stoking of this poor old woman's hopes. *You child. You fool. You absolute ninny. Did you not think for a moment that a letter from a war zone could have something besides good news?*

Martha lowered the paper, revealing Mrs. Chauncey's expectant face gazing up at her. Her eyes fixed her with the rapt attention of a child engrossed in a story. Martha opened her mouth to speak, but a croak came out instead. A sticky film glued her tongue to the roof of her mouth. She worked up saliva at the back of her throat and rinsed it about her mouth until she was able to speak. This fixed the problem, but drove home afresh that she had no idea what to say. In desperation, she blurted the first words that came to her head.

"Dear Grandma Evelyn," she began. Her eyes drifted across the spaces between the text, careful not to focus on any one word lest it trip her up and muscle its way unbidden into her improvised sentences. "I hope all is well with you. I am doing well over here in England. The weather is fine and there has been little fighting. I miss you a lot and think of you often. It will be a happy day when I am home and can visit you. Let us pray that this war ends soon! With much love, Tobey."

Mrs. Chauncey beamed. "Why, wasn't it nice of him to think of his old grandma!"

"He's a fine boy for sure, Mrs. Chauncey." Martha clutched the letter to her chest, the text facing inward. "Shall I put the letter with your effects? I'd hate for you to lose it."

"Yes, yes, please do keep it safe!"

Martha staggered away on knees of gelatin. She dabbed the letter on her dress, drying the smudges left by her sweaty fingers, folded it along its existing creases, and tucked it back into the envelope. This she stuffed in the front pocket of her apron-like uniform, a design that seemed odd to her at first, but whose utility she'd come to appreciate.

You're a cad, Martha Donnelly. A cad and a liar.

The rest of Martha's mail delivery duties passed in a haze. A jab of terror greeted the opening of each envelope. What fresh misery might coil inside them, to burst forth at the moment the paper seal was broken? She knew this was ridiculous—bad news was not ubiquitous, and any that came wouldn't be her fault—but the near-miss with Mrs. Chauncey had scraped her raw. Her whole body sagged as her fingers relinquished the last missive to a wheelchair-bound old man, who tore it open and read it quickly before tossing it aside with a scoff.

"My old union, wantin' contributions from pensioned members for a dispute. Some pension I got, windin' up here! You'd think they'd know better, them bein' the finks who cheated me."

Martha offered a sympathetic coo, though inside she heaved a sigh of relief. Patient gripes she could handle, even if they were directed at her. It was their grief that made her tremble. Funny that tending to the dying didn't bother her at all—it wasn't a joyful thing, but it was honest, needed work, and she did it proudly—but the cold announcement of a death overseas died a death of its own on her lips. She went to Nurse Tremblay to get her next task—hopefully something to occupy her hands and not her head—and opened her mouth when another voice spoke in her place.

"Hey, Tremblay."

Eloise's face hardened at the sound of her name. Martha turned to see who had spoken and recognized the orderly from her first tour of the asylum. He glanced at her with mutual recognition and flashed a lupine smile.

"*Nurse* Tremblay, if you please, Mr. Fox. We are professionals, yes?"

"Sure. Verloc—sorry, *Doctor* Verloc—just did intake with a new patient. Diagnosed him with neurosyph. Says treatment starts this afternoon, so one of your girls'll have to get on it."

"Thank you for the message, Mr. Fox. Tell Doctor Verloc that I'll be with the patient shortly."

Fox cocked a salute and walked off, sparing Martha a final glance as he went. Eloise watched him go, eyes narrowed, and muttered under her breath. *"Casse-toi, espèce de cochon."*

"Uh, Nurse Tremblay?"

"From you, Eloise is fine, *ma choupette*. What would you like to ask?"

"That man, is he a relative of Doctor Verloc's?"

"Not to my knowing," said Eloise. "Why do you ask?"

"Well, it's just that I saw him...behaving inappropriately while Doctor Verloc was giving me a tour, and he didn't do much of anything about it."

"And you wondered why Verloc allowed this, *oui?* But if the good doctor fired him, who would he hire to replace him? He can only choose from those who apply. With the war, there are few young men left. And for those who remain, why would they earn a dollar here when any factory would pay them triple for less? When a position must at all costs be filled, it is the Foxes of the world who will fill it."

"A sad thing to say about a place of healing."

"*Oui*. But in such a place we do what good we can. And you will do more good if you stay far from Mr. Fox and his friends. Though I am guessing I need not tell you this."

"No indeed."

"Wise girl. Now, come. This new patient is waiting for us. I suppose it is time to show you the fever cabinet."

***

Eloise made sure that they arrived at the treatment room before the patient did. There were two reasons for this, she would later explain: first, there was the practical matter of allowing herself time to educate Martha on the process, including its risks, without having the patient overhear.

Second, it meant that when she first encountered the machine, the patient wouldn't see her face.

It was not an outwardly menacing device—Martha had seen and even handled tools of a far more macabre bent in her years as a nurse. The real issue was in what Eloise would call its symbolic dimensions, for it resembled nothing more than a coffin. True, there was a padded hole at one end where the head poked free, and a mechanized bellows that fed the far end with a tangle of rubber hoses, but look past the details to the object as a whole and the resemblance was unmistakable.

"This is the fever cabinet," said Eloise. She ran her fingers over the smooth grain of its lid. "A bit scary to look at, no? But it is really a very simple device, and is used only for patients with neurosyphilis. Such patients are unlike the others, whose illnesses reside in the mind but spread out and effect the body. For them, the disease is in the body, and seeps into the mind. It is a germ that causes this madness. Kill the germ, and the body may heal."

"I see," said Martha. "But how exactly does this device kill the disease?"

"Actually, it does no killing on its own. The patient's own body does it, in the same way bodies always have. Through heat. What is a fever, after all, but the body cooking away the invaders that wish to do it harm? In the past, doctors have caused deliberate fevers by infecting them with malaria, but this is a risky procedure, as you will likely guess. The machine is better, because it gives us more control. Steam from the boiler heats the air, which is pumped into the chamber. Slowly, the temperature of the patient will rise until it is as if he has a high fever. He stays this way for several hours. The heat kills the virus, much as with a true fever, although the risk here is lower because we can control how hot and how long."

She unhooked the metal clasps and swung open the lid. "The patient climbs inside and gets comfortable. You cover his exposed skin with wet towels, close the lid, and pull the switch. From there, your job is to monitor their temperature, and to keep them comfortable, hydrated, and calm. Many patients panic during their time in the machine. It is not so comfortable inside, though we do our best. The heat makes it hard to breathe. Some feel they are suffocating. You must reassure them that they are safe, and that the treatment takes time. Speak with them of other things, their childhoods, their families if they have them. Anything that carries the mind far away. It is your ability to keep them calm, more than anything else, that will determine the success of the treatment."

Eloise demonstrated the machine's controls, highlighting the temperature dial, explaining the various gauges, and pointing out common things that could go wrong. None were life-threatening, she insisted. As long as the patient's vital signs were monitored regularly, the machine was perfectly safe. To die from it would take time and a level of discomfort no patient would tolerate.

"There is one other thing to show you. Follow me." She led Martha to a door at the back of the room. Unlike the wooden door that led to the hallway, this one was solid metal. A padlock above the doorknob fastened it shut. Eloise drew a key from her pocket, undid the padlock, and hung it from the latch. The door was well balanced and opened easily despite its considerable weight. Eloise set a built-in doorstop with the heel of her foot and ushered Martha inside.

The room beyond the door was cramped, dark, and humid. Lead pipes clung to the walls and crisscrossed overhead, rattling beneath watery payloads and giving off a damp, sinister heat. Their presence turned an already narrow walkway into a claustrophobic passage little more than a shoulder's-breadth wide. Most of the pipes fed into one of several main lines at the backmost end of the room, stout columns of iron-banded lead that ran down to the boilers in the basement. A maintenance cart stood wedged between two of the mains, its rusted-out casters a clear sign that it hadn't been moved in some time. Atop it rested an adjustable wrench, various pipe fittings, and a number of other tools and parts Martha couldn't identify. Unlike the cart itself, these tools seemed to move fairly often—Martha saw clear drag lines in the dust across most of the workspace. Likely the maintenance crew left them here to avoid lugging them back and forth.

"The pressure is highest in this area," explained Eloise. "So we must be very careful. The valves must be handled gently. Here is the line that feeds the fever cabinet." She pointed to a valve next to Martha's head. "We must turn this a few minutes before we run the cabinet, to give the lines time to prime themselves. It looks big, but turns easily for its size. Try it."

Martha studied the valve. Its handwheel was large, maybe six inches in diameter, and shaped like a ship's wheel, while thick globs of lead held the bonnet in place. The stem, however, seemed disproportionately thin, and Martha feared an errant blow of her hand might bend it. She reached up and fitted her hands between the prongs on the handwheel, noting the heat that radiated through the metal. She spun it counterclockwise and was surprised at the ease with which it turned.

"You're right," said Martha. "Nothing to it."

"It is very important to close this valve again when the treatment is finished. It may look small, but it holds back tremendous pressure. The lines further down are not meant to contain such volume for long, which is why the cabinet has a release to bleed away buildup. This works as long as the cabinet is running, but if you shut it off and leave this valve open, the lines could eventually burst."

"I'll be sure to remember."

They left the boiler room and shut the door behind them. Martha had questions, but before she could ask them the front door opened and the patient stepped inside. He was fortyish, square-shouldered, with black hair crudely barbered and shadowy stubble covering the lower half of his face. His skin bore the scars and splotches of rough living, though he seemed well-muscled and healthy despite his yellowish pallor and the purple bags beneath his eyes. Martha knew him at once as a laborer—not just from his size, but from the loose-shouldered way he held his body and the delicate clumsiness of his movements, as if every object he ever handled was brittle enough to snap if he wasn't gentle. It was a look that reminded her of her father and brothers, and the lads who manned the factory lines back home.

He shuffled over to her, hands clasped in front of him, and spoke with a polite nod.

"I am sorry, they told me I am to be here for treatment. My name is Roland Hellmich. I am...a patient here." He stumbled over the last words, as if learning of their meaning only as they left his mouth.

Eloise took Roland's hand and guided him further into the room. "But of course, Mr. Hellmich. Please come in. I am Head Nurse Tremblay. Nurse Donnelly will be administering your treatment. I know this machine looks a little strange, but please do not be alarmed. I will explain."

Eloise gave the man a tour of the machine much as she had for Martha, though she tempered her descriptions to match the man's education and comfort with English. The change was subtle but evident, glimpsed in a shift in weight towards the ends of words, a pruning of technical details, a greater reliance on gesture. It simplified and left no residue of condescension. Martha could see the man relax a little as Eloise spoke. She wondered if she could ever convey the same air of medical authority.

Once her explanation was complete, Eloise told the patient to undress and climb into the machine. She offered him a towel to cover himself. "Nurse Donnelly and I will wait outside. Let us know when you are ready and Nurse Donnelly will begin the procedure."

They stepped out into the hall. "This procedure, it is not always the easiest thing to watch. I would stay with you, but the afternoon rounds..."

Martha gave what she hoped was a reassuring shake of the head. She knew Eloise was stretched thin as the skin of a soap bubble, even without the added burden of training her. Asking her to dedicate several hours to a procedure that consisted largely of observation would be a criminal misapplication of resources. Martha was a trained nurse. She could twiddle a few knobs and take a man's temperature.

"I'll be fine," she said, speaking with a certainty she didn't feel. "You showed me everything already."

Eloise brushed a stray hair from Martha's forehead. "I could use twenty more of you, *ma choupette*. If you run into any trouble, shut off the machine and come find me—and do not forget the auxiliary valve."

Eloise's swift stride clicked down the hall. Martha listened to its echoes receding in the distance until they disappeared beneath the undergrowth of groans and shuffles and muted chatter sprouting from the neighboring rooms. A hospital was never completely silent until the day it closed for good. An asylum even more so. She left the hall and returned to her patient, who lay beneath a towel in the fever cabinet.

"So, Mr. Hellmich. We'll be here a while, so we may as well get to know each other. What did you do before your spell with us?"

Roland smiled at the euphemism. "I worked on the docks, loading ships. Before this I was a machinist by trade, but this job I lost. Since then, I do what I can, where I can. Mostly this is on the docks. There is still need for strong hands and strong backs there."

"Hard work, I imagine. But at least you are outdoors, breathing fresh air. The lake is lovely."

"This is true. I would do more of it, if I could. But jobs are not so easy for me this last year. Feelings have changed, since the war."

"How long have you been in Canada?"

"Twelve years."

Martha gave an appreciative whistle. "Seems to me, you're more Canadian than German after that much time."

"If you would tell the foremen this, I would thank you."

Martha blushed. Roland spoke without any obvious bitterness, but his frank admission made her uncomfortable. "I made the crossing myself nary a few months back. Quite a voyage. Three weeks in a hold sleeping two to a cot. I suspect for you it was much the same."

"We had no cots, but yes. You are coming from England?"

"Ireland. County Cork."

"Ah. Some in my *Zug* would say you were going to join our side and fight the British from the rear. Such foolish things soldiers get in their heads."

She smiled. "I suspect there were some back home who were tempted. You were a soldier?"

"*Ja*, in the *dreiundzwanzigste Abteilung*. A bunch of silly boys raised on silly stories about the Fatherland, fighting a war we had no chance of winning and no reason to win."

"Most wars could be described the same way."

Roland paused a moment to reflect on this. "Perhaps. I think there are some wars which must be fought. Wars which could not be otherwise. The war we fight now is one."

Martha felt herself bristle at these words. She knew better than to discuss politics with patients—nothing could fracture a healing relationship faster—but the question banged on the back of her teeth, demanding to be asked.

"Are you a supporter of Hitler, then?"

Roland laughed. "When I left Germany, Herr Hitler was a silly little clown of a man, always shouting. When I learned he was seeking the Reichstag, I laughed. Is that not what clowns are for, to make us laugh? Who would vote for this man, with his Charlie Chaplin moustache and his failed coup? He was not even a German. When he won, no one in this country was more surprised than me." His smile faded. "I read the papers often, in the library. It is good practice for my English, but it keeps me also informed of home. There are days when I read things, and I do not recognize the country of my birth at all. Other days I read the same things, and I recognize it all too well."

Martha nodded. "Aye, I know what you mean. I've not been gone near as long as you, but already Ireland feels strangely distant to me."

"What made you come to Canada?"

"I've an aunt who came here in '22 with her family. Her son—my cousin—and his wife passed in the spring. Left three boys in my aunt's care, and she's too ill to work much besides a little sewing at home. None in my line had fare enough to bring them all back home, so I came over to keep things afloat for a time."

"A hard turn. But this is a noble thing you do for your family."

"Oh, I don't know. T'wasn't all noble airs brought me here. I'd always wanted to see the New World, heard stories of it since I was a little girl. About the skyscrapers and the open plains. Everything was bigger here, they said, grander."

Roland smiled. "They said much the same in my country also. Now you are here. Do you think it's true?"

Martha tugged on her lower lip. "In some ways, aye. But not the ones I expected. Things are less set here, less history holding 'em all down. Seems easier for things to change. Ideas. Inventions. People. Coming here, it almost felt like I got to the part of my life that wasn't written down yet. I suppose that all sounds a little crazy."

The turn of phrase struck her ear as if spoken by an outsider, and she winced at the inadvertent meaning. Roland noticed it as well, but seemed to find it funny. He laughed softly to himself.

"You are, I am guessing, in the right place for saying crazy things."

She responded with a polite chuckle, more out of gratitude than genuine humor. Her embarrassment receded before it reached high enough to drown her, but she could still feel it lapping at her ankles. "How are you feeling?" she asked, both to monitor his progress and steer the conversation towards more amenable ground.

Roland's gaze turned inward, as if he were pondering a difficult question. "Actually, I am feeling a bit unwell. I suppose this is normal?"

"Is it quite bad, the heat? Would you like a cold cloth on your head, or some water?"

"I am not so sure this will help. It is not the sort of heat one finds on summer days. It is a heat from the inside out."

"Miss Tremblay told me it could be uncomfortable. We have to raise your body temperature in order to kill the germs. I'm sorry, I wish there was a better way."

"*Nein*, it is not my body that burns. It is deeper, as I say."

"I'm sorry, I don't understand."

Roland's head started to swivel back and forth, a slow but insistent negation directed at an unseen speaker. His words came out as moans, barely understandable. "*Nein, nein.*" The shaking grew faster, travelled down his shoulders.

"Mr. Hellmich, are you all right?"

"*Mir geht es nicht so toll. Es is zu heiß hier drin. Zu heiß. Hilfen Sie mir bitte! Es ist zu heiß!*"

Roland's head whipped from side to side. Flecks of white foam oozed through his clenched teeth and collected in the stubble on his chin. His arms yanked at the leather restraints hard enough to shake the entire cabinet. Martha feared he would break the whole thing to pieces, feared even more that he would die before he got the chance.

She turned off the machine and ran around to the far side to undo the clasps holding the lid in place. The hot metal singed her fingertips and she drew back, hissing at the pain. She hiked up the hem of her dress, folded the material a few times over, and set it between her palms and the clasps. The heat still pressed through the fabric, but was muted enough to tolerate. She heaved and the clasps came free with a snap. A curtain of steam rose from the crack between the lid and the wall. She shouldered it open, taking care not to touch any exposed skin to the wood.

A gust of humid air singed her cheeks. She squinted through the pluming mist and saw Roland's body, its spasming muscles gone limp. His skin flushed the furious red of boiled lobster. The sour metal stink of sweat and antiseptic clawed her nostrils and prodded the corners of her eyes. Gagging, she knelt and grabbed the steel basin of water that attendants used to soak the towels. Her lower back squealed at the weight of it, but she bit her lip and forced her body to lift. The basin came free with a scrape of metal on ceramic. She hoisted it up, tottered beneath its bulk, and with a final grunt of effort spilled it over Roland's prostrate body.

Roland convulsed like a hook-snagged fish. He flailed against the sudden flash of cold water, twining left and wriggling free of the fever cabinet. A gasp of pain and mingled relief spilled him supine on the tile floor, bare belly heaving. His towel bindings had come free in the ordeal, and Martha draped one afresh over his genitals as she lowered her head to his face to check his vitals. His heart raved and pounded in his chest, his breath hitched and gasped, but a hand on his shoulder settled him gradually to a state that, if not calm, was at least reeled back from panic. His fear-fogged gaze cleared and settled on Martha's face, brow furrowed in delayed recollection. He glanced past her at something overhead and the fear returned, leeching the last corpuscles of color from his ashen cheeks.

"Das ist unmöglich," he said, his voice a whisper. *"Ich konnt' es nicht gewusst..."*

"What? I'm sorry, I don't understand."

Martha traced his line of sight to figure out what he was talking about. The answer, such as it was, told her nothing. After his tumble from the fever cabinet, he'd worked his way partly under its chassis, and was now staring at a small brass plate affixed to its undercarriage, which read *Made in United States, 1939.*

"Come on, let's get you off the floor."

Kneeling down, Martha slipped an arm underneath the hollow between Roland's neck and the floor and levered him into a sitting position. He was a lot bigger and heavier than she was, but she'd worked with big male patients before and knew how to make the most of what strength she could put to bear. She gave him an encouraging tap on the side, signaling he should help, and waited for life to flow back into his limbs.

Together, they hobbled over to a recovery cot at the side of the room, where she helped him lay out and covered him with a blanket. She took his temperature and was relieved to find it had already fallen back to 101 Fahrenheit—in the range of a fever, but not a dangerous one. He'd pushed 105 on her last observation before his fit, and at such heights small shocks could be fatal. She covered him with a sheet and dabbed his head with a cool cloth, partly to further lower his temperature and partly as an excuse to stay nearby, in case he grew agitated again. Patients in delusory states could go from catatonic to flailing in an instant, and she wanted to be on hand in such an event to keep him from hurting himself. The recovery cot had thick canvas straps at the shoulder, waist, and knee level, but she was hesitant to use these. Her infirmary training remained foremost in her mind, and she'd yet to acclimatize to the asylum's liberal use of restraints—nor was she certain that she would ever want to.

Luckily, Roland showed no signs of growing agitated. He was still in distress, but it was distress of a quiet sort: limbs limp, head lolling from side to side, lips forming the same words over and over: *"Ich konnt' es nicht gewusste, ich konnt' es nicht gewusste..."*

"Just stay put, okay? Don't go trying to stand up on your own. I'm going to fetch Nurse Tremblay."

She moved towards the doorway but paused before she got there, remembering what Eloise had told her. She doubled back into the boiler room and shut off the valve that fed the fever cabinet. Steam thrummed through the pipe, the force of it rattling a loose bolt in one of the nearby fixtures. The sound ceased as the valve swiveled shut.

When she emerged, Roland remained where he was. His head continued its restless swiveling from side to side while the rest of him remained motionless. He repeated the same few German words in a thin, parched voice, oscillating between a whisper and a moan. They struck a somber note as they rang against the room's tile walls, a rosary incanted against a dark and looming force. Martha pushed this morbid image from her mind and left to fetch Nurse Tremblay.

5

THE FEELING HAD seemed to leap upon him in an instant, vicious and unprovoked, but even as it sank its fangs into his belly he realized it had been stalking him for days. He saw the lurking smudge of its shadow all around him, portents backlit by the harsh glow of hindsight. It stalked him in the train yards, where its voice echoed up from the depths of a greasy cookfire. It stalked him through the streets of Queenstown, casting hallucinations on the walls of passing buildings. It stalked him through the halls of the asylum, strutting resplendent in finery sewn from the pelt of his scalped and still-dying hope. And now it pounced on his chest, and its weight was the weight of all things, and its claws parted bone as easily as air, and he writhed like a mouse in an eagle's talons until the vessel of steam and suffering capsized and spilled him to the floor.

He lay there for a quantity of seconds too numerous and hazy-rimmed to count, a rain-sodden watercolor of time, until his eyes happened upon the cabinet still on its perch, and he wondered how he could have fallen with such violence yet left it precisely where it had always been. He tried to stand and couldn't, wondered why, and found he was already standing. The transition was instant, a flipbook with only two pages. He staggered, reached for the cabinet to catch himself, and fell clean through it.

The floor, at least, remained solid. He turned onto his back and stared upwards at the cabinet's smooth pine undercarriage. A brass plate affixed to the wood read *Made in United States, 1939.* The words centered him somehow. Such a prosaic detail seemed out of place in a hallucination. He tried standing again, this time keeping careful track of his every movement. His body worked as it always had, but the air around it was slipperier, its resistance vanished. He felt like a man who'd spent a lifetime in manacles suddenly cut loose, his unfettered limbs clumsy with unfamiliar freedom. It was a sensation so odd that he forgot for a moment how he'd managed to fall through a solid object just moments before, an occurrence that only returned to his mind after he ducked to keep from banging his head as he crawled free.

As he examined the cabinet, he realized that it wasn't empty. A figure lay where he had moments before, a man of his stature but with features blurred beyond recognition, edges warping and flickering like the corona of a distant star. A second figure sat on a wooden chair he'd originally taken as empty. It bore the same indistinct smudginess as the figure in the cabinet, but the size of its frame and the color of its outfit pegged it as the nurse who'd been overseeing his treatment. He reached out and touched the apparition's shoulder. His fingers passed through it as if it were mist.

A peculiar hum emanated from the wall nearest the hallway. Roland approached it, drawn and afraid by turns, and laid his hand against the wall. Like the floor, it was tangible. Roland assumed this meant he hadn't died and left his body as a phantom, and wondered why he felt comfortable making this assumption. Surely there were rules for such things, and the living had no cause to understand them. His hand found the doorknob—also billowing its strange mist-sound, also tangible—and turned. The door opened and Roland stepped out of the fever cabinet room and into hell.

A great abscess of stone and fire devoured the building's interior, a multicameral twining of caverns and cliffs ballooned to impossible size. Such a vast abyss shouldn't have fit in ten asylums, yet here it was crammed into one. Rivers of molten fluid sludged along channels hewn in blackened bedrock and poured into a vast lake whose churning waters spumed a reek of blood and sulfur into the sticky, humid air. The heavy stink of it settled on Roland's tongue and packed his nostrils until he gagged.

The place was bad, a nightmare made manifest, but worse than the setting were the people who populated it. They hung from iron chains bolted into stone walls, quivered in cages, writhed in metal confinements forged with a twinned passion for innovation and cruelty. The sound of their lamentations rang off the cavern's vaulted ceiling and raked Roland's ears with the incessancy of unoiled machinery. He staggered back, hands clamped over his ears, and leaned against the wall to keep from collapsing.

A shrill note pierced the air, cutting through the moans and wailing as if it were nothing but quiet chatter. The waters around the edge of the molten lake distended and hulking grey figures emerged from its depths. They shrugged the liquid from their massive shoulders and strode ashore, their toeless feet flared like the crude base of Doric pillars. Seen from the back they appeared headless, though as they turned Roland spotted hunched projections jutting from their chests Their faces were dull and featureless, the sort of half-images one saw in random assortments of rocks or clouds. Only their eyes, flecks of onyx deep-set in boreholes, betrayed signs of sentience.

The golems each carried with them an apparatus resembling a long-necked bellows, which they manipulated with a dexterity belied by their great bulk—Roland was not a small man, but two of him stood shoulder to shoulder would not match the breadth of a single creature. Striding up to a man strung chained to a nearby boulder, the golem thrust the tip of the bellows into his mouth and drew forth a cloud of some vital essence. The man struggled as the operation began, but it was over in a few seconds and left him half-conscious and pale, blood dribbling from his lips. The golem trundled over to a large capsule and sprayed the bellow's contents into it through a rubber aperture. The capsule, a seamless ovoid of polished silver metal, rested on tracks that led along the bank of a molten river into the becraggled distance.

More golems followed the first, and soon the capsule was evidently full, for two golems took crouching stances and with their immense shoulders forced the container along its track. Their pace was slow but relentless. Despite his horror, Roland couldn't help but feel a grim fascination at the exhibition of this strange industry. What were they taking from those poor souls? And where were they taking it?

One of the golems swiveled its upper body until its cantilevered head jutted in Roland's direction. It raised a knobbled finger at him and issued a low, rumbling hoot. Others followed its gesture and soon a small crowd gazed up as one at Roland, who recoiled from the exposed edge and crouched against the wall out of sight.

For a moment terror pinned him in place, rationalizing that it was best to stay low lest he be spotted again. But in his heart Roland knew this was ridiculous. There was no denying the creature had spotted him, and whether the sounds it made were language or merely grunts, it had made its discovery to the others clear. Staying put would accomplish nothing. He forced himself to his feet and, keeping one shoulder tight to the plaster-walled remnants of the asylum, ran down the hallway in search of escape. The sensation of plaster against his fingertips grounded him. Without it, it would be too easy to dismiss the whole thing as another hallucination—a proposition he couldn't accept, no matter how much he wished it to be so.

Thunder scaled the wood-and-plaster cliff-face of the asylum, and soon a pack of golems had reached Roland's ledge. They moved with a heavy, lumbering stride whose individual motions seemed slow, even ponderous, but added up to a relentless pace that human legs couldn't match. Roland learned this lesson too late, as he found himself pincered by golems on both sides. He dove for the nearest door, yanked it open, and hurled himself inside.

The room was dim and brooding, its vast window emitting no light, its ornate desk and expansive bookshelf lending no opulence. Everything about it was slightly off, as if some sloppy accounting had shortchanged its angles a couple of degrees, small deficits that aggregated into a lopsided whole. Dread wafted from its walls, chilling Roland in a bone-deep way even the golems hadn't managed. He didn't like this room, and the fact he couldn't say why made it even worse. Yet there was no leaving the way he'd come, so his only choice was to find an alternate exit.

He dashed to the window, ready to hurl himself through the glass if he couldn't pry up the sash, but stopped when he witnessed what lay beyond. He'd held no hopes of seeing the landscaped grounds of the asylum, and would have ventured once more into the hellish caverns he'd just escaped, where hopefully he could seek a quiet spot to hide. But the realm opposite the glass was neither earth nor hell, but a smeary blankness that contained nothing at all. Its emptiness was so absolute that for an instant Roland perceived it as a flat and featureless barrier, but even a brief glance revealed the undeniable yawping madness of its depth. The plain wasn't simply vast; it was infinite.

Roland backed away from the window, hands raised in an appeasing gesture, as if the eternal nothing beyond the glass had eyes and had noticed him. He pressed his shoulder against the walls, hoping for a return to his intangibility, but none gave any sign of yielding. In desperation he tried yanking books off shelves in the fevered hope that a false one might trigger the release of a hidden door—he'd seen as much in movies, and it was all he had left. But while the backing on the bookshelves remained as solid as the walls, the books slipped like fog through his fingers. He groped at the stack, seeking anything that might help him, and dislodged a single volume. It fell to the floor with a thump and spread open.

The words squiggled and bled before his eyes, wriggling with the restless illegibility of text in dreams. He picked it up and squinted at its contents, but no amount of concentration could hold them in place. He shut the book and noticed the green glow emanating from its jacket. It grew in intensity as he watched, forming an emerald corona that baptized his hands in cold ethereal light. He stared at the object, transfixed, until a golem thrust its fist through the door behind him.

Splinters of wood showered the room's grey carpet. The sharp crack of the door's destruction was followed by the low, pained grinding of the jamb against the golem's intruding shoulders. Its bulk strained against the narrow aperture, rending hanks of wood and plaster from the frame. Cracks spread across the wall, thickening as the golem forced its way farther and farther inside. One shoulder burst through with a triumphant roar of shattered lumber. The second would follow soon.

Roland watched the beast approach, book clutched to his chest. He had no weapon to defend himself with, and nothing in his imagining could stand against such a foe anyway. He swallowed a hard lump of fear and waited for the doorway, its rectangular shape already contorted into a squat ovoid by repeated pounding, to yield altogether.

A cable of cold white steel cinched tight around the ridge of bone between Roland's eye sockets. He felt a moment's itchy discomfort before the cable retracted and yanked him forward. The book flew from his stunned fingers. His feet left the carpet and he was soaring, first at the golem and then through it, and finally into a howling vortex from which no light shone.

***

The cot sagged in the middle and the covers itched where they touched bare skin, but the quiet was nice. Roland lay with hands folded across his stomach and savored it as best he could. A few moments passed pleasantly, but images of chain-bound serfs and hulking golems skulked in from the periphery of his vision, filling the room with their phantom forms and etching their ghastly moans on the silence. He shut his eyes, plugged his ears, and muttered his mantra to better block out the nonexistent noise: *"Es ist nicht echt, es ist nicht echt."* The visions faded, sinking back into the mire of whatever realm had birthed them. Roland sighed and tossed his head back against the pillow.

He'd lost consciousness shortly after being seized by whatever force propelled him from the golem's grasp, and it took a while for him to piece together what exactly had happened to him—or, rather, what outside observers said happened to him. The fever cabinet had affected him more acutely than anticipated, triggering an epileptic fit that resulted in the abrupt cancellation of his treatment. Post-treatment observation—completed in a dimly lit but tidy infirmary tucked into an annex at the back of the hospital, as if in afterthought—revealed no obvious cause or trauma. As an explanation, it made sense, and he took it as true.

But the vision remained, stubborn as a greasy thumbprint on an otherwise flawless photograph. He'd expected it to dissolve with time, crumbling in the daylight with the volatility of dreams. But unlike the delusions that had landed him in this place, which he could recall only as blurry snapshots robbed of their import, his recollection of the asylum's hellish abscess had sharpened with time. It seemed almost that he could see the place in his mind's eye with more detail now than he could when he was there in the flesh—or the mind, or the spirit, or through whatever impossible means he had been so transported. He could count the pebbles littering the cliff edge atop which he'd studied the horrors below, map with exactitude every bend and swell of the roiling river, decant from its stink the precise molecules of sweat and blood and sulfur. He saw it every time he closed his eyes, and the image lingered upon opening, a phantasmal overlay of the sort that over-bright lights branded on unshielded pupils.

The vision nagged at him, posing conundrums that his fever-bruised mind had neither the energy nor inclination to ponder, but toiled at anyway as if marshalled into action at gunpoint. His body didn't leave the fever cabinet until Martha aborted the treatment. And yet he, by his own recollection, had. The only explanation was that he had left his body, but that was no explanation at all. Roland was a Christian, not a spiritualist. He believed in the soul, but as a facet of one's humanity that could not split from the body until death. That one might send it on its own temporary voyage like some astral emissary was not only ludicrous, but sacrilegious. If he set such heretical explanations aside, the only logical conclusion was that he'd hallucinated the whole thing.

But then how had he known about the plate under the cabinet? There's no way he could have seen it on his way into the room. It wasn't until afterward that he'd been in any position to glimpse even briefly at its underside. Yet he recalled with absolute clarity.

A dour nurse of indeterminate age oversaw care in the infirmary. Unlike the other nurses, who flitted from place to place and job to job as necessity dictated, she made the infirmary the sum and total of her domain, venturing from it only on short missions to demand more resources. She treated her patients without warmth, but with a grim efficiency that Roland couldn't help but respect, even as she jabbed a thermometer under his tongue and frowned in silence at the results.

"Normal. That's 24 hours' observation. You can go."

"I am still feeling a little bit dizzy. May I please rest a bit longer?"

"Tremblay said 24 hours, you got 24 hours. Other folks need these beds too. This ain't a hotel."

Not a prosperous one anyway, thought Roland, eyeing the several empty cots nearby. He said nothing of the kind, as he suspected this nurse would not be above calling in orderlies to drag away any patient foolish enough to go against her edicts.

After being discharged from the infirmary—though "evicted" seemed a more accurate description—Roland muddled his way back to Wing B. He found it strange how much freedom patients had to wander within the facility. All exits were carefully guarded, and trips outside were all but forbidden, but within the confines of the building itself, there was little supervision. Such a level of trust was refreshing, though Roland suspected it had more to do with the asylum's limited manpower than anything. When you have one orderly for every seventy-five patients, your policing of movement can't be all that expansive.

He found Harvey at his usual place, chatting with a cheerfully demented woman about her past life as Mata Hari.

"You still got it, honey," he said, flashing a smile. "I don't care what those fancy doctors say."

The woman giggled, twirling a lock of matted hair around a boney finger. "They had to change my looks, acourse, after they smuggled me out. Not even the prime minister knows the truth. He did, he'd be keen to crack open my head and feast on the secrets I've got in there. I could tell you a thing or two, believe you me."

Roland stood politely by and waited for her to finish her monologue, after which she tottered over to another table. Harvey glanced at Roland as she left, shooting him a sly grin.

"It is not so kind, I think, to feed her delusions like that," Roland said.

"What d'you think she'd rather hear? That she's a shriveled up old prune and ain't ever to see the kind side of her twenties again? There ain't no kindness in honesty of that sort, friend."

"The truth is always best."

Harvey shook his head. "You're a good egg, friend. Most fools are. Say, what happened to you anyhow? I heard tell you had to spend a hot minute in the infirmary."

"Yes, there was some trouble with my treatment. I had a...bad reaction."

"Don't blame you for that. Those hothouses are no joke. You're lucky, maybe they'll push your next go back a few more days."

"My next go?" During his recovery, Roland's thoughts had been so focused on the visions themselves that they'd leapt over the event that caused them. Would his second stint in the fever cabinet send him back to that place? He turned to Harvey, burying his fear as best he could. "How many such treatments does a patient usually get?"

Harvey shrugged. "I'm no expert on it, but I recall a fella 'bout your age a few years back went through I think six or seven goes before they discharged him."

"And they worked?"

"They discharged him, didn't they? It ain't like the high and mighties here ever make a mistake." Harvey chuckled at this.

Six or seven. Roland contemplated six or seven encounters with the hellscape carved into the asylum's interior, six or seven tussles with the golems and their nightmarish bellows, six or seven serenades by the unholy choir of suffering that rose from those depths of fire and stone, and recoiled like a man who'd toed the crumbly edge of a vast and yawning abyss and looked down. Such a fusillade of encounters would surely be fatal—if not physically, then to his mind and spirit, which could endure such torture no more than his body could withstand being crushed by a ten-ton block of iron.

"I do not wish to do this, Harvey. What can I do to stop it?"

Harvey barked a single hard laugh. "Friend, you'd just as soon try and turn back the tide. Verloc ain't one for taking orders from patients. We ain't his customers, we're his charges, and his say-so is law."

"But perhaps he would reconsider."

Harvey fixed Roland with a pitying look. When he next spoke, his tone had softened, though the message relinquished nothing. "Verloc ain't a man known for reconsidering. Once he gives a diagnosis, it's the Lord's truth, far as he's concerned. Being second guessed by a patient—one sent up here by the courts, no less—ain't gonna sit well with him. Sorry, friend. T'ain't fair, but nothing in this place is." Harvey's eyes snapped to the left. His face darkened. "Case in point."

Roland followed Harvey's gaze to the doorway, where Fox and his compatriots slouched in. They seemed always to be together. One would think that in an institution as understaffed as this one, the orderlies would be distributed as widely as possible, but the trio moved as if conjoined, and yet scarcely performed more work than a single person. The biggest of the three dragged a mop behind him in a wheeled bucket, its casters squeaking. Fox carried a broom, but he held it down near the bristles and swung the pole swordlike in front of him, as if he'd never seen how such a tool was actually used and had no inclination to learn. He spotted Roland and swatted the larger man with the broom handle to get his attention.

"Well, lookee here, if it ain't the Kaiser. Heard you were all dinged up in the infirmary. But, since you're better, I've got something for you. Hey, Pluck, hand the mop over to Jerry here."

Pluck stepped forward, dragging the mop behind him. The squeal of the casters on their ungreased axles seemed amplified against the tile floor. He stood in front of Roland and extended the mop handle to him. His lips widened into a grin that fit strangely on his face—it wasn't that it seemed phony, so much as that his face was one unsuited to large displays of emotions, its heavy features moving with the sluggish reluctance of tectonic plates.

"Hang on a minute," said Harvey. "This fellow is your patient, not your employee. Best I recall, mop and bucket duties are for orderlies only. That means you and tall, dark, and handsome over there."

"Institute policy, old timer. Occupational Therapy. Just cause your wrinkled ass is too broken down to benefit, don't mean Jerry here shouldn't be given the chance."

"Call it what you want, it looks a lot like shirkin' to me. And I don't recall you bein' fit to prescribe treatment."

Fox fixed Harvey with a sour smile. "And it looks to me like you're in the wrong wing. Shouldn't you be slurpin' up tapioca in C with the other geezers?"

"It's a common area, junior. Thought you'd understand that well enough, bein' the very definitions of common yourself."

"Real funny, wise guy. But I ain't talking to you." Fox turned his attention to Roland. "Pluck, give him the mop."

Roland looked from Pluck, to Fox, to MacCruiskeen, and back to Pluck. All three stood frozen, eyes locked on his, awaiting his acquiescence. They made no outward threat, but refusal didn't seem like an option. Cringing at his cowardice, Roland reached for the mop.

Harvey grabbed him by the wrist. His grip was firm and unexpectedly strong.

"You don't gotta do that, friend. You give an inch here, they'll have you wipin' their heinies and shakin' their peckers dry after they piss before long. Lord knows they could use the help, but you ain't the man for it, all I'm saying."

"Stay out of this, old man," said Fox. "This ain't none of your business."

"You don't know a damn thing about my business, son. All I see here's a few young bucks tryin' to finagle their way out of a bit of honest labour—labour my tax dollars pays for, no less."

Pluck yanked Roland's arm from Harvey's grip and settled his hand on the mop's handle. Roland felt the smooth grain of the wood against his palm. His fingers tensed instinctively around it, loosened, and shoved the mop back.

"I will work if asked," he said. "But not by you."

Harvey clapped Roland on the back. "Attaboy. Sorry, fellas, looks like you'll be swabbin' the deck your own selves. I'm sure a trio a' clever boys like you'll figure it out eventually."

The last drops of humor wrung free of Fox's face, leaving a dry and bitter mask that glared at Harvey. He stepped forward, pushing Pluck aside, and grabbed him by the scruff of his shirt. Harvey stared back at him, unimpressed by this show of force.

"You gonna hit an old man, out here, in the open? You go ahead and try. I know Verloc keeps you around cause every young fella with enough brains to work a broom got scooped up in the war. But you're out here bouncin' between the guard rails like they ain't never gonna break. Might be you wanna get your goings a little smoother, though, 'cause those things only hold until they don't, and after they bust loose it's a mighty long fall."

Fox weighed these words, gave a final yank on Harvey's shirt, and shoved the old man away. His wheelchair listed on its left wheel, but Roland caught the handles and righted it before it toppled. Fox snapped his fingers and the other two skulked off behind him, the mop bucket marking their passage with a prolonged squeal of its casters.

"Do you think it was wise, speaking to those men in such a way?" asked Roland.

"Don't care," answered Harvey. "Felt good. At my age, that's about all you can ask for. But returnin' to your questions 'bout your treatment, you ever thought a' asking the nurse what saw you have your fit to weigh in? No way Verloc's gonna heed a patient, but a nurse might maybe have half a chance."

The sudden shift in topic threw Roland off balance, and he struggled to catch up. "I... Yes, this is a good idea. Thank you, Harvey. I mean not just for the advice, but for your support with...them."

Harvey waved the thanks away. "Please, I ain't about to let those knuckleheads go about pretendin' like they run the show. The thing you always got to remember is: this is our home. It ain't theirs."

Roland thought over Harvey's words long after their conversation was over. He realized that the older man was right: this *was* his home, for now at least, and if he was going to live here, he might as well try to make the situation as bearable as possible. Whether a vivid hallucination or something stranger, the visions brought on by the fever cabinet were not something he could endure more than a few times without going mad. He would need to do whatever he could to get them stopped. So resolved, he left the common area in search of Nurse Donnelly.

6

THE FOOD CART jerked and zigzagged, its pitted wheels locking against their axles and catching on the grouted border of every tile. Cups of watery orange juice sloshed over their brims, dampening the crusts of the ham sandwiches stacked nearest the drink tray. Martha settled the cart in a location roughly central in the common room, engaged the brake with her heel—as if such a cumbersome thing could roll anywhere on its own—and opted to circulate the food tray by tray.

Over the weeks, she had settled into the routine of food delivery, and developed a good knowledge of which patients could order from the set menu—consisting today of ham sandwich, egg sandwich, and tapioca—and which lacked that capacity, of those who could handle solid food and those who required a special nutritionally enhanced porridge—despite, in some cases, their protestations to the contrary. She handled each exchange with a pleasant smile, shrugged off the insults of the demented, and calmed frayed nerves with a few words in an exaggerated rendition of her Irish brogue, which she found had unexpected sedative effects on most patients.

Near the end of her rounds in the geriatric ward, Martha realized that she hadn't encountered Mrs. Chauncey. This was strange, as the older woman was relentlessly social and scarcely found anywhere but in the common areas. Martha wondered if she might have taken ill. She resolved to check the dorms after she'd finished handing out lunch when Roland approached her. A worried, awkward look hung about his eyes, dragging his gaze downward where it skittered among the dust motes and smudges marring the tiles.

"Nurse Donnelly, I'm afraid I must ask a favor of you. I am worried about my next treatment. I do not wish for the same thing that happened last time to happen again."

"Yes, of course. I don't blame you for an instant, Mr. Hellmich. That was awful, and I'm terribly sorry it happened. I've spoken with the head nurse since to explore what might've been the cause, and we've come up with some guidelines to reduce the risk of another febrile seizure. If you'd like, I'd be happy to go over it with you during your next session."

Martha hoped the suggestion would bring him some relief, but if anything the anguish on his face only deepened. He ground his slippered toe against the floor. "I appreciate this offer, nurse. But it would please me more if there were a way for me to not have the treatment at all."

Martha bit the corner of her mouth. "I'm sorry, I really don't get much say at all in the sort of treatment you receive. All of that is decided by Dr. Verloc. I issued a report to him explaining your reaction, but nothing he's sent back suggests he wants treatment stopped. And unless he explicitly changes his recommendation, there's nothing I can do."

"I understand. But perhaps if you spoke to him..."

Martha paused a moment, hoping to stumble across a polite but unambiguous way to tell Roland what he certainly didn't want to hear: that Dr. Verloc probably hadn't even read the report, and any negative result short of death wasn't going to change the man's prognosis. She hadn't been working at Walpole for all that long, but a few weeks' observation was enough to glean that Arnold Verloc was not the sort of man to be swayed by his subordinates.

She opened her mouth to speak, still uncertain of what to say but aware that every moment of delay sank a dagger of hope a little deeper into Roland's belly, but before she began she registered the look of hollow-eyed terror that haunted his face. Before her stood a man whose fear seemed to go deeper than simply squeamishness over an unpleasant procedure. His was the look of a hunted mouse in a naked field, frozen in the instant before an owl swoops down and nabs it. Martha's teeth resumed their contemplative gnawing on the side of her cheek.

"I can't make any promises," she ventured. "But I suppose, since he never responded to the report, it couldn't hurt to ask. Just to confirm his stance."

The owl soared by, its shadow passing, its eyes locked on other prey. Roland relaxed, his hunkered shoulders unfolding. "I would be most grateful if you would do so," he said.

We'll see how long that lasts, Martha thought, *once Verloc gets through with us.*

***

"I must really stress to you, Mr. Hellmich, how unlikely it is that this will work," the head nurse said. She stood before the closed door, one hand raised to knock, the other performing minute adjustments to the hem of her dress. "Dr. Verloc, he is not one for changing his mind, and he believes most strongly in the fever cabinet as a treatment. It was, after all, very expensive for the institute to purchase."

"I understand this," said Roland. "And I thank you all the same for trying." He said this looking first to the head nurse and then to Nurse Donnelly, who stood to his left and answered him with a shy smile.

The head nurse pursed her lips and nodded. It was clear to Roland that she found the proposed meeting pointless, perhaps even counterproductive, but she did not disagree and, apart from the reluctance she couldn't help but telegraph, she made no sign of resentment or annoyance about it. Roland wasn't sure whether she was doing it for him or simply on Nurse Donnelly's request, but in either case he was grateful.

With a final huff of indrawn breath, the head nurse rapped her knuckles against the door. The sound echoed down the empty hall, carrying a finality that Roland found unnerving. A muffled voice called for entry. The head nurse heeded it and stepped inside, Roland and Nurse Donnelly behind her.

Dr. Verloc's office loomed over Roland with a heavy atmosphere belied by its simple furnishings. The room wasn't actually his main office, but a mere satellite situated in the public ward. It had functioned as the director's main office at the time of Walpole's founding, but once the newer and more opulent private ward was built, the director and his secretarial staff moved there. The old office remained, but was used only intermittently, and served as much to store old documents as it did for actual paperwork. Consequently, nothing inside was designed to impress or intimidate. The desk was little more than a table, a slab of pine with fluted legs, a shallow undercarriage that housed drawers, and a skirting of thin panels to hide the occupant's legs from passersby. The chairs were upholstered in mismatched fabrics, the stitching loose in spots. The window was a simple mullioned foursquare, bereft of the sweeping glass or panoramic views of more stately offices. Only the bookshelf was at all impressive, and that was more from volume than quality. Row upon row of leather-bound tomes ran the room's modest length, their titles branded in a gold print that was intended to imply opulence but wound up all but illegible in the room's dim light.

And yet as Roland followed the two nurses inside, he felt as if he'd stepped into a chamber of sinister grandeur, the axis on which some vast and horrid mechanism spun. He chalked this up at first to the man behind the desk, who peered over his glasses at the trio of interlopers standing opposite him with a look of undisguised impatience. Certainly Verloc's countenance was not one that inspired welcome. But the feeling flowed over the man, rather than from him, a constant presence niggling at the back of Roland's neck. He would have turned around and left without another word, had his two reluctant companions not come solely on his behalf.

"Ah yes, Head Nurse Tremblay. You wished to speak with me?" Verloc's tone was no more cordial than his expression. His gaze returned to the document on his desk before he'd even finished speaking. The head nurse answered, undeterred.

"*Oui*, Doctor. There is a matter concerning Mr. Hellmich's treatment. As you may recall, he reacted badly to the fever cabinet. A febrile seizure."

"Yes, such incidents can occur when the patient is inadequately monitored. A more stringent approach should rectify the issue."

"Perhaps. But it is also not unheard of for some patients to be more susceptible to these seizures, particularly if they had them often as children. In such a case, it could be that continued treatment poses danger for the patient."

Verloc twiddled a pen between his thumb and forefinger. "Interesting. And you're basing this conclusion on the results of your personal research?"

The head nurse lowered her gaze. "No, Doctor."

"But you *have* read extensively on the matter? Peer-reviewed studies assessing the risk posed by fever treatment on a subset of neurosyphilis patients with histories of febrile seizure?"

"No, Doctor."

"Really? Then what, precisely, are you basing this recommendation on, nurse?"

"Only my observations, Doctor."

Verloc fixed her with a heavy-lidded smile. "Your observations. You are a skilled manager and clinician, Nurse Tremblay, and I do not doubt that your years of experience afford you a certain level of confidence that approaches, in some select areas, that of a qualified medical resident. But unlike you, I have studied the latest research on psychiatric therapy, and have come to the conclusion that fever treatment is the most effective approach for patients with Mr. Hellmich's condition. I thank you for your input, but in the future please leave the diagnosis to qualified professionals."

"Yes, Doctor."

"Good," said Verloc. He resumed his paperwork. "You may see yourselves out."

Arms at her sides, the head nurse motioned for Nurse Donnelly and Roland to leave with a small fanning motion of her hand. Roland tried to signal an apology to both women, but their eyes were elsewhere and he could only shrug helplessly at the discomfort he'd imposed on them—all of it completely pointless, it would seem. He turned to leave when a glimmer of emerald light caught his eye. It flickered on one of the lower shelves behind Verloc, its source a slim green volume that appeared out of place with the other denser tomes. Roland's gaze struck it like a match to a fuse, and its fluttering luminescence soon exploded in a fireball of green light. Beneath its unflinching emerald glare, the room transformed, its shadows realigning into the misangled chamber in which he'd sought refuge from the golems. Roland's knees unlocked at the discovery, sending him reeling to the side. A swift grab for the doorjamb just barely kept him aloft. Verloc watched his near collapse with disdain.

"Nurse Tremblay," he said. "Kindly bring your patient back to the ward, as he appears incapable of doing so himself. I've no further need to examine him, nor am I especially interested in his company."

"*Es tut mir leid*," Roland muttered. Once to Verloc, who eyed him the way one might an insect squirming within sight of one's dinner, and again, with more sincerity, to the head nurse and Nurse Donnelly, who helped him from the room and settled the door softly shut behind them.

"I'm sorry about that, Eloise," said Nurse Donnelly. "That was...unpleasant."

"No worse than expected," the head nurse answered. "I'm sorry, Mr. Hellmich, but there is nothing more we can do. All decisions on your treatment fall to Dr. Verloc, and as you were involuntarily committed, you have no recourse to lodge a complaint."

"I understand. Thank you for trying. I am sorry you had to go through that for nothing."

The head nurse waved the apology away. "I have thick skin. Dr. Verloc's barbs ceased to prick me long ago. Nurse Donnelly, could you show Mr. Hellmich back to the ward? I must attend to some paperwork."

"Right away, ma'am."

They walked silently for a time, accompanied only by the syncopated clatter of their footsteps. After a minute or so, she spoke, prefacing her comment with a surreptitious glance over her shoulder.

"He'd no right to speak to you that way."

"It is fine. It is much as Missus Tremblay said. I too have gained a thick skin over the years."

She shook her head. "That's not the point. You're a patient here, and patients should always be treated with respect. That's how I was taught, anyway."

"Would that all doctors thought as you do."

"I'm a far cry from a doctor." The nurse passed the comment off with a chuckle, but beneath the levity Roland sensed a deep wound, the kind that scabs over but never truly closes. He stopped walking and took her hand in his.

"A doctor is a person who seeks to heal others. In this, the word fits you far better than him." This said, he released her hand and continued walking, lest she think his announcement preceded some additional urge. Her footsteps resumed after a couple of seconds, increasing their tempo to catch up. She reached his side and kept pace, but the two resumed their earlier silence. Roland didn't mind. His thoughts had turned to Verloc's office, and the glowing book on his bottom shelf.

***

The lid of the fever cabinet shut with a slow and ponderous thud. A waft of damp air gusted across Martha's face, carrying the faint sour odor of human sweat. She fastened the clasps binding the lid to the casing, feeling as she did more like a jailer than a nurse. It was hardly surprising that the cabinet's design favored utility over aesthetics, but could its makers not have made it look just a *little* less like an instrument of torture?

By the look of it, Roland's thoughts lay along similar lines. He stared upward, face set with the grim resolve of a man contemplating a barefoot walk across burning coals. Martha checked the dials and readied the machine, but paused before releasing the steam through its metallic innards.

"Before we begin, I just wanted to let you know, we'll be going about things more gradually this time round. I'm to take your temperature at ten-minute intervals, and ensure we gain no more than one degree every half hour. I'll keep close watch on your pulse as well. I intend to see to it that we don't have any repeats of last time."

"Thank you," Roland said, though any comfort he may have taken from her words did not show on his face.

"I don't blame you in the least for your reluctance, Mr. Hellmich. Why, after your episode—"

"It is not having another fit that worries me, nurse."

Martha didn't expect this response. "It's some other effect that worries you, then?"

A look of pained indecision darkened Roland's face. Over her years in nursing, Martha had grown adept at guessing a patient's thoughts from their looks and gestures, and it was clear to her that Roland was holding onto words he both did and didn't want to say. She read it in the downcast wrinkles at the corner of his mouth, the uneasy seesaw of his floor-bound gaze, the nervous tug of lower lip between eye teeth. She saw these things and waited, knowing that the pressure would build on its own, and any efforts to extract it prematurely would only tamp it down.

"Something happened to me, in my first treatment. It...awakened something in me. Something that had already been stirring." He swallowed, mouth working a few silent syllables before venturing on. "It is as if there is a door in my mind that was long left shut. In the past few months, it has opened a crack, but the fever cabinet threw it open all the way. Through it I saw things, troubling things. Things I do not wish to see again."

"I understand," said Martha. "Hallucinations during a fever state are fairly common, and I know they can be very upsetting. I think the approach we're taking—"

"These were not hallucinations. They were something else, something...deeper."

"Meaning no disrespect, Mr. Hellmich, but the hallu— *visions* you speak of are the reason you're here with me today. They're the sickness we're trying to treat. Blaming them on the fever cabinet would be a bit like blaming aspirin for a headache."

"I suppose I cannot expect you to think otherwise. But is there no room in your reasoning for things that science cannot explain? For psychic phenomena, out of body experiences?"

"I would pay little heed to the psychics," Martha said. "And hallucinations can take many forms, including the one you describe. Just because one feels different from the others doesn't mean it has a different source."

Roland shook his head, his frustration bubbling upward. "But there is a difference. I know this, because my earlier visions, they all spoke to...to a dark time in my life. They were memories given flesh."

"Perhaps it would help to share them with me, then."

"It is painful to speak of," replied Roland. "I do not wish to relive it."

"That's your decision, of course. But it sounds to me like you relive it an awful lot anyway. Perhaps speaking these memories aloud will clear them from your head for a time. You've naught to fear from me. I've no cause to go reporting what you say."

Roland closed his eyes. Martha couldn't tell if he was reflecting on her words, or choosing merely to ignore her. She thought about probing him again when he spoke.

"Have you lived through a war, Nurse Donnelly?"

"Aye. As a wee girl I saw the Civil War, though I admit it didn't touch me much. Lean times at supper, but the fighting was mostly far away. And I was neither soldier nor battlefield nurse, so I've not your experience."

"Then let me tell you a secret. Much of who wins a war is up to luck. This is a truth the generals will never speak, as it makes scrap of their fancy medals, but it is true. A war is won by luck and numbers, and the winner is he who can bear the most bad luck without breaking.

"By the summer of '18, there had been much bad luck in Germany, and every man and boy on the ground knew it. Oh, we'd had our *Kaiserschlacht,* but none I knew believed it would last. America stood against us now, and from all we heard the might of the New World could not be matched.

"In the closing days of a war, a man's mind goes one of two ways. Some feel only despair, and will do whatever they can to stay far from the front. Desertion, malingering, falling back at the start of every charge. It is not just death they fear, for death was always there about us, but death in the war's last days. I saw men who had rushed headlong against enemy guns without a thought that spring freeze in terror come the fall, when all seemed over but the fighting and every man dreaded catching the final bullet of a four-year war.

"But there are others who seek glory with the same lust as the first man's fear, who do not dread death at all, but a homecoming without enough medals on their chests. The commander of our *Zug* was the second type. *Oberleutnant* Wilhelm von Schober, a young Junker from a military family. For him, victory was as much a birthright as his land and his riches, and for a time it looked as if he were about to inherit it.

"The Americans had not yet arrived in large numbers, and British forces were spread thin. Across a hundred and fifty meters of mud and barbed wire sat a British trench with only a single machine gun nest to guard it. One nest with two gunners was enough to stop our charge, but if the guns were gone, the Tommies would be helpless. It was just one trench among thousands, no better or worse than any other, but to my commander it was the very heart of the British Empire, and seizing it would kill the beast that had plagued his country for half a decade. To do it, he needed only one man with a grenade and an arm to throw it. That man, he decided, was me.

"The plan was very simple. In the dark of night, I would sneak beneath the barbed wire and crawl up to the nest. I would toss a grenade inside, killing the gunners and destroying the guns. The others would charge the very next instant, before the British could fix their post, and swarm the trench. I had done such creeping-crawling work before, though never did an entire attack rest on my shoulders. Still, I was young, and more aligned with Herr von Schober's views than many of my brothers. I pictured the medal I would receive, the stories I could tell when I returned home, how I had taken an enemy bunker single-handed. For a young machinist's son, such glory was a path to bigger things, and I craved it.

"The night was cloudy and cold, colder than a summer should be. The mud stiffened into clumps, which made passing over it easier but more painful. I can still feel the hard clods digging into my knees as I crawled, inch by inch, through cratered earth. Bodies lay half-buried in the mud, the smell of them dampened by the cold but still putrid. No matter how tight I shut my mouth, the dirt still got inside. It had a copper taste which I knew to come from blood.

"I moved slow, as I was trained to do, every motion carefully planned. It is only when you try this that you realize how much of what we do is done without thinking. To walk across a room, to grab a glass and drink, it seems a simple thing, just so and done. But there are a hundred motions inside each action, all of them the work of many muscles together, and on that night, each was its own private task. I crossed in two hours a span I could have walked in two minutes. When I reached my position, I felt as if I'd scaled a mountain.

"The machine gun nest was to my right. Two meters or so, maybe less. Close enough to see the stitching on the sandbags, to hear the heavy breath of the gunners at their perch. I looked back the way I'd come, afraid I would spot some sign of my passage, pleased when I could not. The men in my *Zug* appeared to be on active guard, the position of their sentries no different than any other day. In truth, I knew that every man was crouched in secret behind the outermost rampart, ready to leap up and attack the moment they heard the explosion of my grenade.

"During my crossing, I was not at all nervous, but when I hefted the grenade, I felt that cold nausea of fear building in my belly. The lives of every man in my *Zug* depended on the accuracy of my throw. I'd brought half a dozen grenades, but the first blast was the signal. If it went high or wild, it would take precious moments to prime and toss the second one, if I even survived long enough to do so. A second is an age in the height of battle, and in such a window of time two machine gunners could rip fifty men apart.

"I thought of this and my hands, always steady, began to tremble. Their shaking scared me more than the guns did. I was a soldier, a perfect instrument in the Kaiser's war machine. I performed my work smoothly, with precision. I was not some herky-jerky contraption, full of shaking! Yet the more I told my hand to steady, the worse the shaking became. The tremors crept up my arms and down my legs, and soon my entire body was caught in an endless shiver. Fighting it seemed useless, so I chose instead to wait for it to pass. The men in my *Zug* did not know my exact progress, after all, and a couple of minutes would make no difference to the plan.

"What a terrible price I paid for those two minutes. For in that time, it seemed the British had decided on their own forward charge. It was a desperate bid, as their equipment was meagre, but those months were a desperate time. The first mortar landed a dozen meters to my left—a terrible shot, falling far short of our line, but most unfortunate for me. The blow knocked me senseless, and I awoke some seconds later in a pit of ruined earth. The sound that brought me back was the distant cry of *Oberleutnant* von Schober as he led the charge from our trenches.

"I still wonder if he truly thought the sound he heard was my grenade. They are different noises altogether, a grenade and a mortar shell. Even a novice solider could tell the difference. But von Schober's blood was up, and perhaps he thought it was then or never. Calling off his attack would have been to him unthinkable. Perhaps he assumed the shell masked my own successful attack. In any case, he chose to risk it, and the risk cost him everything.

"The machine gunners were clever men. Even now, I marvel at their calculating calm. They waited until the men of my *Zug* were halfway across the field before opening fire, ensuring no cover or easy return to the safety of the trenches. In stories, it is the screams of dying comrades that stay with you, but I heard no screams, for the machine guns rattling overhead deafened me. The clamor did not last long, perhaps two minutes, and by then it was over. Silence returned, or as near to silence as my ears could gather, for I was half-deaf for some time afterwards.

"The British charge that followed was fast at first, but the Tommies soon learned that anyone who would have resisted them had died in the mud, and their coming grew almost casual. They made no effort to tend to the wounded or identify the dead, for by that time in the war sentiment over such things ran very low, even for one's own men. We had simply seen too many dead bodies for them to remain the totems of mourning that civilians saw in them.

"And so they left me as they did the other bodies, and I made no effort to alert them to my presence. Shrouded in a crater, half buried in mud, I made a most convincing corpse. At some point I became aware of a pain in my side, and realized with some astonishment that I was wounded. Shrapnel from the mortar shell had torn up my side and back. The wounds were puckered but shallow, and the bleeding stopped on its own. Otherwise I would not be here.

"I lay there in the mud and filth for a day, perhaps more. Time was hard to know, but I recall the rise and setting of the sun, and it was not until the following dawn that a contingent of my comrades retook, with considerable effort, what the British had taken a day before with little more than a stroll. It was Germans who found me, at the end of a long battle, and who extracted from me the story of my *Zug*'s destruction—minus, of course, my ignoble role in it all. I cast myself in my telling as one more young soldier in an ill-fated charge. They sent me from the front, and I saw no more of the war.

"No one questioned my story. Why would they? The attack had happened, plain as day, and no one, soldier or civilian, wanted stories of German cowardice. We were all Teutonic warriors, defending the Fatherland against the wily British and barbaric French. I was even decorated for my valor, awarded an Iron Cross. Me, a man who could not even throw a grenade. I kept it in a drawer for many years, until I sold it to help pay for my passage across the ocean. It fetched barely one-tenth the ticket price, which was still more than it was worth..."

Orbs of sweat rolled languid, sticky paths across Roland's forehead, catching on wrinkles and nesting in the bristle-stiff hairs of his eyebrows, pausing on the precipitous ridge of his temples before plunging downward. Martha soaked a cloth in a basin of ice water, wrung out the excess, and dabbed it on Roland's face. The heat of his skin shocked her. Touching him felt like placing a hand on the side of a furnace. She soaked the cloth again and let it settle on his skin still dripping, her fingers working gentle circles over the terry cloth.

"You mustn't hold your actions against yourself. The only true sinners in war are those who start them, knowing it's not their blood that will be spilled. You were just a boy."

"Perhaps. But to my country, to my *Oberleutnant*, to my *Zug*, I was a man. A man they trusted. And I failed."

Once more Martha soaked the cloth and laid it across Roland's forehead. She recognized his words in the men who'd come back from the Civil War—not that they'd spoken, but the meaning fit the folds of their faces, the masks that grief had hammered into place. Countries at war made of men tools to pursue their own ends; should the source metal crack or buckle, such was the cost of pursuing victory. And should the metal escape the forge no weaker than it entered, unscathed but changed to suit a new and violent purpose, little effort was paid on peacetime to bend it back into its previous shape. For there was always fresh ore to be mined in the tenements and country hovels. Is that what she'd be, when the latest war in Europe ended? A frazzled blacksmith hammering rust-eaten swords back into ploughshares?

These thoughts so consumed her that she almost failed to notice as Roland's eyes rolled up into his head. His body tensed, its every cord pulled taut, and fell limp. Martha flew from her chair and pressed the side of his neck, where she felt the butterfly flutter of a pulse against her fingertips. *God take me for a fool, he was right.* The slow, measured increase in the cabinet temperature, the status checks and monitoring, none of it had mattered. *Two know-it-all nurses and a know-it-all doctor, all telling him pretty lies. And he knew better than all of us, and even told us so, for all the good it did.*

A few moments passed and his pulse slowed and strengthened. An ear held to his mouth revealed deep, steady breathing. She left him long enough to cut the flow of steam to the cabinet. Her hands paused over the clasps. Opening the lid would cool him down quicker, but the shock could also do more harm than good. His pulse was fair, and while he'd lost consciousness, the crisis didn't seem acute the way the first one had. She soaked a rag in cold water and bathed his forehead with it, resolving to do so until he woke or turned for the worse, at which point she would need to fetch Nurse Tremblay.

Another sword lay bare on the anvil. She could only pray that the metal held as the fever banged it back into shape.

7

ROLAND'S SECOND DESCENT into hell was more graceful than his first. He passed through the fever cabinet as easily as before, but his short voyage to the ground was less a plummeting than a sinking, the air a buffeting, viscous presence against his back. He moved his arms in expectation of resistance, but found them unencumbered. The floor held firm as before.

He stood up, not bothering on this occasion to crawl out from beneath the cabinet. The feeling of his head passing through solid wood and metal was unpleasant: a jostling of the belly, as if dropped from a great height. There was no physical sensation, however; his discomfort was wholly psychological. Once standing, his waist protruding from the head of the cabinet as if he were some improbable chimera of flesh and wood, he felt no discomfort at all— that was, provided he didn't look down. A glance at his hybrid state opened the floodgates to nausea anew. Closing his eyes, he stepped free of the cabinet, resolving to save such experiments for a later time.

Part of Roland had hoped his peculiar transportation would be a one-time event, but in his heart he hadn't really believed it. Being back here was thus a disappointment, but not an unexpected one, which made it a little easier to handle. He'd thought through what to do if such a situation arose, and decided that the best course was to stay put. He'd eventually returned to the land of the living last time, and there was no reason to think that venturing into the halls expedited the process. If anything, it only put him in greater danger.

He found a comfortable spot and sat down. The wall felt cold and strangely insubstantial against his back, the firm enamel of its tiles gone spongy. The floor had a similar texture. He didn't worry about falling through it, but it yielded to his touch like a crash mat, dimpling where his fingers pressed in. He experimented with this for a while, applying different levels of pressure and drawing figures in its viscous surface. With concentration, he found he could sink his hand in deeper. Lifting a chunk of floor as if it were mud proved impossible though—it passed through his cupped hand on extraction, intangible as mist.

Bemused by his discoveries, Roland looked up and noticed a strange thing: the wall leading to the hallway was growing transparent. He glimpsed figures on its far side as if through a heavy fog, dim shapes that flickered in and out of view. The longer he watched, the more solid they grew. Color drained from the tiles, leaving wan slabs of yellowish glass through which the vaulted nightmare of stone and lava could be seen. He hunkered down, afraid the wall's newfound translucence worked both ways, but a grim fascination kept him from turning away entirely. He watched as the tiny rag-clad figures went about their torment, their anguish met with indifference by the titanic strides of their granite overseers, who only stopped ignoring the captives for the few instances it took them to shove a bellows down their throats and withdraw whatever essence it was they harvested.

An arched doorway led up from the cavernous depths on the far side of the rocky valley, and from its curtained darkness staggered an old woman. She wore the usual asylum attire, its plain-spun cotton stained with dirt and freshly torn in places. A golem loomed behind her, frog-marching her forward with nudges from his enormous outstretched hand. She looked up at Roland, her eyes met his, and the distance between them collapsed like a telescope pressed shut. She was no closer than she had been a moment before, but he saw her as he would someone standing mere inches from his face. Every mole and wrinkle stood in abject clarity before his magnified gaze. He could chart the twitch and tug of muscles beneath her skin, the shift-slide of confused terror into comprehending panic.

"Help me!" she pleaded, and it was as if she'd rammed her lips against his skull and bellowed directly into his ear canal. "Call someone, please! Call my Tobey! Call Nurse Martha! Those boys did something to me and now I'm—"

A shove from one of the golems cut her sentence short. She fell flat, face slamming into an outcrop of stone, and her words dissolved into meaningless wailing. The golem lifted her up and fitted her with chains, moving her this way and that as if trying to fathom the workings of some stubborn appliance. The intimacy of his perception vanished, and she was once again a vague and distant figure, though Roland felt her suffering no less acutely. His hands shook as he pressed them against his chest to better quell the frantic rattle of his heartbeat. She could *see him*. Through walls, across a vast and torrid expanse, she could see him. And if she could see him, there was no reason to think the golems couldn't.

Waiting no longer seemed like such a prudent option. He needed to get free of this place. The only question was how. He circled the fever cabinet, studying the billowing mist-flicker of its edges, the fuzzy insubstantiality with which his fingers passed through its wooden grain. Here stood the vessel that brought him to this place. Was there a way to coax it into bringing him back? *A difficult task, if I can't even touch it.* True, but if a solid wall could morph into putty, perhaps an intangible object could turn solid.

Drawing slow, measured breaths, Roland held his hand over the cabinet, palm down. He lowered it towards the lid, willing his fingers to meet resistance. His fingertips hovered a quarter inch above the grain, shaved the distance to an eighth, a sixteenth. He told himself that the cabinet was a solid, physical object. The distance closed until it was so small that he could not tell by eye whether or not he was touching it. Only feel could guide him, and he felt nothing. He closed his eyes, spread his fingers, and forced every muscle in his hand taut. Tremors of exertion skated from his fingertips to his elbow. He gritted his teeth, inhaled once through his nose, and rammed the heel of his hand downward. It moved less than a millimeter before striking solid wood.

His eyes flew open. He watched his fingers tiptoe along the cabinet's lid, the pads of flesh opposite their nails pressing flat with each step.

He rounded the cabinet to the side with the clasps and flicked them open. They worked exactly as he would have expected in a normal situation, the slight resistance of the springs followed by the loose swing of bronze hinges. Part of him could even have believed that he was standing in the waking world, the cabinet's momentary intangibility a mere figment of his imagination.

The sight that greeted him as the lid swung open convinced him otherwise. For as the one lid swung open, a second, identical lid remained fixed in place. He couldn't budge it, but it didn't much matter since his hands passed clear through it anyway. As he probed the cabinet's strange doppelganger, the wood grew translucent, taking on the same hazy appearance as the walls in the moment when he'd first spotted the old woman. It was as if his effort to open the lid had split its very being in two, the half on his plain swinging open while the half in the waking world remained—figuratively and literally—out of reach. As troubling as this notion was, the contents of the cabinet that he sighted through its lid disturbed him still further.

It was him.

Roland wasn't sure of the last time he'd looked in a mirror, but he knew his own face well enough to recognize it, even with its eyes shut. The head itself had been exposed the whole time—the cabinet enclosed him only from the neck down—but before he'd opened the door, it had possessed the faceless anonymity of an unfinished doll. With the lid open, detail flowed across the empty expanse of the occupant's face, removing all doubt that the being in the cabinet was him.

Well, sure it is. Who else would it be? Roland supposed there was logic to this, but that didn't make seeing himself through his own disembodied eyes any less unsettling. He glared at the face dozing beneath him, entranced and repulsed by turns at the peculiar, onanistic intimacy of seeing himself with his eyes shut. It was a firsthand sight he'd never before been granted, one that, by definition, should be impossible to obtain. He studied the lines of strain radiating from the corners of his eyelids, the pale lips drawn thin atop a clenched jaw shadowed with stubble, the dappled iridescence of sweat beads quivering beneath fluorescent lights.

Placing his hands on his doppelganger's shoulders, he swung one leg over the lip of the cabinet and placed it inside, where he was both surprised and relieved to find it made contact with the padded interior. He pulled his other leg in and shimmied down, his limbs passing through those of his double. A few adjustments brought him level with the body, so that they became as one man with two torsos: one unconscious and supine, the other levered at the hips with elbows braced on the cabinet's rim. He closed his eyes and lowered himself into the cabinet, feeling like a man willingly climbing into his own casket.

As his back pressed against the cabinet's cushioned base, he felt a momentary tug at the base of his skull, not unlike the fleeting sense of falling that sometimes accompanies an aborted transition into sleep. His body tensed, his eyes flew open, and he found himself back in the realm of the flesh, a patient hand smoothing a damp cloth across his forehead. He looked up at Nurse Donnelly, who heaved an audible sigh of relief at his waking.

"Oh, thank the Lord," she cried. "I was afraid you'd made a liar out of Nurse Tremblay and me. All that talk about things going better this time. Are you feeling alright?"

"I am fine. I went there, once again. To the place I told you about. It was much the same, only there was a woman. Old and frightened. She saw me, though I hid, and..."

"It's okay," Nurse Donnelly said. Her hand traced slow arcs across the furrowed expanse of his forehead. "Mother Abigail always said there's cure in the telling."

"She saw me, and she cried out, in terror and in pain. She asked for help, from me, and from two others. One was a man named Tobey. The other was you."

The nurse's hand paused in its course. The cloth withdrew, leaving a damp and ghostly chill on his skin. "You've no right to say such things."

Roland looked up at her. The nurse's gaze had hardened, her once soft irises now chips of flint. "I don't understand. You asked me to tell you what I saw—"

"You're speaking about Mrs. Chauncey, a kind old woman who wouldn't hurt a soul. I've no idea why you'd choose to make up such morbid stories, but I must tell you I don't appreciate that sort of thing."

"I do not know this Mrs. Chauncey, but I can only tell you things as I witnessed them. Whether vision or madness I leave to you to judge, but I speak truly, and with no ill will."

Her gaze softened as he spoke, though reluctance still flitted around its edges. "I s'pose it's unfair to assume unkind ends on your part, but there's no sense in it. If what you saw truly is a..."—she groped for the word—"a vision of someplace beyond, then Mrs. Chauncey has no place in it. She's alive and well."

Roland opened his mouth to respond, but before he could speak, a faint glimmer snagged the corner of his eye. He turned in its direction and saw a nebulous green figment rippling the plaster wall to his right. The figure shrank, its hazy borders firming into tight geometric lines. It formed a rectangle, spun on its long edge and opened in a fanned panoply of pages. As he realized what he was seeing, Roland performed a quick mental sketch of the asylum's layout, and after a few seconds confirmed what he suspected in his gut all along: a straight line drawn from him to the ghostly tome projected on the wall would, if extended far enough, point straight to Dr. Verloc's office.

***

For the rest of the treatment, Roland didn't speak. In his silence Martha sensed no anger, but rather a deep and brooding preoccupation. Asking after its cause brought no meaningful response. Occasionally he would shrug, or mumble something inaudible before returning his attention to the wall, which had in some unfathomable way captured his interest.

Martha took no offence to his indifference, but it did worry her a little. So intense was his gaze that she once again considered halting the treatment, taking his focus as a possible sign of brain damage, or at least delirium. But the more she observed and probed, the more it seemed that there was nothing fundamentally off in his thinking. He was simply lost in thought.

She made a point of maintaining her polite disposition, reinforcing it in places to show that she was still providing him the best possible care. His sudden mentioning of Mrs. Chauncey had rattled her, and she'd struck back with more force than she intended. While there was no doubt in her mind that he'd incorporated her into his hallucinations, she felt the accusation that he'd done so deliberately was unfair. In their interactions thus far, he'd given no reason for her to assume that sort of malice from him. It was far more likely that he'd observed her exchanges with the older woman at some point, either directly or through some passing second-hand comment, and absorbed them unconsciously into his delirium. Dreams, after all, were magpie nests of the mind, built from the stolen fragments of our daily thoughts and gleanings. Surely hallucinations were no different.

Only when the machine was shut off and the cabinet door opened did Roland once again acknowledge her. He gave a curt nod of thanks and dropped his gaze to her feet.

"I am sorry if I caused you distress. Please know I only spoke honestly of what I saw."

"Please, think nothing of it. Patients have been known to say all manner of strange things in the cabinet. The heat, it plays tricks with the mind."

"Of course. Tricks."

After cooldown and recovery, Martha escorted him back to the ward and resumed her duties. Mostly this consisted of flitting from one place to the next, absorbing complaints and spotting ailments and doing her best to alleviate each. The hours bled away and she soon found herself behind the supper cart, grateful for the set tempo and simple ritual of food service.

As she ladled out bowls of tepid rice porridge, she became aware of a dull anxiety rumbling in the lowermost regions of her belly. She looked back across her day, searching for a reason for her worry, and recalled the detail from Roland's strange vision in the fever cabinet. Probing it sent a fresh burble of unease through her.

Strangely, part of her managed to find this reaction funny. The poor fellow was suffering from an illness whose primary symptoms included delusion. His hallucinations were a cause for pity, not fear. The good Lord alone knew why or from where his brain conjured images of Mrs. Chauncey, or how exactly he connected the old woman with her, but the possible explanations were as many as they were mundane. And unlike many delusions, this one was fairly easy to disprove. She wondered if it would be therapeutic for Roland and her to have a short chat with Mrs. Chauncey. Seeing her might reassure him that the visions he received in the fever cabinet were nothing but waking dreams, but confronting such dissonant ideas might cause him distress. It might even push him deeper into paranoia, send him scrambling for rationalizations that would cast her in a more malicious role, as deceptive oppressor instead of clueless caregiver. She would have to ask Nurse Tremblay what she thought. The head nurse had no shortage of experience dealing with troubled patients, and she could likely offer her some guidance on how to put Roland more at ease. She would need to speak with Mrs. Chauncey, too, before suggesting anything. Not that the older woman would be able to give any sort of clear assent, but Martha could at least gauge her initial reaction. Perhaps she would mention something next time she saw her.

As the proposal crossed her mind, Martha realized that she hadn't seen Mrs. Chauncey during her rounds serving dinner. This in itself wasn't a big deal, as more than one nurse offered meals and it was possible that she'd simply been sitting in another part of the dining hall. But she hadn't seen the older woman at breakfast either, and that *was* odd, since her mornings were fairly well regimented and she tended always to sit at the same table.

None of it meant much on its own of course, but the anxiety, tamped down a moment prior, resumed its previous discontented burble. Shaking her head at her silliness, she crossed the ward and tracked down the other nurse, Valery, who'd done dinner duty. A middle-aged woman with frizzy black hair, she had one of those jaw-busting surnames from Eastern Europe that Martha, to her shame, could never remember properly. Styzyk or Stirzinsy or something to that effect. She dreaded the day when circumstance would require her to speak it aloud, but for now she used the woman's Christian name, which leant her an outsized familiarity that the other nurse didn't seem to mind.

"Ah, Mart'a," she said, her tongue skidding over the *th* sound, "is all well? You have a pale look."

"Oh yes, I'm quite fine, thank you. I just had a question for you if you don't mind. Do you know Evelyn Chauncey?"

"Of course, a nice lady. Alzheimers brings out always the trut' in a person, and hers is a good trut'. Is she unwell?"

"Not that I'm aware of. I didn't see her at dinner and was just wondering if you did."

Valery shook her head. "Not t'at I recall. It is possible I forget, t'ough. After so many bowls, one blends into another, yes?"

"Of course."

"If you are concerned, you could check the infirmary. Perhaps she has caught a bug."

"I'm sure you're right," Martha said, and thanked her.

Only Mrs. Chauncey wasn't in the infirmary. Neither was she in her cot, nor receiving hydrotherapy or any of the other specialty treatments meted out, depending on the intensity of the machine and the disposition of the operator, as either cure or punishment. Martha checked the daily sign-out log and saw no mention of her there, which was hardly a surprise. She had no family to speak of apart from her grandson Tobey—and given the contents of the black-bordered telegram Martha had read, it was clear he was in no position to be taking her out for lunch.

Eventually she could no longer ignore the fact that her search was cutting into her duties, and so she gave it up for now and went about her day, assuring herself that she would stumble upon Mrs. Chauncey when she least expected it, to no small private embarrassment at her overreaction. It was a humiliation she welcomed, for at least it would resolve her uncertainty.

When her shift ended and Mrs. Chauncey still hadn't appeared, she decided to swing by the master registry in the private ward, which housed details on the admission and discharge of every patient. Unlike the internal records, which comprised the sloppy and imperfect jottings of nurses and orderlies during moments stolen from their half a dozen other jobs, the master registry was purview of the reception secretary, and maintained with meticulous accuracy. Its contents were subject to public audit, and errors were not tolerated. If Mrs. Chauncey had left the hospital—through discharge, through sign-out from a caregiver, or even through death—the exact time and nature of her egress would appear on those pages.

As a nurse assigned to public charges, Martha had no cause to enter the private ward in her day-to-day activities, and hadn't been since her first arrival when looking for a job. She was struck anew by its tidy opulence, lent greater radiance by contrast with the drab and ramshackle public ward. It wasn't quite a palace, but the disparity was stark enough to jump out at her: the tiles gleamed, their grouted gutters clean and smooth and devoid of the flecks of black mildew no amount of scrubbing could scour free; the windows glistened, their transparent surface unmarred by smudges or cracks, offering views of the outside unimpeded by checkerboards of safety wire threaded through the glass; metal fixtures snagged ribbons of fluorescent light along chrome junctures. Nowhere could she see rust crudely concealed beneath daubs of paint, cracks puckering beneath haphazard swabs of plaster, stains half-scrubbed, floors half-swept, deep-set smells masked by clouds of antiseptic. The whole place looked ready for a photoshoot or tour from a prominent citizen at any moment, a state that the public ward had never for one instant attained in her tenure, and by all accounts not for many years before either.

The master registry lay off the front atrium in a snug annex. While patients of suitable capability manned the reception desk in the foyer itself, the registry office was helmed exclusively by paid staff. For liability reasons, patients were not allowed inside, and even frontline staff like Martha couldn't enter unattended. Fortunately, the secretary on duty was a bright and cheery girl about Martha's age, who greeted her with a smile and had no qualms about allowing her a glimpse through the master registry, though the patients' individual files, in which items from the registry were filed each night, was off limits to non-clinical staff.

"Take your time," she said, swiveling a hefty leather-bound ledger across the desk.

Martha flipped to the latest page and worked backwards. It didn't take her long to find what she was looking for. There, on the second-last page, stood the name Evelyn Chauncey, voluntarily discharged into private care. Martha ran her finger along the entry, looking for more information, and found it by the right margin.

She closed the book. Around her the office seemed to wobble, as if built from cheap canvas sets beleaguered by an unexpected gust of wind.

"Find what you needed?" the secretary asked.

Martha nodded. She performed some contortion of her lower face that she hoped resembled a smile, thanked her, and left. The image of the book hovered before her eyes in ghostly calligraphy, the sort of lingering phantasmagoria imparted on the pupil by bright lights.

Patients in Mrs. Chauncey's condition could not discharge themselves on their own. They required a signatory, someone who had the legal authority to take them under their care. For wealthy patients, a representative from a private clinic could play this role, but in nearly all cases the signatory was a member of the family. And so it was here. For on the line indicating "patient is discharged under the care of:" a familiar name had scrawled his signature.

Tobias Chauncey, her grandson, who had died over the English Channel last month.

IF THE PUBLIC ward's decrepitude could be said to have an upside, it was perhaps that the paucity of staff meant patients were given a certain level of autonomy to roam within the confines of the sealed wing. This privilege was given not through beneficence or as a sign of trust, but simply because the asylum lacked the staff needed to enforce overnight lockdown. Catheterizing incontinent patients and cleaning bedpans for the bedridden already taxed the nurses and orderlies almost beyond endurance; adding dozens of unnecessarily befouled containers each night was out of the question. It was easier to let patients with sufficient physical and mental capacity go to the bathroom on their own. Those with psychosis, delirium, or other potentially disruptive conditions were already segregated anyway, and even people who, like Roland, had been admitted via the legal system remained patients rather than criminals.

All of this added up to a certain level of trust, however reluctant, that Roland was hesitant to abuse. The asylum's skeletal staff allowed some freedoms as an expediency, but it also precluded any half measures for those who pushed boundaries too far. There would be no closer eye kept on him if he were discovered skulking about where he didn't belong—there were no free eyes available to do the keeping. Instead, they would simply toss him in a padded cell and slide his food to him through a slot in the metal door. Roland had seen these chambers on his desultory rambles through the halls—there was little else to do to pass the time—and could recall with hateful clarity the claustrophobic dimensions of canvas-clad brick in the empty rooms, and the howls and the furious, futile banging of skulls on steel that rattled from those already occupied.

And yet, however strong his fear of the padded rooms might be, the draw of the green book was stronger still. He had begun to see it whenever he closed his eyes, an emerald glow that cut through steel and wood and stone and burned itself onto the inside of his eyelids. Its pulsing, amorphous shape resembled the throbs of color that sometimes hung before his eyes after exposure to bright lights, but unlike such phantom fireworks, the green splotch retained a fixed position no matter which way Roland moved. With his eyes shut, he could turn a complete circle, and the image would drift steadily across his field of vision, disappear beyond the periphery, and reappear half a rotation later on the opposite side. He tried shaking his head and turning rapid circles, but the color could not be budged. It simply hung there, silent and tantalizing.

After a couple of days of anguish spent trying whatever he could to ignore the green glow, Roland succumbed to its call and decided, for better or worse, to inspect it. It was for this reason that he found himself, in the dead of night, standing before the locked door to Dr. Verloc's office, forcing his frantic breath into a steadier rise and fall. He held in his sweat-slick right hand a butter knife secreted from the dinner cart that evening. As an implement it was hardly lethal, but nevertheless contraband outside the dining area, and if discovered on his person yet another potential ticket to a padded cell. He tried to ignore this thought as best he could as he slid the blade into the gap between door and jamb and shimmied it behind the latch. The blade's dull serrations snagged on the latch, strained and slid home, pressing the wedge of sloped metal into the backset and letting the door swing free. Here was yet another way the building's antiquated fixtures benefited him: Verloc's main office in the private ward, which unlike his satellite office housed objects of monetary value, would doubtless count among its renovations a modern and less pickable lock.

Roland wasted no time before stepping inside and easing the door shut behind him, and in an instant found himself amidst the silent shadows of an empty office. A half-moon strung between tattered grey clouds slanted pale beams through the window, providing enough light to see by. With a soft, deliberate tread, he made his way to the bookcase and crouched down.

He gazed across the lower shelves, hunting for the distinctive green spine he'd seen on his first visit and a thousand times since in the miniscule *Kino* projected onto his eyelids. His first couple of passes were fleeting, almost casual, so confident was he that the book would reveal itself as it had days before. On his third scan his eyes moved slower, appraising each spine individually rather than waiting for the color to leap out at him. When that didn't work, he began to grow frantic, running his fingers along the leather spines and pulling books out at every whim. The color had been sharp and unmistakable before, but in the moonlight every book lay shrouded in a wan alabaster hue. He held his clenched fists to his temples and closed his eyes, willing himself to recall as best he could the book's location.

A band of green luminescence flared across black canvas in the lower right field of his vision. On instinct his hand reached out unseen towards the light, grabbed stiff ridges of leather, and pulled. He opened his eyes and found himself clutching a slender tome, its emerald binding more muted than in his memory, but unmistakable.

His first impulse was to snatch the book and run, skitter to some private corner like a mouse with a bit of absconded cheese. In his eagerness to flee the office as quickly as possible, the proposition was an appealing one. But taking the book came with its own dangers, which together tallied far higher than the risk of staying put and inspecting it *in situ*. Where in the asylum would he find a spot with sufficient privacy to read it, and where would he hide it in the meantime? What if an orderly or nurse found it among his effects? Or what if Verloc noticed it missing and demanded a full search? No, however much his gut longed to flee, it was much more sensible to stay put and read it in the confines of Verloc's office, where it belonged and could thus not be missed. It was a logical choice, and it cost him dearly.

Squatting on his haunches, Roland turned the book in both hands and studied the cover. Arabesques embossed in gold framed the title: *A Compendium of Eminent Personages from Queenstown and the Greater Niagara Region, 1678 to Present.* Roland puzzled over the words. Despite the archaic language and his own imperfect English, he found their plain meaning clear enough. It was simply not the sort of title he expected for a book that had summoned him with such mystic fervor. He wasn't sure, on reflection, exactly what he *had* expected, but a compilation biography of Queenstown's notables certainly wasn't it. Something a bit more arcane would have suited better—a text in Latin perhaps, or a grimoire smuggled from some ancient coven and scrawled with whispers of occult practice.

The clatter of approaching footsteps drove disappointment from his mind. Shoving the book back into its place on the shelf, he scurried to the desk and ducked out of sight, knees curled to his chest. The footsteps grew louder, trailing in their wake voices that bandied and cackled to one another. Even before their words grew clear, Roland could tell their source. The trio of orderlies, Fox, MacCruiskeen, and Pluck. While their presence brought an instinctive revulsion, it also came with a certain relief. Whatever they were up to—their nightly rounds, perhaps, or more likely shirking whatever meager duties the shift nurse managed to assign to them—they had no business in Verloc's office. They would soon pass by, and then he could leave, green book be damned.

As if to taunt him, the footsteps swerved closer and stopped before the office door. There was a pause, followed by some mumbling, and the click of tumblers turning over. The door swung open, spilling a wedge of light across the floor and drenching the desk. Roland pulled his feet back and wriggled deeper inside.

"You really think he's got some in here?" said Pluck. Roland was slightly disgusted with himself for being able to tell their voices apart, as if the knowledge were an unsightly stain heretofore hidden beneath a rug.

"Of course he does," said Fox. "You know how much brandy the guy downs on a daily basis? No chance he doesn't keep a little tipple stashed all over this place. Come on, get looking already."

A pair of legs appeared in the opening. Roland watched with helpless dismay as they hunkered down, bringing their owner's chest level with his head. He held perfectly still, praying that through some divine intervention they wouldn't see him. But it was hopeless, and a moment later Fox's eyes locked with his own. A flash of startled terror seized his face, which he quickly swept away in favor of an amused smirk.

"Well I'll be damned," he said. "Those frigging war effort posters weren't lying. There really *is* a kraut hiding under every rock. Hey, Mac, Plucky, come take a look under here."

Their faces hung above Fox's shoulders, smiles lupine in the moonlight.

"What you doing under there, Jerry? Planting bugs for the Fatherland?"

Roland ignored the jibe. "It seems to me," he said, "that we have both of us caught the other doing something they should not. You have found me outside my quarters, and I have overheard your search for Dr. Verloc's private stores. Perhaps it would be best for all of us to simply forget we saw one another."

"Please, pal. You think Verloc's gonna listen to some syph case's story over three of his trusted orderlies? Way I remember it, old Pluck here heard some commotion in Verloc's office, and we came over to investigate."

"I always did have good ears," agreed Pluck.

"Door was open, and inside what did we find but a sneaky little kraut, scrabbling about for pills or cash, whatever he could get those Kaiser-loving mitts on. I sell it right, I might even get a raise out of the deal."

Roland exhaled, head bowed. "I will do whatever you ask of me. Wash floors, scrub toilets. Any job you dislike, I will do it without complaint. Just let me return to my room."

"You really want us to keep mum for you? Fine, we will. On one condition."

"Name it."

"Fight me."

Roland scrutinized the words Fox had spoken. Surely he'd misheard, or else there was some idiom he was missing. He looked up at Fox, brow furrowed. "I'm sorry, I don't understand. You wish...to fight me?"

"That's right. First to the floor loses."

"And if I lose?"

"When you lose, you mean? You drag your sorry ass back to the dorm, case closed. Nothing riding on it, I just got itchy knuckles and you look bulky enough to take a few punches without breaking in half. What d'you say?"

Roland shut his eyes. The green light was still there, burning at the edge of his vision. He rubbed his face, crawled from beneath the desk, and stood.

"Where shall we do this?"

They walked him to a quiet courtyard away from the dormitories, marching two abreast and one a step and a half behind him. Running would serve no purpose for him, so he wasn't sure why they were taking such precautions. He figured it was the same reason they did just about everything else: because it amused them.

The night air settled like a wet towel over his shoulders, raising fields of gooseflesh from shoulder to wrist, but there was also something pleasant in its bracing coldness. He wondered how long it had been since he'd last been outside. Weeks, probably, though it felt like years.

Brick surrounded them on all sides, broken only by a doorway and banks of narrow windows reinforced with thick wires. Within the four walls stretched a couple hundred square feet of grass. Bald patches marked common footfalls between the doors, and an untended garden squatted in one corner, its meager crops swallowed by weeds.

Fox took position near the center of the courtyard. Pluck and MacCruiskeen led Roland to his own station. They drifted off to separate corners, leaving him alone to face down Fox across ten feet of crabgrass and broadleaf plantain. Roland sized up his opponent. He was smaller than Roland by a few inches, but leanly muscled and unencumbered by the slow erosion of twenty years' labor. Yet youth, Roland knew, was a strength and a weakness. The trick would be to suppress the former and exploit the latter.

He realized with surprise that he actually wanted to win this. On the march over, his mind had focused mostly on how to end the fight as quickly as possible without Fox accusing him of throwing the match. Now, with the stiff bristles of night air scouring his nostrils, and Fox's smug grin dyed silver by moonlight, he wanted nothing more than to teach this arrogant little bully that the asylum was his workplace, not his kingdom.

You'll gain nothing by winning, a voice cautioned. *He wants a bit of playtime, not a contest. Creatures like Fox don't show magnanimity in defeat. If you bruise his pride, he'll come at you with everything.*

He knew it was true. But in the moment Roland didn't much care.

There was no formal beginning to the fight, no bells or buzzers or announcers signaling the start of combat. Fox simply came forward, fists raised to his chin, and started circling. Roland circled back, reaching back to the distant outposts of his mind where his army training resided. They'd done a fair bit of close quarters combat in his *Zug,* and Roland had been among the better soldiers at it, but he'd stored the memories without care and not looked on them since, and most were moth-eaten and rotten. He rolled his shoulders and hunched into his best approximation of a boxer's stance, testing his footwork and seeking out a good place to land a first blow.

Fox gave him no time to plan. He came at Roland with a right hook that scythed through his guard and grazed his nose. Had his reach been an inch longer, the fight would have ended right there. Instead Roland barged forward with forearms crossed and shoved Fox off balance. The orderly's feet skidded over dew-slick grass, giving Roland a free moment to pummel his abdomen. Fox took the punches with a taut belly and though it was clear from the rasp of exhaled breath that they stung, they failed to knock the wind clean out of him. He recovered and warded Roland off with a few stiff jabs.

They pulled back long enough to get their footing and circled in again, neither man showing any eagerness to shy away. Both had their blood up now, and there would be no stopping until one of them lay face up on the ground—and perhaps not even then.

Roland shrugged off his pretense of technique and threw his weight around instead, muscling forward with arms crossed before face and belly, absorbing punishment until he was close enough to dish out some of his own. Fox's footwork was defter, his punches more polished, but he lacked the raw power he needed to knock Roland to the floor. Roland knew it, and in his current state he didn't feel the punches at all. He would learn of them later through a secondhand summary of aches and bruises, but in the moment, they landed like distant, muted things, shells fired at a neighboring barracks.

Though any impartial referee would have called the match for Fox—he'd landed more blows and taken fewer by far—this was no sanctioned fight, and his lack of tangible progress showed in his face. His smile grew flat, its smug curves wilting into a sneer before splitting in a snarl of pent-up frustration. His punches came faster and harder, but also sloppier. He forgot his footwork, stopped maintaining the poise needed to recoil from Roland's onslaughts. Roland saw this, and waited until the younger man looked about to blow.

The moment came after a lucky jab split Fox's lip. Blood darkened the spaces between his teeth, turning his gritted sneer into something vulpine and hungry. He roared and came at Roland with windmilling fists, his discipline cast aside. Roland watched him come, chambered his right shoulder, and, shrugging off his smacking blows, hurled a cross directly into Fox's face. Roland felt the distinct quiver-snap of cartilage compressing and giving way as Fox's nose imploded. Blood spumed out of collapsed nostrils, followed by thick cords of runny crimson mucus.

Fox tottered backwards like a child on stilts, his every step precarious. His joints became a collection of loose hinges. He managed two staggered steps before tumbling, so disheveled by the blow that he couldn't even brace himself in the fall. His head struck hard earth. Roland stood over him, fists half-raised with caution, and worried for an instant that he may have killed him. He crouched down, ear cocked an inch above Fox's mouth, and heard the reassuring rasp of his breath.

"Can you stand?" he asked. "Let me help you up."

He wasn't sure whether Pluck or MacCruiskeen landed the first kick, only that he was soon on his back and the two of them were stomping on his chest. He rolled to his side, one arm draped across his face in a protective shawl, the other cocked across groin and belly. Feet pummeled him from both sides, the intensity of the attack making it impossible to stand.

Fox hauled himself to his feet and joined in, taking up position directly over Roland's head. Roland looked up through splayed fingers and saw Fox glaring down at him. A slick of snot and blood covered his face from nose to chin. Strings of mucus stretched between lips split in a wild, mirthless grin. He raised a foot high enough for his sole to blot out the moon overhead. Roland watched as it descended until its rubber treads filled the world, and all was darkness and pain.

9

IT WAS TWO in the morning and Harvey had to piss. It seemed to him that, if he ever needed a quick way to summarize old age to an incredulous youth, that sentence could serve as well as anything else he was liable to come up with. He hadn't slept a night through with kidneys untapped since his back gave out in '29. You'd think things might loosen up a bit as a body got on in years, build a bit more capacity. His pecs had withered into sagging teats and his balls drooped halfway to his knees, yet somehow his bladder bested gravity and snugged up while everything else stretched out. How was that for justice?

But truth be told, it wasn't crying kidneys alone that had been keeping him up lately. Things had been a little lonely around the ward these days. He missed having Roland to talk to. The big lummox wasn't the snappiest conversationalist in the world, but he was a decent guy with his head screwed on the right way, and such things counted for a lot in here. Hard to believe they caught him thieving from Verloc's office. He didn't seem the type. Course, that was only the official line, and between the official line and the truth a body could sometimes fit enough open space to play a decent game of touch football.

The dormitory was unlit save for the shards of moonlight that strained through the wire mesh across each windowsill. Stale air rattled and wheezed with the sonic detritus of eight aged and infirm bodies, a raspy chorus of farts and snores and muttered toothless dreams. Harvey tossed aside the fibrous cotton wafer they called a blanket and swung his legs over the bedrail. He grasped his wheelchair one-handed and dragged it into position, not bothering to unlock the brakes. Below the waist, he may have been as withered as a pole bean vine in December, but his hands remained as strong and nimble as they'd ever been, praise the Lord.

Lifting himself with his forearms, he waddled into position and vaulted into the chair. Rusty axles squealed beneath the sudden addition of his weight. If he'd been any fatter, Harvey was sure he would've cracked the hunk of junk clean in half by now. As it was, he was grateful to have a working chair at all. More than one patient at Walpole had become bedridden not through age or injury, but simply through a lack of usable wheelchairs.

The squeak of his wheels grew audible in the otherwise silent hallways, a sound usually swallowed by the steady swell of ambient noise during daylight hours. A few blue-tinged lights stood sentinel in key junctures along the hallway, guiding the asylum's assorted insomniacs to their midnight destinations. Harvey barely needed them. He'd wheeled down this hallway so many times he was confident he could do it even when the milky haze of cataracts finally thickened into an impenetrable scum, as it inevitably would. Thinking of his impending blindness didn't bother him as much as other people thought it should. Even he was sometimes surprised by his own fatalism. But it seemed to him that there wasn't much in his life worth seeing anyhow, and if the good Lord saw fit to set scales in his eyes, perhaps there was a good reason for him to do so.

A shadow broke free of the wall and drifted in front of Harvey's path. He hasped his palms over his tires to slow himself down. Rubber scraped against calluses thickened by years of similar maneuvers.

"Off to drain the lizard, huh?"

The shadow moved forward. A beam of blue light washed the darkness from the figure, revealing the young and eminently punchable face of Fox the orderly. Someone had clearly taken the face up on its offer, as a wad of gauze secured with white surgical tape stretched across his nose. Harvey laughed.

"Boy, he sure did a number on you, didn't he?"

Fox smiled. It was a good effort, but Harvey could tell it was forced; a certain tension about the eyes gave it away. "Sure, but you haven't seen what *he* looks like."

"Oh, I'm sure your boyfriends paid him back for uglying up that pretty little mug of yours. That why they ain't hangin' 'round you now? Looks ain't what they used to be?"

"You'll wanna check your sources, old timer. Weren't no one else but me, Pluck, and MacCruiskeen there. You should just thank God it was us that caught that maniac, and not someone more delicate."

"I reckon I'll wait to hear his side of it, just the same."

"Syph cases don't get sides. Just wrist restraints and a rubber room."

Harvey scoffed, though the comment cut him deeper than he let on. He didn't like the thought of poor Roland bound hand and foot in some musty old cell, punished for an infraction that was surely inflated or contorted in the telling, if it even happened at all. He couldn't say for certain what *had* happened, or even precisely what was alleged to have happened—rumors bled and shifted in the gap between mouths and ears of even the most faithful tellers, to say nothing of the cracked, leaky pitchers that held water in an asylum—but he would bet his last dollar that whatever story Fox and his cohorts told, it was bent to cast them in the best light possible, regardless of how far it deviated from its original shape.

"I've got to get this dead weight off my bladder. Shouldn't you be workin'?"

"Matter of fact, I was just about to get started." Fox snapped his fingers.

A tight band of misery cinched across Harvey's windpipe. He reached up instinctively and felt a thin steel wire digging into the wattled flesh of his neck. His fingernails scrabbled at the cord, but they could get no purchase and managed only to slash bloody divots in his skin. Dank air sour with halitosis buffeted the back of his head and drifted in humid plumes across his cheek. Each gust paired with the sound of a simian chuckle.

Though instinct drove him to dig ever deeper at the wire, he forced himself to let go and move his grasp to the hands that held it. His fingers dug at bulbous knuckles, wormed into the puckered gap between thumb and palm, but he had no more luck there than he had with the wire itself. A voice spoke behind him, not from the choker but from another standing nearby, but Harvey's ears could make no sense of the sound. His senses collapsed into a jumble of disparate inputs, the effort his brain would have spent assembling them diverted to the more pressing task of moment to moment survival.

A ragged darkness closed in from the edges of his vision, narrowing the hallway to a knothole through which only Fox's laughing face was visible. Harvey opened his mouth to lob a final curse at the man, but his lips would make no sound. A patch of warmth spread across his lap, and he realized he'd wet himself. *Lord, couldn't you've waited 'til I punched out to loosen my pouch? Ain't I earned that much?*

With this thought, the knothole closed and darkness settled in around him, hot at first but quickly plunging into cold.

***

Beneath the tiled floors and slotted drains of the Erasmus Walpole Institution for Mental Hygiene ran a network of tunnels, cellars, and catacombs that comprised the asylum's sprawling multilevel basement. Unlike the upper floors, which even in the pauperish public ward made some basic effort to appear clean-lined and sanitary, the basement offered no sop to clinical order whatsoever. The floors were rough cement, the ceilings a nest of pipes and cords beneath steel girders that jutted out like the ribcage of a starving man. The walls were built from concrete blocks or else simply borrowed from naked stone, natural formations that made clean lines and symmetry impossible. It seemed like a place less built than unearthed, a long-sealed cavern of shivering refuge for a forgotten Paleolithic race, its sooty walls encrusted with their fears and ghosts and cook-fire smoke.

Verloc looked around at the rock walls and shuddered. He disliked the basement in the best of circumstances, but the odious—and far too frequent—business that brought him down here made his presence all the more uncomfortable. He pulled his coat tighter around his bulk and shivered against the cold, which seeped from the stone walls and burbled up from the floor like water squeezing through a ship's hull. Every part of the basement was cold—except for the boiler room, which sweltered with a sooty heat that raised blisters on Verloc's skin whenever he visited for more than a few minutes—but no spot was colder than the recessed chamber in which he waited now. Here the last vestiges of the hospital fell away. The floor wasn't even concrete, but merely raw stone scraped into as level a surface as possible. A single craggled vault formed walls and ceiling alike, rising in a battered and sagging parabola from the rock floor. In spots the room reached lofty heights of twenty feet or more, in others little more than ten. There were no pipes, no fixtures, no furniture apart from half a dozen rusting gurneys, their threadbare mattresses reeking of mildew. The only light came from an oil lantern on an iron stand, the reservoir of which Verloc topped up on every arrival.

The distant squeak of unoiled wheels echoed through the crypt. Verloc tensed, grateful that his wait was almost over and yet dreading what was to come. He spent the moments as the sound approached working the anxiety from his features. Each wrinkle of worry smoothed away, every tensed muscle flattened, as if his face were a sheet freshly ironed. When the gurney wheeled into view there was not an ounce of uncertainty in Verloc's expression, only impatience and a touch of disdain. He looked at the man wheeling the gurney and glanced down at its contents, which lay obscured beneath a pale cotton sheet.

"I have been waiting for some time," he said. He motioned to his pocket watch as if its ticking hands provided a precise catalogue of the man's tardiness.

"Hey, it's like they say," said Fox. "You want it done fast, or you want it done right?"

"I suppose I shouldn't be surprised that both together would be beyond your capabilities." He sneered down at the shrouded object on the gurney. "Well, let's see your handiwork."

Fox pulled back the sheet. An elderly man lay on the gurney, his russet skin already waxy with death. A faint smell of corruption arose from his innards, largely masked by the much more prominent ammonia stink of urine. Verloc inspected the body from head down, pausing before too long at the purplish abrasion snaking across his neck.

"I told you very clearly that there must be no clear sign of trauma on the body," he said, frowning.

"Yeah, and I did as you told. No bashed skull, no wounds, no cuts. Guy's clean."

"And the broken skin and contusion around the neck? Surely even an ignoramus could tell that this man has been garroted."

Fox shrugged. "Well, I tried givin' him a heart attack, but what can I say? The old guy didn't scare easily."

"I'm glad you think it's funny. In the future, I trust you'll develop more delicate methods."

"I've never been in the business of delicate. What you want me to do? Ask him nicely?"

"You've never heard of poison? Or even a subtler form of asphyxiation? A sheet of rubber over the face works wonders, or so I'm told."

Fox leaned over the body and squinted at the bruising along its neck. "Honestly, you can barely see it. Just swab some makeup over it or something."

"Yes, I'm sure a dab of foundation will fool the coroner. You were, at least, discreet enough not to tell anybody about this?"

"Please, you think I'm an idiot?"

Verloc restrained himself from his desired reply. "So no one knows about this? Not even those two scofflaws you spend so much time with?"

"Hand to God, Doc. I did this one solo. I got no more interest in getting a call from the cops than you do."

"I'm pleased to hear it."

Fox tilted his head. For perhaps the first time in their association, Verloc noticed the younger man attempting some form of self-restraint. It failed, of course, and Fox posed the question he'd clearer thought it may be better not to ask.

"What do you want these guys for, anyway? You harvesting organs or something?"

Verloc shot Fox the most withering look in his arsenal of expression. "I've made it quite clear that anything beyond the immediate task is none of your business, nor will it ever be. Content yourself with idle speculation to your heart's content. But say nothing to anyone. Any word you breathe will be steadfastly denied by far more credible sources, and ramifications will return to you alone. Do you understand?"

Fox raised his hands in mock surrender. "Hey, have it your way. I could give a shit, right?"

"Quite. Payment will arrive with your regular cheque in two pay periods' time. The filing will be under overtime with hazard pay. Something along the lines of cleaning out the boiler lines would suffice. I suggest you find a day that fits and block it off in whatever calendar you keep. Clear records make for a sounder sleep."

Fox tipped him a two-fingered salute and left. Verloc waited until the sound of his footsteps petered out into silence, and paused another five minutes to ensure he didn't try and double back. When the time passed with no noise but the ambient hum of transformers and the distant rattle of water through pipes, he set the oil lantern on the foot of the gurney and wheeled it to the back of the crypt. He reached into a crevice along the rock face and triggered a switch hidden among the shards of granite.

A latch slid free deep in the stone, and what had appeared to be a solid chunk of earth swung effortlessly outward, revealing a space still more sunken and ancient than the tunnel that served as its outsized atrium. Verloc still recalled the day when he first discovered this place, the mingled fear and curiosity, slathered atop a greedy anticipation that beckoned him onward with an almost audible call. It had seemed to him inevitable that such a chamber would hold treasures beyond imagining.

Oh, how right he had been. How right, and how terribly wrong.

He eased the gurney through the hidden doorway and into the chamber. It cleared the jamb by no more than an inch on either side, but Verloc moved with the grace of much practice and slid it home without a single graze of steel on stone. The lantern cast greasy yellow light on the granite walls, catching on jags and skimming over the shadows that pooled in its pocks and craters. With the light drifting before him, Verloc felt like an oarsman navigating the waters of a subterranean lake. It was a sensation that never failed to unnerve him. He struck a match against his pantleg and touched it to the rag-swaddled head of a torch to his left. Flames spired around the pitch-soaked cloth, pressing the shadows back to the corners of the room, where they regrouped and nattered silently to one another, planning their inevitable reconquest of a land that was, morally and historically, theirs by right.

In the center of the room rose an altar hewn from black stone. Unlike the sooty granite craggles that surrounded it, the altar was smooth as marble and polished clean of every blemish. It seemed not to reflect light but to swallow it, leaving a rectangular hole in the earth that descended forever into some terrible yawping chasm that knew no bottom.

He wheeled the gurney round until it lay flush with the altar lengthwise. The altar stood about an inch higher, which made transitioning the subject a chore, but Verloc had developed a system that worked for all but the largest bodies. He shimmied his hands under the body's shoulders and, pushing with his legs, hoisted the back and head onto the altar. As he did every time he performed the ritual, he felt a moment's subconscious dread in the instant his fingers brushed the altar. Each time a part of him worried that his hand would fall clean through the darkness, and the membrane, once punctured, would unleash a vacuum that would suck him to oblivion. And yet, each time they hit hard cold stone and the sensation vanished, leaving him vexed at its specificity and ashamed of its strength against all evidence. He did not fancy himself as someone who was superstitious or prone to phobias. Though really, if ever there was a man justified to fear the supernatural, surely it was him.

He performed a similar maneuver with the feet, forming a saggy V-shape—this worked best once rigor mortis had set in, but for reasons of odor Verloc was happy to be performing it with a fresher body. A nudge and a grunt shunted the rest of the body onto the altar. He removed the sheet and tossed it beneath the gurney for laundering.

Rounding the altar, his hand traced the stone lip until it came upon a recessed compartment. He reached inside and withdrew a stout onyx dagger. He took the dagger in both hands, blade pointed downward, and stood over the body. His hands tightened around the handle. He breathed in once, deeply, and spoke the words that rose unbidden from his lips, escaping with a voice and cadence he hardly recognized as his own.

"With this blade, I sever your essence from the aether into which it was woven. With salt and blood and fire I call you, with salt and blood and fire I bind you, with salt and blood and fire I place you in thrall to Emperor Erasmus Walpole, First and Final of His Line, Supreme Ruler of the Second Plain."

These words spoken, he plunged the dagger into the corpse's chest, pulled it free with one hand, and with the other reached inside and withdrew the heart. Its ventricles twitched and puckered like the mouths of fish dying on a sea trawler's deck. He placed the heart in a brass bowl and returned the blade to its station. There was no need to wipe it; the polished stone remained clean. By the time he looked back at the body, the wound he'd made had closed. He couldn't tell by looking, but past inquiries had confirmed that, to any suspicious coroner, the heart would remain where it had always been, intact and quite undamaged. Exactly what he'd taken he was still not sure, but it was not a physical organ.

He watched as filaments of grey smoke twined upward from the belly of the brass bowl. The threads widened, splitting at their ends and felting into thick plumes. An abrasive sizzling resounded against the brass, the sound of water flicked into hot oil, and the heart began to burn. Or rather, "burn" was the best word Verloc had to describe it. For the flames that licked across the heart were unlike any earthly fire he had ever seen. They were black, giving neither heat nor light, and consumed in a manner less of combustion than expedited decay. Tongues of dark fire lapped at collapsing muscle, each undulation peeling back layers of tissue until there was nothing left but a smudge of greyish residue. A whiff of sulfur itched his nostrils, followed by something deeper and darker, the ugly-sweet stink of corruption beneath healthy skin.

At the far fringe of the torch's glow, the shadows began to twitch and sway like curtains before an open window. Random at first, the motion took on a steady undulation, tendrils forming warp and weft and weaving into a single entity stitched of darkness. It started simple, a plain black obelisk, before shaping itself into a man in a spiked helm and a flowing robe. Though his form was only a silhouette, bereft of depth or shade or color, Verloc could nonetheless make out the arcane runes that crowned the helmet, and spot each fold and ripple of the robe. This discrepancy of sight and knowledge made looking upon the figure painful, and Verloc kept his eyes cast mostly downward, a genuflection that seemed always to please the creature, and was quite possibly intended.

"Long have I waited, servant, for your latest show of fealty. I grow impatient in your absence."

Verloc bristled at the chastising tone, but kept his annoyance beneath the surface. "It's been scarcely a week, Master, since my previous sacrifice."

"Yes, the old woman with fading memory. Nary a wisp of vital essence to her. A truly uninspired offering. And what have you brought me today?" A hand formed within the shadowy mass and reached out, grasping the heart and drawing it up to the figure's face. "Hmm, more life in this one, but the vessel was old as ever. Much of its strength has already leeched away. Better, but still inadequate."

"Old people are less suspicious acquisitions, Master. Death among their number is taken as a matter of course. When virile young men die with no obvious cause of illness or injury, it raises questions."

"I trust one has sense enough not to draw my ranks from noblemen. I care not for the pedigree of my subjects. Only their vitality."

"Things have changed since the days of your asylum's founding. Even the poorest and most wretched must be accounted for. There are authorities charged to check records and interrogate staff. They cannot be turned aside at the door, nor can unexplained deaths be dismissed with a shrug and a nod to unbalanced humors. My work has grown more challenging than it was for my predecessors, and I must move with a commensurately greater caution. If I cannot mask what goes on here from the law, I'll go to prison and your asylum will be shut down. There'll be no new souls then."

"I require no lectures from the likes of you, apostle. I know my business, and my business needs souls."

As if I couldn't tell between an entrepreneur and an addict, said a voice in Verloc's head, though he pushed the idea away before it had fully formed. He was even now unaware of the full extent of Erasmus' powers, and had no desire to test them with such perilous experiments.

"I am merely suggesting prudence, Master. My methods are chosen to ensure your security, and my own."

"Perhaps. But I sensed no such reluctance in your young procurer. There is much vitality in that one."

Verloc felt stung at this, and ashamed of his own jealousy. "Fox is not without his uses. But his recklessness will be his undoing. If I do not watch over him closely, it could be ours as well."

The shadow gave a curt nod. "I grant you your knowledge in the matter, and will follow your recommendation. For now. But there is another matter that requires tending. One of your charges has begun to gain The Sight. His glimpses have been fleeting so far, kept mostly in states of heightened attunement to other plains, but the window is growing."

"Such visions have occurred before, Master. Surely it is nothing to fear. Anything he says will not be believed. Such is one of the chief advantages to presiding over a madhouse."

"I care not about his ramblings. It is the occurrence itself that disturbs me. Such creatures are a greater danger than you realize. I wish the man found, and disposed of."

Excellent. Another death on the ledgers. "Tell me what you know of him."

"He is a large man, neither young nor old. A strong essence, but wounded. He nurses much doubt inside him."

Verloc nodded. "I will watch for signs on my end, and if it is required to remove him, it shall be done. Though there is a chance his vision will fade on its own. Such has happened before, as you know."

"There is no need to remind me. I will tell you more of him as it is revealed to me."

The shadows began to unknit, resuming their stochastic sprawl about the cavern. Panic cinched tight around Verloc's belly. He spoke, hating the urgent weakness in his voice, but unable to excise it.

"And, Master, my payment? There has been nothing for some time, and..."

Even with its absence of features, the shadow figure somehow managed to smile. "Fear not, my apostle. Your scrying glass has been replenished. Your appetites will not go unsated."

Rage smoldered red and shameful across Verloc's cheeks. Erasmus always made him beg. He gritted his teeth and said nothing as the figure dissolved back into shadow, leaving him alone in the chamber—apart from the corpse strewn across the altar. He dragged it back onto the gurney and maneuvered it into the crypt where it would await the coroner, his worries once again flooding across his thoughts.

Under Erasmus' insistence, the number of deaths in the asylum was fast becoming untenable. If the pace kept up, the Province was bound to intervene. Verloc had reduced the pressure somewhat by "discharging" certain patients whose relatives were too distant or indifferent to follow up, but such a maneuver couldn't be sustained forever. He was robbing Peter to pay Paul, and he knew it. Eventually some inquisitive relation would come calling, and the errors in the registry would be as good as a smoking gun in his top drawer. He needed a plan for such a contingency—a pliant clerk to act as fall guy perhaps, or a convenient fire in the registry office. Each idea had its flaws, but it was Verloc's nature to plan, and charting his options in the wake of every eventuality calmed him as little else could.

His plotting occupied him until he reached his office—his true office, not the seedy bolt hole in the public ward with its chockablock tomes bequeathed by directors past—and slid into his leather chair. He opened the bottommost drawer and with trembling fingers withdrew a silver slate. Clamshell patterns crimped its edges, but its surface was otherwise smooth, yet strangely non-reflective. A cloudiness infused the metal, as if irrevocably tarnished over decades of careless use.

Verloc gazed into the tray. The vaguest semblance of his reflection looked back at him, little more than whorls of muted color. He looked deeper, urging himself through the thickets of tarnish with a sweaty, desperate hope that troubled him in its intensity. *He lied,* insisted a voice. *He sensed your mockery and is punishing you by withholding his end of the bargain.*

He needs me as much as I need him. He wouldn't dare.

Oh? And what are you going to do if he does?

Verloc winced at this realization. For the answer, of course, was nothing.

Just as his hope dwindled, a spark of nebulous red light struck against the center of the tray. It flickered, faded, and returned, widening as it spun into a gyre of radiant color. A speck of shadow opened in the gyre's nexus. As it grew, the whorls of color deepened, transforming from a flat disc to a funnel. Verloc reached into the aperture, sinking fingers into the spongy walls of the tunnel, and climbed inside.

The walls tightened around him, squeezing him forward in peristalsic bursts. They shaped him as he went, remodeling his features as if they were clay, and he emerged in a body quite unlike the one he'd had on entering. The bulk around his middle had shrunk, pressed into dense pads of muscle that lined his chest and arms and shoulders. Black hair tumbled across his once bald pate. The sagging jowls beneath his jaw stretched to drumskin tightness.

He stood, savoring the easy dexterity of his burly limbs, and eyed the cacophonous cavern with distaste. People were so unimaginative. Erasmus hadn't made his realm this way; his captives had. They forged it with their minds over the centuries, a thousand thousand images of a punitive underworld hammered by suffering into indifferent stone. Verloc wondered if, through concerted and combined effort, they could shape the place into something less outwardly horrific, or if the die had been cast. It would be ironic if they could, a horde of prisoners in shackles built from their own lack of imagination. They would still be prisoners, he assumed, but prisoners in a prettier cage. That wasn't nothing.

In any case, the broader expanses of Erasmus' domain didn't interest him. His private chamber lay through a door to his left, and he entered. Inside, a four-poster bed filled over half the room, its plump mattress rippling with downy pillows and satin sheets. Amidst the tumble of bedding lay a trio of young women. Whiffs of sheer fabric cradled their curvy bodies. They gazed up at Verloc and cooed with joy at his approach. The iron bands about their wrists offered the only hints to their captivity. They seemed otherwise eager for him, quivering with a lust that was no less tantalizing for being manufactured. Erasmus may have bent these particular souls to their task, but Verloc couldn't criticize the man's handiwork. He chose a nubile redhead and eased her onto the sheets, hands resting on her shoulders before sliding downward to more enticing domains. He smiled as her deft hands undid his belt and eased his pants down his hips.

And there it was. The shame, bobbing like an ugly little piece of flotsam on the otherwise pristine sea of his pleasure. He pushed it down beneath the waters as if to drown it, though he knew the relief such an action proffered was only temporary. It was a horrid little nugget of truth, and the truth cannot drown. It would wait beneath the waters, patient, until his grip faltered and the inexorable force of its buoyancy brought it once again to light.

But for now, his grip held, and the kernel of shame could only bide its time in the stifled darkness of the vast still sea.

10

THE ROOM KNEW neither day nor night, but only a dusky non-time that stretched eternal in all directions. Hours seemed not to pass in orderly procession, but to hang about in a humid cloud, dissipating only by the caprices of some vast and uncharitable weather.

Roland sat within his fog of stagnant time, heaving eternities by the lungful and watching eons in the inscrutable shift of dull shadows on the wall. In the moments where his thoughts could dredge themselves free of the sluggish mire that entombed them, they turned inevitably to the book in Verloc's office.

He'd held it. He'd actually held it in his hands, and like a fool he'd let it go. The momentary disappointment he'd felt on reading its title had vanished, replaced with a certainty in its importance that he could only hold in retrospect. To make things worse, its emerald glow had become visible even with his eyes open, and his every moment was tainted with its mocking presence. He could find relief only by turning his back to it, and even then, he remained aware of it, its glow transcribed into a greasy spot of heat on the back of his neck. Still, the feeling was easier to take than the vision, and in time he learned to ignore it. Things became manageable.

That was, until the ghosts appeared.

They were little more than figments at first, the sort of vague human shapes one sometimes sees in clouds. But as time passed in its inimitable way, they gained shape and heft and color, and soon they staggered fully formed into his cell, dressed in rags, bound hand and foot by chains, faces miming cries of silent anguish. He couldn't hear them, which was a small mercy, but the sight alone was unbearable, and his dread of them grew so great that the moments of their absence became almost worse than their presence. A time came where he could take no more, and he began to shriek at the phantoms, face red and raging, fists pounding on the padded walls of his cell.

"Hau ab! Hau ab, ihr verdammten Geister! Ich will euch nicht sehen! fahrt zur Hölle, und nimmt dein verdammt grünes Buch mit!"

The clang of a fist on the cell's metal door silenced him. A voice he didn't recognize bellowed at him through the slot.

"Pull yourself together, Jerry. You've got a lady here wants to see you, but I ain't lettin' her in 'til you stop that damn caterwauling."

A visitor? Who would come to see him? He fell silent at once, hoping whoever it was hadn't been dissuaded by his ravings. A key turned in the lock and Nurse Donnelly stepped inside, followed by a lanky young man in an orderly's uniform. He paused at the doorway and eyed Roland the way one might size up a mangy and potentially rabid animal.

"You want me to keep watch here?" he asked.

"That won't be necessary, James. Thank you."

James nodded, his relief poorly hidden. "Right. Give a knock when you want me to let you out." He closed the door.

"Nurse Donnelly," said Roland. "It is very nice to see you. To what do I owe the pleasure of this visit?"

"Officially? I'm here as your caregiver, to see to your welfare and arrange your ongoing treatment."

"But unofficially?"

Martha's gaze drifted to the corner of the room. "I need you to tell me how you knew."

Roland waited for clarification, which didn't come. "I am sorry, what is it I knew?"

"...About Mrs. Chauncey. How did you know she was gone?"

"I have already told you this, to the extent I myself understand it."

Nurse Donnelly closed her eyes. "Yes, I recall your visions. I mean, how could you have *truly* known? Did you overhear other patients speaking of it? Did you inquire of another nurse?"

"I did none of these things. It is only as I have said, nothing more."

"But it's possible you overheard and simply don't recall, isn't it? That your subconscious noted it and dredged it up again later in...in your fever dream?" Her voice took on a pinched urgency as she spoke, as if invisible fingers pressed harder and harder on her larynx.

"It is possible, yes. But is it any more plausible than my own explanation? To a scientist, perhaps, as it breaks none of their laws, but to one who considers probabilities?" Roland shook his head.

"And what, precisely, is your explanation?" Nurse Donnelly asked.

"That something in my treatment changed me. It granted me something, or at least awakened it from where inside me it had long slept. In either case, it is awake now, and its strength grows every minute."

"But Mr. Hellmich, such things simply aren't possible."

"Such a handy word, 'possible.' One can use it to fix just about anything to one's liking."

The nurse pinched the ridge of bone between her eyes. "And was it these visions of yours that led you to attack three orderlies outside of Doctor Verloc's office?"

Roland smiled. It was intended as a sardonic gesture, but he was surprised to find real humor in it. "Is this what they say happened? That I rushed them like some *wütender Stier?* I had expected a bit more art to the telling. Perhaps this was naïve on me, given the tellers."

"If things didn't happen as they say, then what exactly did? They certainly didn't drag you out of bed at four in the morning, others would've seen that."

"There is...a book." As he spoke the words, a green flare erupted in the space beside Nurse Donnelly's leg. It was only at that moment that he noticed the image had gone dormant while he was speaking to her, and that the ghosts that had plagued him enough to shout were also absent. Had they left deliberately, banished by her presence? Or had his sight of them simply gone dim?

"A book?" prodded the nurse, nudging his derailed train of thought back on track.

"Yes. I first noticed it when we went into Dr. Verloc's office to discuss my treatment. Since then, it has grown more prominent in my vision. I see it even now, a sort of beacon leading me forward."

He told her the story, making no effort to hide his planned theft or downplay the bloodlust that had seized him in the first moments of his fight with Fox. The nurse listened with pursed lips. When he finished, she burst with pent-up outrage.

"But this is an appalling breach of conduct. Even for them. To deliberately instigate a fight with a patient—no, not just instigate, extort—I can't even imagine. We need to tell Dr. Verloc at once."

"Do you think he doesn't know already? If not the exact truth, then its general flavor? The story Fox told was lazy because it need not be otherwise. Verloc is not a stupid man. He sees who he has hired, and he does not care."

"But why? Why doesn't he care? Fox and MacCruiskenen and Pluck, they're no kin to him. Near as I can tell, he doesn't even like them. Why let them run roughshod over patients, when all it could earn him is a lawsuit from the Province?"

"I can think of only one place where the answer might be found. Perhaps I am mad to think it so, but think it I do."

The nurse looked at him quizzically for a moment before realization dawned. "The green book, you mean."

Roland nodded.

***

Verloc read the letter three times. With each reading, he hoped to find some nugget of optimism to assuage his fears, to stumble on a parsing that cast the letter in a kinder light and loosened the belt of panic that cinched ever tighter around his chest. But the closer he studied the words, the more ominous they seemed:

Dear Dr. Verloc,

The Erasmus Walpole Institution for Mental Hygiene has come to our attention. Patterns of morbidity, convalescence, and discharge have emerged that appear out of step with the broader trends found in the Province.

To identify any irregularities, and potential areas where improvement is warranted, we request a full copy of your patient intake and discharge records over the last five (5) years, in addition to a signed and notarized letter from you stipulating to their accuracy. Following our assessment further steps may be required. You will be notified of any necessary actions on your part at this time.

Please respond to this letter with the requested documents, sent by courier or mail, by no later than December 7th. The address for sending is included in the attached documentation.

We look forward to corresponding with you further, and hope that our assessment will help you implement changes that improve the care outcomes seen at your facility.

Regards,

Winston Bishop, Senior Auditor for the Ontario Minister of Health

He set the letter on his desk face down and covered it with a few stray documents, as if afraid that without such encumbrances it could sense his guilt. He'd known a day like this was coming, had known for years, but a part of him always suspected that his careful and creative documentation could hold the hounds at bay until his retirement, at which point some other poor fool could drink from the poison chalice that had sat, full to the brim, on his desk all this time.

Grabbing a book of stationary, he penned half a dozen letters offering as many excuses for delay or cancellation of the audit—destruction of some records from a burst waterpipe, poor bookkeeping by an easily scapegoated secretary (the ones who spoke poor English were best), personal health issues—and threw all of them into the wastebasket next to his desk. The exercise was pointless. Auditors did not accept excuses. Destroyed records, however convenient and plausible the excuse, would invite in-person investigation, and once those eager fingers started scratching at the wallpaper, it wouldn't be long before the whole rotten edifice lay naked in the light of day. The records were better, as he'd taken care to fudge them elegantly, but his long-held confidence in his abilities evaporated the instant the ink from the letter stained his fingers. He was a neurologist, not a forger. His trade was the revelation of internal truths, not the construction of falsehoods.

A knock on the door dragged him back from his ruminations. It was a welcome return, but he felt annoyed nonetheless and barked out a reply. "Who is it? Come in if you're coming in."

A nurse from the public ward opened the door and shuffled inside. She was a bit mousey, with pinched cheeks and dowdy brown hair, but her hips were ample in their roundness and he suspected her matronly uniform hid a pair of soft and lovely breasts. He let his eyes slide up her as he met her gaze, looking in a manner that seemed inattentive rather than lascivious. His years of work among young nurses had made him adept at this, and he sense no discomfort in her gaze when their eyes finally met.

"Begging your pardon, sir. One of the elderly patients has a blockage in her bowel. It needs to be flushed out. Head nurse told me you've some reference guides on colonic irrigation in your office on the public ward, and I wondered if I might borrow the key."

"Head Nurse Tremblay couldn't have provided you with one?"

"She's off duty, sir. And I didn't know she carried one besides."

"In the future, she would be the better point of contact. But for the time being, you may use mine." He pulled a keyring from his pocket, unthreaded a stout iron key, and slid it across his desk. She grabbed it just as it skated over the side, fumbled it through her fingers, and caught it with her elbow against her belly, an action that elicited a not unpleasant bit of jiggling. She nodded her thanks and left without another word. Not terribly astute—none of them were, truly, apart from Tremblay—but she seemed to have enough sense not to waste his time unduly. He amused himself for a moment by working her through a few favorite wardrobes and postures in the theater of his mind, before a voice yanked the curtains closed and spilled him back to the present moment. It came from the bottommost drawer of his desk, a bit muffled but still clear.

"I require your attention, Apostle Verloc."

Verloc closed his eyes and drew a slow, inhaled breath. It was a gesture that steeled him without giving outward signs of insubordination—he remained uncertain as to how much Erasmus could see into the realm of the living. Once composed, he opened the drawer and withdrew the scrying plate, in which he could see Erasmus' crowned and jagged silhouette.

"I serve at your pleasure, Master. Please tell me what you need of me."

"There is but one thing of value you can provide me, and the time has come to deliver it."

Verloc bit back a sigh. "I'm sorry, Master, but now is not the time. Our situation has just become significantly more delicate. The Province has smelled something amiss, and are about to set their bloodhounds to sniffing about our records. The most recent set must be spotless. Any death even the least bit suspicious—"

"I am aware of your concerns, apostle, as you never fail to bring them to my attention. But there are dangers beyond the talents of mere clerks to calculate, and they grow by the hour. The seer is gaining strength. I have not seen one of his vitality in an age or more.

Fortunately, his growing power has made him easier to identify, and I have found him."

Erasmus' form disappeared from the plate. Blobs of color swirled in its absence, coalescing into the image of a large, unshaven man in a padded cell. His eyes darted back and forth beneath the unkempt thicket of his hair. Verloc recognized the man without difficulty.

"Him? That immigrant fellow who came in on police escort last month? Master, this man is exactly the sort of patient we cannot afford to lose at this moment. Despite his diagnosis, he remains otherwise healthy and bereft of physical symptoms. These will come in time, but they cannot be reliably faked. He'll be a candidate for a pauper's grave in due course, but should he die now, we may as well invite the chief of policy down to the catacombs for a personal tour."

"You overstep your authority, apostle. You would do well to remember that you serve at your post at my pleasure, and as things stand, I am fast growing displeased. Should your services be deemed unnecessary, I can assure you, you would not like the result."

"My services will become unnecessary if the asylum is shut down. Master, I mean no disrespect, but I beg you to heed my words. I do not deny that there are risks that remain quite outside my ability to identify, but there too exist risks to which I am the more attuned. The patient is imprisoned and all but forgotten. Give me just a little time to ensure our safety before we act."

"I have not reached out to you for counsel, but for action. I will ask you one more time only. Will you carry out my dictate?"

Verloc sighed. "Of course, Master. In a few weeks' time..."

"Not a few weeks. Not a few days. Today."

"I'm sorry, Master. It pains me to fail you, but I simply cannot. You will understand when you see how close we skirt oblivion."

Verloc put the scrying plate back in his desk. He expected the muffled voice to berate him, but Erasmus apparently found such an outburst beneath his dignity, for he gave no further reply. Verloc smiled. The act of rebellion had been a challenge, but there was a certain pleasure in its execution that could not be denied.

It would likely be some time before he was once again granted a visit to the Second Plain. But so be it. Someone needed to protect Erasmus from his own worst impulses, and the job had fallen to him—if not for Erasmus' sake, then certainly for his own.

11

MARTHA STOOD OUTSIDE the hall leading to the secure rooms for several minutes. Reticence bolted thick bars across the threshold, preventing her crossing. She studied the object in her hands, hefted it, and hoped she was doing the right thing by bringing it along. There was reason to think that, by probing the lowermost reaches of Roland's unhealthy fascination, one might identify its source, and sweep away the rotting origins of his warped thinking. But there remained risk of backlash as well, as he could seize any trifling coincidence as proof of the accuracy of his visions, cementing his believe in them still harder.

The bars gave way, sawn through by her resolve, and she cleared the short distance to Roland's quarters with purposeful strides. A teenage orderly picked at pimples on his chin while thumbing a Tijuana Bible crudely hidden in the jacket of a Book of Common Prayer. Martha thought the ruse might have been more convincing if he'd chosen something less suspiciously pious as cover.

"I'm here to see a patient," she explained to the boy. "Roland Hellmich."

The boy cocked a thumb in the direction of Roland's room. "Key's hangin' on a hook near the back of the hall."

Martha raised her eyebrows, surprised by his indifferent acquiescence. She'd prepared a detailed justification of her visit on clinical grounds and was both relieved and a little disappointed that she had no cause to use it. Probably she could have walked by with a knife in her hand and the boy wouldn't have lifted a finger to stop her. She gave the boy a prim nod of thanks that he didn't acknowledge, grabbed the keys, and unlocked the door.

The asylum frowned on calling its secure rooms "cells," but there was no other term Martha could think of that didn't feel false and euphemistic. The chamber was a sad, dim cube, its every surface upholstered with a once-white fabric that had faded to a piebald yellow in the few places unmarred by stains. A lone bulb encased in a hemisphere of shatterproof glass clung to the ceiling, providing the room's sole source of light apart from whatever scraps could squeak through the gaps in the door. There was no furniture to speak of, apart from a raised slab of padding in one corner that constituted a bed. It was there that Roland sat when she arrived, back straight, legs crossed, eyes fixed on some arbitrary point on the opposite wall.

"Well," she said. "I've brought it for you."

To Roland's credit, he did not attempt to snatch it from her nor demand to see its contents. He merely nodded, his interest evident only in the intensity of his gaze. Martha brought it over and sat down next to him on the bed, trying her best not to show the revulsion she felt at the mattress' spongy dampness. She knew its current state wasn't Roland's fault, since in her limited dealings with him she'd always found him to be stringently clean, and there was no sense reminding him of the squalor into which the asylum had foisted him.

"So, this is the book your vision led you to. *A Compendium of Eminent Personages from Queenstown and the Greater Niagara Region, 1678 to Present.* I'm afraid I don't see the significance."

"I had the same thought. Open it, please."

She turned to the table of contents. The entries consisted of dozens of names of prominent figures associated with the region, almost none of whom Martha had heard of. The dates of their births and deaths, given in parentheses, suggested a certain chronological ordering, though the entries were also grouped by field, with batches of names appearing under various headings: "Explorers," "Political Figures," "Sports," "Literature and the Arts." Under the final section, "Religious Leaders and Mystics," a single name caught Martha's attention: Erasmus Walpole. She looked at Roland, who had clearly noticed the name as well. In unspoken agreement, they turned to the identified page and began reading.

Erasmus Adolpho Walpole, 1721-1804 (disputed). Erasmus Walpole counts among the founding fathers of Queenstown, being among the earliest settlers to the township in 1769. He established the first house of worship in the area and oversaw it as minister, claiming he had been ordained in the Anglican church and served as a parson in Hawkesbury England. However, subsequent records from Hawkesbury show no sign of a man named Erasmus Walpole, and the tiny hamlet bears scant resemblance to the prosperous and bustling mill town he described in letters and surviving writings, suggesting he had never actually visited it.

Whatever his origins, Walpole proved an adept minister, and his congregation swelled, dwarfing that of the Catholic church founded two years later—a substantial achievement, given that the predominant number of settlers at the time were of French extraction. He quickly became a popular figure in the town, gaining frequent mention in letters as a forceful and resolute man of God. This perception remained for many years, though slowly shifted over time, as Walpole's more peculiar tendencies began to color his reputation. Houseguests reported strange occult tomes among his bookshelves, and whispers began of queer rituals held in the rectory. One citizen, a blacksmith named Hal Orson, even accused Walpole of witchcraft, saying the minister recruited him to forge strange sigils for use in satanic rituals. The accusations were not corroborated.

The few extant sermons preserved in regional archives show a forceful and gifted writer, but also one with apocalyptic predilections and a self-image that bordered on the messianic. Descriptions of end times, shocking in their gruesome detail, peppered his pronouncements, and conclude generally with an emphasis that he alone could lead the faithful to salvation through God. In his later sermons, his imagery drew less and less from direct biblical sources, recounting instead strange and nightmarish visions taken from other writings, or perhaps his own imagination.

Because of this change in focus, or perhaps simply due to the shift in his reputation over the intervening years, Walpole's congregation began to dwindle. With a flourish of martyrdom, he announced a pilgrimage into the uncharted wilds to the northwest of the city, where he claimed that important visions would be revealed to him.

When he came <u>back</u> to the city several years later, he did so with a vast and mysterious fortune, which he promptly began spending with a generosity that placed him firmly <u>back</u> in the bosom of the community. He funded the construction of bridges, buildings, and other public works, paid for the maintenance and beautification of parks, expanded the city's ramshackle shoreline into a bustling wharf capable of supporting substantial industry (a boon that benefits the city to this day), and established bursaries for the children of clerks and laborers to attain higher education. His greatest contribution, however, and the one into which he poured the predominance of his vision, was the hospital for the mad. Built on a slab of unforgiving bedrock on the outskirts of the city that had long been deemed useless, its soil too parched and sour for farming, its earth too rocky and rough for housing, it dwarfed in size everything built in the region to date. For its construction, he relied principally on labor imported from outside of the village. Indians from the surrounding tribes were the most frequently recruited workers, many of whom began attending his services upon <u>conclusion</u> of their day's work. When the hospital was completed, most of these men stayed on as groundskeepers, orderlies, and maintenance men, while Erasmus himself became director. It was a role he took to with aplomb despite an absence of medical training,

Erasmus' beneficence erased much of the discomfit his quirks had generated, though there remained some chatter about how exactly he acquired the money to fund such lavish philanthropy. Some men said he'd invested in the slave trade, then blossoming into a mercantile force. Others that he had used gambling, liquor, or other sinful acts to attain his wealth, and his generosity was thus a form of atonement. A few whispered tales far stranger and darker still, stories filigreed with the occult, but these were generally discounted.

At the <u>end</u> of his life, Erasmus was rarely seen outside of the hospital grounds. He is presumed to have died on or around June 14th, 1804, as no one beyond this date could provide any clear description of his whereabouts, but as with much of the life that came before, its <u>end</u> remains shrouded in mystery. No clear cause of death was ever provided, nor was his death officially recorded by the coroner's office. He appears simply to have vanished.

Though a reclusive and enigmatic figure, Erasmus Walpole made an indisputable and indelible mark on his community. The scope of his deeds has echoed through the ages, and can be heard even today in many of the amenities Queenstown's fortunate residents take for granted—not the least of them the hospital that became the focus of his later years, which has operated without pause for over 50 years.

When they finished reading, Martha set the book down and turned to Roland.

"An unusual man, to be sure, but I must say I see little in the way of revelations here. What did we learn, really, besides some local history and a couple of rumors?"

Roland scratched at his chin. "There is something strange here."

"Well, aye, he was an odd duck, and no mistake, but—"

"I do not mean with the story itself. I mean with the text. Look, some of the words have been underlined."

Martha skimmed the passage, and saw what Roland meant. In several places, a meticulous hand had drawn a thin black line beneath the text. She gripped the corner of her mouth between her teeth and chewed it lightly.

"Notes, I suppose. By a medical student, or a scholar of some kind. It's common enough for astute readers to mark passages."

"But these are not passages. They are simply words. Look, here. 'End.' 'Back.' 'Conclusion.' This is not a collection of notes for later study. This is a message."

"A message saying what?"

Roland looked at Martha. "This is your mother tongue, nurse, not mine. I would think you would grasp this sooner. All these words are synonyms, are they not? They hold the same meaning."

Martha flipped to the back of the book.

"See? Nothing here either. Now can we... Hmmm..." Running her thumb along the lip of binding, Martha noticed a peculiar lumpiness behind the paper backing pasted over the stiff bound cover. She slid her thumbnail into the seam between paper and binding. The backing came free with a crunch of ancient adhesive. She took the aged backing between thumb and forefinger and slowly peeled it. There, tucked between the binding and the outer cover, was a sheet of age-yellowed ledger paper. With a ginger tug of her fingers, she eased the paper from its hiding place and smoothed it against the front cover of the book.

A dense, cramped script filled the paper from end to end. There was no margin, no spacing, letters stood one atop the other, the dangling tails of gs and ps tangling with the upper stalks of fs and ts. Despite these limitations, the writing was clear and legible. Each letter appeared carefully composed—far from a hasty jotting, but rather something intended to be read.

Martha and Roland looked at one another. Silently and together, they began to read.

To my successor,

I write this on the Twelfth of April, in the year of our Lord 1885. It may be many years hence until this message is found, if indeed it is found at all. If I have succeeded in my task, I will destroy it unread by any eyes beyond mine, so if you are reading these words, know I have failed.

My name is Eugene Owens. I am the Head Physician at the Erasmus Walpole Asylum for Lunatics, a position I have held for thirteen years. From a young age, I felt a calling for medicine, and it was with no small amount of pride that I accepted my doctorate from McGill College in the spring of 1871. I emerged a young and—if I may in this most personal confession eschew any false modesty—talented physician in search of a venue suited to my gifts. In what appeared a stroke of fortune, I soon found an opening at Walpole, for the previous director and head physician had passed away abruptly and left an urgent need for continued stewardship. What I lacked in experience I made up for in education and verve, and after a short interview with the board I was granted the position. It was the greatest triumph of my young life, and also perhaps, I would one day discover, the greatest tragedy.

Not long after my directorship began, I found myself led by a strange and inexorable impulse to the darkest recesses of this building, where the corridors of an old but unremarkable basement gave way to a sunken catacomb in which I found an altar of great antiquity. It was here that Erasmus first revealed himself to me.

As a man of science, educated in reason and empirical medicine at one of the greatest universities on our vast if underpopulated continent, I did not and do not consider myself one susceptible to superstition or the occult. I long scoffed at reports of the supernatural, considering them defects in human perception and memory. It therefore humbles me to admit how quickly, effortlessly, even eagerly this skepticism fled in the face of the shadowy figure that rose from that altar.

I do not write this account to seek absolution for my actions, but I should make some small effort to explain my eagerness. You see, I am a man beset by forbidden impulses, unnatural thoughts which I prefer not to dwell on, but which must go unfulfilled by dint of the law. Erasmus saw these desires in me, and he showed me in his sorcery the means to grant these desires to a degree I never in even my most debased fantasies thought possible. In exchange for these wonders, all he asked was for me to grant him occasional services in matters he insisted would be anything but onerous.

I wish I could say I first rejected these impulses, that it was only through months or years of guile that my defenses wore away, but the truth is I accepted at once. He saw in me things I could tell no one, and far from turning away in disgust or horror, he embraced them. And so I trusted him. How naïve I was! How great a fool is the man I see in these words as I read them back to myself now! For though as he said, the deeds he required were hardly taxing to my body, they took a far steeper cost to my mind, and my soul.

His request at first was thus: whenever a patient in the care of my institution should die, I was to escort the body that same night to a chamber in the building's lowest catacombs— the very room where Erasmus first revealed himself to me. There, I performed a certain ritual which I shudder to describe, before conferring the body to its proper resting place in the mortuary. He assured me that no one who observed the cadaver would ever know of its desecration, for he commanded powerful illusory magics that would render to any inquisitive hand or eye a form unchanged in any way from the normal course of decomposition.

I did not enjoy these actions, but they seemed a small price to pay for admission to the dew-gilded valleys of pleasure that Erasmus opened before me. However, time passed, and the terms of our agreement began slowly to change. One day, Erasmus informed me that the rate of mortality in my institution had slowed to an unacceptable degree, and I must make up the shortfall however I saw fit.

There is, of course, but one way to render freshly dead bodies when nature or circumstance does not provide them, and the name of this method is murder. I recoiled from this request, as a physician and as a man, but the gates to my paradise closed before me, and it was not long before I found myself in the room of one of my patients, a terminally ill man with a severe and intractable case of lunacy. I administered him a fatal dose of opium, telling myself I was ending the suffering of a miserable creature, and the access to my Eden was once again granted.

This first fatal transgression led to others, each resting on shakier and shakier equivocations. I told myself that I was easing suffering, that I selected only the most wretched among my patients and ushered them beyond this fleshy realm of misery and pain. But Erasmus favored the young and healthy over the old and ill, and my rationalizations soon grew untenable. In truth, they all were. For I took an oath to first and above all things do no harm, and yet a great deal of harm I had done all ready, and a great deal more I was still to do.

Until this time, Erasmus gave little guidance on the subjects he wished for sacrifice, other than a general insistence on youth and vitality. But the day came where he called to me in my office, his voice like the scratching of rat claws on the rafters, and told me the exact person I must deliver to him. Her name was Constance, and she was eleven years old. She was a shy little wisp of a thing, below a normal height and weight for her age, but intelligent, with a keen, inquisitive mind and a cheerful smile. Her condition was tragic, the stigma it bore confining her to our asylum, but nothing about it was terminal, and there was a chance that her fits could grow more manageable with time.

I asked him why this girl in particular should be sacrificed, and he told me that the girl's condition granted her the ability to see beyond the mundane world around her, and peer at times into his own realm—a skill he referred to as The Sight. This power was growing, he told me, and would soon be joined by an ability to manipulate the rules of his realm as he did. Such an occurrence would spell disaster, threatening his realm—and, of course, my own garden of forbidden delights. Once I would have scoffed at claims of psychic or paranormal ability, but clearly my attitude towards such things had changed. Now my reaction was not at all about the bizarre nature of his claims, but of the moral implication of his demand.

I must be clear, as much as it pains me to unbandage and bare the naked wound of my sin—she was not a terminal patient. Barring unexpected illness or terrible misfortune, she would live to adulthood and many years beyond. Even if fate in its cruelty did not allow her to ever leave the asylum, she would still have had a life. The nurses had taken it upon themselves to teach her reading and figures, and she had a deft hand with pen and ink, producing images of depth and complexity far beyond her years. She was the very definition of promise and innocence, and it was my duty to crush her beneath my heel.

And so I did. I can say no more of it, for the memory pains me too greatly, but know I did all I could to ensure she did not suffer. I say this not to earn your forgiveness or pity—I deserve neither—but to assuage, in some small way, the anguish of my trodden and tarnished soul.

With this black deed behind me, I felt no relief, only a dull nausea of anxiety. For I understood by then that there would be other demands, some of them even more appalling than what I'd delivered so far, and that the time would come where my only choice would be to heed them and become a monster, or refuse them and be destroyed. It occurs to me now that, at the moment of this realization, the time for this decision may have already passed.

And so, on a last dalliance to the garden two weeks ago, I ventured beyond its sylvan walls and peered at the larger realm Erasmus had made. What I saw haunts me still.

There, I saw each of the men and women I had brought to the altar, chained and clothed in rags, their tortured forms wracked with incalculable misery. Among them were each of the patients I delivered unto him, including Constance, the young girl with fits and a talent for ink drawings.

I have spent the intervening period in the library of Holy Scepter and the city's many bookshops, reading what I could of the sort of tomes Erasmus favored when he was merely a man, and not something both more and less than that. Through this, what I saw, and my own judgement, I believe I have now grasped, in rough detail at least, exactly what he has done.

The impetus for Erasmus' sinister scholarship remains unknown to me. Certainly, he bent his abilities to the accumulation of an immense fortune, though any lust for gold he may have had was long since vanished, and I suspect the money was always a means to an end rather than an end in itself. If vengeance drove him, it is unclear to whom or for what. Rather, I think it was power itself he craved. Erasmus glimpsed the devil, and in him found neither a villain to oppose nor a master to serve, but a blueprint to follow.

In the course of his infernal study, he learned of a dark art through which he coaxed back the souls of the recent dead. With spells of binding he made them his thralls, and on their backs he built an afterworld. In this place, those wretches snared by his sorcery are cut forever from the grand fabric of God's creation, and may gain neither eternal life nor divine punishment as meted out by their Creator.

But even Satan is a part of God's plan, and without purpose Erasmus grew dissatisfied. He needed something from his thralls beyond mere possession, a utility that would lend savor to his acquisition. He found it in the simplest and most ancient of pleasures: consumption. And so his hell became a farm, and the souls he enthralled his livestock. He crafted servants whose granite skin and great stature reflected his perceptions of his own strength, and drove them to syphon, piece by piece, the essence from his captives, until nothing but husks remained.

But Erasmus' innovation became his prison, for his need to own and acquire did not vanish when his need to consume emerged. The more he ate, the less he owned, and the more he kept, the less he could eat. He became cursed with two competing hungers, and to sate one was to starve the other. The only way forward was to acquire an ever-growing stock of souls, and for this purpose he has me—as, I suspect, he had the director before me, and the one before him. There is no telling how long this nightmarish practice has gone on, nor how long it will continue. Unless, that is, I am able to stop it.

Through my actions on Erasmus' behalf, I had rendered the souls of my patients into the confines of Erasmus' dominion. I have sinned against God and man more profoundly than any human being save Erasmus Walpole himself, and he is no longer human. I am unsure whether my actions can save my soul, but even if I knew they could not, I would take them anyway. My aim is to kill him, and destroy the hell he has created. If there is a way to free those souls I and other weak men have damned here, I will do it. But even if this is not possible, I will do all in my power to at least ensure that no others ever count among their number.

I have performed some reconnaissance, and if there is a weakness in his realm, it lies at the end of the tracks his minions use to cart his meals to him. I have followed them as far as I dare, and learned that the heart of his empire is guarded by a powerful hex, a conjuration of one's greatest fear. Once past this barrier, I believe he is vulnerable.

I dare not leave this letter unconcealed, for while I remain convinced there are limits to Erasmus' powers, their borders are not clearly charted, and he has proven his ability to see things he should not see, and know things he should not know. For its hiding place, I selected this volume, as it was one of the first I read upon receiving the directorship. I can only hope that my successor's mind will be of a similar bent.

Should I fail, my story and my duty shall fall to you. I have told all I know in the hopes it will be of use to you, and that you may succeed where I have failed. Whoever you are, I leave you the account above, and these words: Broker no deals with Erasmus Walpole! For however tempting the offer may be, the terms are false and the payments poison. For thirteen years I have been his thrall, enslaved by his dark sorcery, bound in chains forged from my own darkest desires. Do not let this same fate befall you!

Pray for me, and for those I have wronged.

Eugene Owens

When she'd finished reading, Martha set the letter on the bed and cupped her face with both hands. Roland finished shortly after her, and the two sat together in silence for a time. Of the two, Roland was the first to speak.

"It is more horrible even than I had imagined. Think of it, a hell whose occupants have committed no mortal sin, undertaken no transgressions, where even the blood of the lamb cannot wash them clean."

Martha looked at him with anguish "It's madness, Roland, is what it is. Sheer madness, written by a madman masquerading as a head physician, one who possibly didn't even exist. And worse than that, it's blasphemous! Earthly sins are the flip side of free will, but God wouldn't allow a mere man to trod on the Kingdom of Heaven."

"He has allowed one hell already, with a devil to rule it. Why not another?"

Martha recoiled from the suggestion. "If there is one indisputable fact in scripture, it is that man cannot station himself above God. To suggest otherwise is... It's heresy. It's worse than the golden calf by far."

"I do not question that it is awful. I question only whether it is true."

"Of course it isn't true! You're not well, Roland. Your thoughts are delusional, and they're leading you down a very dark path."

Roland turned his eyes from her. His gaze fixed on a spot in the distance. To Martha, he seemed to be staring at an arbitrary spot on the wall, but the look of resolve that hardened his features suggested that he gazed at something far more ominous. She had no idea what it was, and she was much too afraid to ask.

"I do not expect you to think of this letter as anything but a lunatic's scribbles," said Roland. "I think of it otherwise, but I have seen things you have not, and for that we should both be grateful. If my belief is misplaced, the Lord will forgive me, for he knows my heart and my intentions are pure. But if I am right, and still I choose to do nothing, this he may not be so ready to forgive."

***

Verloc closed his jacket tighter around his waist and shivered. The crypt was never warm, the crags and outcrops on its bare granite walls like greedy tongues lapping up every scrap of heat, but as fall gave way to winter the once-mild cold turned frigid and bitter. This made it a good place to store dead bodies, but those that belonged to the living found it most unpleasant, and Verloc was no exception. His breath emerged from his lips in twists of fog that drifted in the torchlight before dissipating. Numbness nibbled the ends of his fingers. He thrust them deep into his armpits and shifted from foot to foot.

Why was it inevitably *him* down here waiting, and not the mongrels he'd enlisted to serve his bidding? He was director and head physician at Walpole, and in his duties all through the organization overhead his employees met him at his convenience. Meetings began when he entered a room and ended when he left, and not an idle second stood against him. Yet somehow, down here, in the stale and fetid darkness, the rules inverted. Fox was his subordinate, and any crimes committed were by his hand. Verloc held the cards here. It should be *Fox* waiting down here in the cold, shivering like a Cossack peasant, ears cocked for the footsteps signaling the arrival of his superior.

As if summoned by this thought, the heel-toe clop of Fox's soles sounded from the far end of the basement corridor. Verloc listened to their languid pace with growing annoyance. It was bad enough having to wait on a subordinate, but the utter indifference to his time indicative in Fox's stride was the most galling thing of all. It was the sound of someone in no hurry to get where he was going, who knew that his appointment would wait all day for the moment when he deigned to arrive.

Already seething, Verloc's rage darkened further as Fox's silhouette crested the dim corridor leading from the subbasement stairwell to the crypt. For even in the sepulchral half-light, he could see two things that troubled him. Firstly, Fox hadn't brought the gurney with him, which meant he hadn't even yet acquired the body that was the entire purpose of the meeting.

Second, he wasn't coming alone. Two figures strafed him, one small, one large. The light was too dim and the distance too far to make out anything more about their appearance, but Verloc needed no further information to venture their identities. His guess proved correct half a minute later, as Fox finally passed the threshold to the crypt, his dimwitted sidekicks MacCruiskeen and Pluck at his heels. Verloc looked at them and then at Fox, lips pursed with annoyance.

"We had agreed that this was to be a meeting between the two of us alone," said Verloc.

Fox shrugged. "Yeah, well, things change."

"And you think it prudent to invite your...compatriots into this exchange?"

"What can I say? I trust my boys. Whatever we gotta talk about, we can do it in front of them."

Verloc pressed his fingers to his right temple and worked them in slow circles. He could feel a headache taking root there, and hoped the pressure might dislodge it before it grew too large. "Very well, then let's move on to the next of my concerns. I am, as you are quite aware, a busy man with an entire hospital to run. At any moment, there are a myriad of tasks that require my attention and input. For this reason, I choose to delegate certain simple tasks to individuals in my employ. In your case, I require the furnishing of certain items, which I can't help but notice have not thus far been delivered as promised. I trust that you have not wasted my time unduly, and will ensure that said items arrive in due course, and can explain why—"

"Relax, Verloc," said Fox. "We've got your body for you. And it ain't one that anybody's gonna miss, so you've got nothing to worry about."

Verloc glared at Fox, his mouth hanging slightly open. He was used to a certain overfamiliarity and boorishness from the young man, saw it as the inevitable cost of hiring someone of his particular unsavory range of talents, but Fox had, despite his japes and slipshod bearing at his duties, always met a certain baseline of respect that was, for the first time, nowhere in evidence. Never before had he interrupted Verloc while speaking. And while "Doc" was far from Verloc's preferred form of address, it was at least tolerable. To hear his surname pass unadorned from a mouth as boorish as Fox's, that crossed a line.

"You forget yourself, Mr. Fox," said Verloc. "And you overestimate the insubordination, not to mention incompetence, that I am willing to put up with from the likes of you. So, I will ask you, calmly, to explain where the item is, why you haven't yet acquired it, and how soon I can expect to receive it."

Fox absorbed this upbraiding with a lazy smile and half-lidded eyes, arms crossed in front of his chest. He buffed his fingernails on his shirt and inspected them as he spoke—an entirely theatrical gesture, for they were far too dust-caked and dirty to buff.

"You can have it right this minute, Doc, you want it so bad. It's right here in this room with us."

MacCruiskeen and Pluck suppressed chuckles at this pronouncement. For the first time, Verloc's attention moved from Fox to them. He had thus far paid them only a cursory glance or two, but now he studied their expressions in detail, and what he saw troubled him. They had never paid him any real respect, but the grins they beamed at him went well past insubordination to open mockery. The rage building in his chest curdled into dread. With the dawning agony of a traveler who remembers too late some essential item he'd left at home, Verloc played back Fox's words and grew aware of a new interpretation of their meaning. He forced his back to straighten, held every muscle taut, and tamped down any whisper of fear. The slightest sign of weakness could be the end of him.

"I would encourage you to think carefully on your next actions," he whispered. "You may think you can gain something from this, but you will not. I have a being on my side with tremendous power. Kill me, and you'll need to answer to him. Your deaths will make mine look like paradise."

"On the contrary," cooed a voice behind Verloc. "I believe they will meet less opposition than you suspect on that end."

Verloc's stomach transformed into a bucket of ice water. He turned and faced the shadowy apparition.

"Master," he said, his voice quivering. "You can't mean this."

"I mean precisely what I say, and always have. It is you who have failed to understand of late. I have grown tired of your wheedling, your delays, your constant second-guessing. You have forgotten which of us is apostle and which of us is master, and I am no longer interested in trying to teach you what you should have learned long ago."

"I have sought only to advise you, Master. Everything I do, I do it for your protection—"

"I need your advice not at all," Erasmus growled. "And your protection I need even less."

Verloc dropped to his knees. He laced his fingers together into a single fist and shook it, pleading, at Erasmus' feet.

"Master, I beg of you, don't do this. Who will run your institute? Surely you don't think these...these thugs have what it takes to manage an organization of this magnitude? You'll be bankrupt in a year."

"It matters little to me which of you ants is put in charge of the nest. For too long, I have held the assumption that my apostle is best situated at the top of the Institute, but over time I have begun to see the flaw in this thinking. For the skills of a director have little bearing on those I require, and men who grace such positions, learned though they may be, have inevitably lacked the fortitude I need in apostles. Men like your esteemed Fox are much better suited to the role."

Fox tipped an invisible hat at this compliment. "Sorry, Doc," he said. "It looks like you're old news. Mac and Pluck and me, we're the future. Erasmus has it figured out. He don't need administrators or paper pushers. All he needs are a few guys who can get shit done."

Seeing no mercy in his former master, Verloc crawled over to Fox. He grabbed the younger man's pantleg and tugged at it. "You'll go to prison," he pleaded. "All three of you. You must see that. This can't go on! The auditors are already circling, they've requisitioned the patient charts. If we don't do something, all of us will be behind bars."

"Bars are the least of your worries now, pal," said Fox. He raised one foot and used it to scrape Verloc's fingers from his leg. "'Sides, I think you're underestimating your old boss. The man showed us things. Wonderful things. And they're all gonna be ours."

At this, a barrier closed around Verloc's senses. Sound grew muted and dull, and the world went dark. He reached to his face and felt a thin smooth membrane against his skin. His next breath drew no air, serving only to suck the membrane tighter to his lips. He clawed at it until thick, muscled arms pulled his hands away and held them locked behind his back.

"But hey," said Fox. "Thanks for the tip. You're right, a rubber sheet really *is* better than a plain ol' garrote. Won't leave hardly any marks at all!" He kicked Verloc in the stomach, knocking the last bit of air from his screaming lungs. He gasped in silent anguish against the rubber. Spots of fleeting light erupted against the darkmess. *It's all lies!* he wanted to scream. *Whatever he's promised you, the money, the power, the sex, it's all lies! Your pleasures will be empty ones, and the day will come when they end. And more's the pity to you when it does.* But the plastic made such pronouncements impossible. The only sound he could make was an ugly gurgle of bile spurting up his spasming esophagus. A chill sank into him, freezing his skin, his muscles, his bones, inching ever inward until it wrapped its fingers around his heart.

12

"**DR.** VERLOC IS dead," said Martha. "His secretary found him in his office this morning. They think it was a heart attack."

Roland looked from her to Eloise, who had come with her to tell him the news. He nodded once in acknowledgement, his face betraying no hint of surprise.

"It was no heart attack," he said.

Martha looked to Eloise. This wasn't the response she'd expected. It wasn't as if she'd thought the man should tear at his breast and weep, but such a flippant reaction to news of anyone's passing struck her as cold. Yet in his tone she sensed no callousness or indifference, but rather a tired foreknowledge, as if he had received the same sad message a dozen times that day—only that was impossible. Who would have told him?

"There has been no autopsy yet, of course," said Eloise. "But there is little doubt to the cause. Such events, they are not uncommon in men of his, er, dimensions. Especially those who work as tirelessly as he did."

Roland shook his head. "I saw it. Glimpses, only, as if through a thick fog. But there can be no doubt. They strangled him." He looked up at the ceiling. "They will come for me next, I think."

"Who strangled him?" Martha asked.

"Those orderlies. Fox, and the other two. There was another there too, but him..." Roland studied his feet. "I do not wish to speak of him."

Martha and Eloise exchanged sideways glances. Roland's declarations were, almost literally, a textbook example of paranoid delusions. Claimed foreknowledge of death, descriptions of conspiracy, threats against his life. Yet his tone was calm, reasoned, even resigned. He spoke as if of something unremarkable, seemingly indifferent to whether or not they believed him. Martha could take raving, but the declaration of nonsense in such a matter-of-fact way unnerved her. She wondered whether that meant his case was particularly treatable or particularly severe, and how best to address it—to challenge his assertions or indulge them. Eloise favored a third method, ignoring them altogether.

"The asylum board will select an interim director sometime this week. In the meantime, at Nurse Donnelly's request, I am recommending a pause to your fever treatments. The new director, once chosen, will likely review your case and decide for himself, though I will highlight the arising complications and your reluctance to participate, and recommend they be stopped permanently."

Roland shook his head. "I am sorry. I cannot agree to this."

Martha assumed he must have misheard. "Roland, Nurse Tremblay is saying your treatments will be stopped. Temporarily, at least, and quite possibly permanently."

"Yes, I realize this. But the treatments must continue, and without delay."

"I don't understand," said Martha. "You hate the fever cabinet. After your first treatment, you begged me to intervene."

"And I will always be grateful that you tried, and sorry at any difficulty it cost you. But things have changed. And my treatment must go on."

Martha's lips puckered. Sensing her growing disquiet, Eloise spoke before she had a chance to reply. "Nurse Donnelly and I must discuss this between ourselves. Please give us a moment."

Roland nodded assent, and the two nurses stepped into the hallway, easing the cell door shut behind them. As soon as the latch sounded, Martha spoke.

"He's clearly delusional, concocted some mad fantasy about visions and magic. We can't possibly continue his treatment under these conditions."

"On the contrary, the conditions you speak of are precisely what the cabinet seeks to treat, *n'est-ce pas?*"

"Exactly. It was designed to cure madness by killing the bacteria, not to indulge it."

"But Doctor Verloc, he did not prescribe this treatment to indulge anyone's madness." Eloise touched Martha's shoulder. "To speak frankly, the fever treatment has never been my favorite procedure. I have performed many in my time, and have seen small benefit and no miracles. But I have seen little harm as well, when performed responsibly and with diligence. If Mr. Hellmich was still opposed to the treatment, I would be willing to stop it in order to reduce his dismay, for I believe the patient's mindset cures as much as the doctor's medicine. But if he demands, even begs for a treatment he has been duly prescribed, how can I refuse it him?"

Martha placed her hand on Eloise's and squeezed it. "I'm afraid. It shames me, but I am. I've seen his fits, and they're a terrible thing to behold. The next one could kill him."

"Never has a patient died in the cabinet."

"That doesn't mean one couldn't."

Eloise gave her a sympathetic smile. "Human lives are fragile things, *ma choupette*, and we juggle them by the dozen every day. If we dwell on the consequence of dropping one of them, we are sure to drop them all." She took her hand from Martha's shoulder. It wasn't an unkind gesture, but it betrayed a certain finality. "If it will set your mind at ease, I will attend the procedure with you."

They returned to Roland's room. He sat on the edge of his bed, arms folded atop his knees, which reached nearly to his chin due to the inadequate girth of the mattress. Martha looked to Eloise, who nodded at her.

"Nurse Tremblay and I will prep the room. One of us will come down to escort you at one PM. If you change your mind prior to this point, please inform the orderly, who will get a message to us."

"Thank you."

They left the cell and returned to the open wards, walking side by side. As they went, Martha stole glances at Eloise, searching for signs of uncertainty. She saw none, only the steely inward gaze of her running through the thousand tasks that confronted her on any given day. Martha told herself this should be a comfort, that the head nurse did not make careless wagers with patients' lives. But Eloise hadn't been in the room when Roland had his fits, hadn't witnessed the speed at which they spiked and fell, nor the haunted pall that glazed his eyes when they opened afterward. She feared for Roland's body, and for his mind.

And, in a small part of her brain that she wasn't ready to admit to, she feared for his soul.

***

The fever room had a distinct smell, and it was on his third visit that Roland finally placed it. It was an odor he'd last encountered on his trip across the Atlantic. He'd berthed in steerage, sharing a long stretch of the hold nearest the stern—the cheapest of the cheap fares available for passage—with a hundred and fifty other souls. There, in a bed of canvas strung between two rafters, he'd laid awake many a night and listened to the grunt and clang of the engine room, which boiled on the other side of a rough plank wall from his quarters. The air in the hold was hot and sour with steam, tinged with sea spray and a miasma of unclean breaths rising from a hundred and fifty sets of germ-sodden lungs. The same mixture clung to the walls of the fever room, a baked-in odor of steam-warped metal and illness and heat.

He thought back on his crossing as the nurses readied the cabinet, swaddling him with towels and arranging their instruments on a steel tray near his head. The head nurse unclasped the padlock sealing the boiler room and went inside to prime the heaters. Pipes rattled with influxes of pressurized steam, an industrial noise that reminded him still further of his days in the hold. He tried to turn his mind to more pleasant days as the cabinet closed about him, sealing him in another wooden vessel that had carried him to new shores. But unlike with that first crossing, his voyages in the fever cabinet were intended to be round trip. Thus far they had been, and he prayed this time would be no different.

Martha took a seat next to him and began daubing his forehead with a cloth soaked in cold water. In the past they had taken these opportunities to speak, but now Roland preferred to remain silent, and Martha either shared his inclination or simply chose to honor it. Heat crept up him inch by inch, waves of it lapping his skin like the surf from an incoming tide. Sweat prickled his calves, his thighs, his buttocks, a dampness that itched before the towels wicked it away. They'd grow sodden eventually, and the heat, girdled with the weight of accumulating water, would gain sufficient heft to sink below the surface and penetrate to the core of him. In previous visits, he had ignored the sensation as long as he could and fought it when he had no other option. Today, he awaited its arrival, and submitted to it as it came. He threw open the gates and welcomed it into his blood, his bones, his brain. He seized it with the fervor of the newly converted, praised it, showered it with jubilation.

Tremors stormed his muscles but found no foothold, for he was already shaking, a silent, internal rattle like a rain dance of the soul. His mind unraveled, threads pulled this way and that, thoughts unwoven into strands of light and color. He watched with rapture as the room dissolved around him, became a vibrant shifting fog that reassembled into a form that was at once unchanged and remarkably different. He opened his eyes—surprised that they'd been closed, for he'd seen it all perfectly—and stepped from the cabinet, flesh fallen from his spirit like a lumpy chrysalis. He was in the other realm now, not a shipwreck victim cast bedraggled and sputtering onto its beaches, but a traveler, an invader, a conqueror. For he had come to this land with a purpose, and that purpose was no less than regicide.

A mad king ruled here, and Roland intended to slay him.

Curling his toes against the tile, Roland tightened the muscles in his legs—imaginary, but as real in sensation as the slabs of flesh in his jettisoned body—and forced himself to push against the floor. The movement was not a jump but a shove, a deliberate disassociation with an unwanted presence. The floor clung to him for a moment before relenting, and he found himself hovering six inches above the ground. He worked his hands like flippers and sent himself skittering forward. He moved in awkward bursts at first, but the motion was intuitive and soon he was zipping about the room like a hummingbird. He allowed himself one celebratory flight around the room's perimeter before settling down to his business.

He moved to the wall leading to the hallway and pressed his hands against the plaster. It felt cold, firm, unyielding to the touch. He closed his eyes and concentrated, and the wall grew warm and pliant. His fingers sank into the plaster as if into heated wax. He stopped them before they went too far, curled them, and allowed the plaster to cool sufficiently to provide leverage. His grip established, he pressed his face forward and thrust it, with slow but unyielding pressure, through the wall to the other side.

Erasmus' realm remained as he had last seen it, a blistering inferno of misery and pain. Golems toiled among ragged and writhing souls, each bound by confines of black iron, be they chains or bars or crueler implements still. He cast his gaze about the scene, refusing to turn aside, as he believed a weakness succumbed to now would damn him later, when it most counted. He scanned the valley floor until he spotted the railway he'd seen on his first visit. One end wound along the ridge of the horseshoe-shaped canyon on which he stood, snaking along the terraces of its opposite side, while the other ran beyond the valley and into a sparse and shadow-mottled plain, its features swallowed by distance. The railway was Roland's one clue to

Erasmus' whereabouts. As Owens had said in his letter, if this place had a heart, the pair of iron bands would eventually lead there.

He chose a moment when no golems were in sight and passed through the wall, keeping to the shadows and floating lest his footsteps be heard. Beyond the vestiges of the fever room stood a narrow cliffside path overlooking a steep drop, the sort of vertiginous mountain pass one saw when venturing between alpine villages. The path provided cover from the valley below, making it easier to avoid detection, and he followed it as long as he could, but the cliff wended left while the railway carried straight on. If he wanted to follow it beyond the valley and into the plains, he was going to have to venture through open terrain.

Gazing at his hands, he willed his projected form to become dim. He watched as his hands grew greyish and translucent. Invisibility seemed beyond him—no matter how hard he concentrated, a ghostly residue remained—but his appearance was muted enough for him to chance exposure beyond the protective shadows of the ledge. Drawing a single deep breath—physiologically useless, but psychologically invaluable—he propelled himself past the precipice and over the valley below. His stomach lurched at the influx of naked space, but his hands found the correct motion through intuition and soon he was coasting once again.

As he drifted above the thicket of torment, Roland spotted a figure he recognized. Verloc, his glasses gone, his smart attire torn to strips and faded to a lusterless grey as if by a millennium of wear, staggered across a field of hard stones. A chain, bound at one end to a stake driven deep in the earth and at the other to a loop of iron threaded through the center of his thigh, held him at a fixed radius. He ran in circles at the very edge of his reach, beset by a plague of harpies brandishing sticks and daggers. Wizened husks of leathery flesh and muscle, they ran laughing and snarling at his heels. Withered dugs hung to their knees, batted back and forth by each stride, and their spread lips revealed teeth filed to ruthless points. Occasionally one closed the gap enough to jab a spear into his fleshy ass or bite a hunk from his shoulder, but mostly they seemed to content themselves with the chase, cackling to one another and hurling garbled ululations skyward, backs arched back double with the force of their vicious glee. Roland felt a moment's pity for the man, but if his suspicions proved true, the former head physician deserved this fate more than most. With a final glance at the doctor,

Roland situated himself over the tracks and followed them out of the valley.

The land beyond the canyon's walls grew sparse and flat, its crags and spires ground into a grey, featureless plateau. Soil and sky blended into one ash-hued hemisphere, the horizon between them smudged and vague. Only the tracks gave form to the world. Without them, he may as well have been floating through a void. He dropped lower, drawing comfort from their tangibility. As he did, he noticed occasional figures dotting the barren earth to either side of the rails. They were as gaunt and bedraggled as their kinsmen on the valley floor, dressed likewise in rags and beset by chains, but the pain they bore seemed a quiet, more contemplative sort. There was no writhing in anguish, no wailing or gnashing of teeth, no byzantine implements of torture. They simply sat, their backs to the cleft of madness behind them, their grim faces set on an unseeable horizon. Roland watched them with a detached sort of fascination, his gaze trawling over them as he passed, until a wayward glance snagged a familiar visage and yanked him to the desert floor.

Brown eyes, deep set in an aged and hollow-cheeked face, looked up at Roland with recognition. Eyebrows raised beneath a half-cocked smile, a gesture that in this place cost as much effort as rolling a boulder uphill.

"Well, what do we have here?" said Harvey. "You're full of surprises, friend. Flyin' down from the heavens like Superman."

"Harvey. I am sorry to find you in this place."

"You and me both, though I can't say I'm too surprised. Got up to my fair share of sinnin' in my time, and I always figured I had time to get to the repentin' part later. Well, there ain't no later no more."

"You are mistaken. You do not deserve to be in this place. Sin has not brought you here."

"Don't exactly matter why I'm here though, does it? This chain holds either way." He motioned to the iron band clamped around his ankle. Two dozen links, each as thick as Roland's thumb, connected it to a black metal rod pounded into the earth. He shook his leg and the chain jangled, a rasping, ugly sound. "Deserve don't got much to do with it."

"No. It has everything to do with it." Roland grabbed the chain in both hands. The metal felt warm and oily and somehow alive, as if he held the tail of an immense serpent in the depths of its winter slumber. He ran the pad of his thumb along one of the links, willing the metal to soften. *You are ice, and I am fire. You are strong, but through my touch you will become as water, and flow.* He channeled all of his strength into the spot where skin touched metal, willing the link to change, to weaken, to die. But the metal would not change, would not weaken, would not die. It remained just as it was, solid as the truth, and just as cruel.

Harvey watched Roland struggle with a mixture of amusement and pity. "Have you lost your damn mind? You can't break a man outta hell."

"But this. Is not. The true hell." He spoke these terse statements through gritted teeth, each bolt of words punctuated by a grunt as he strained against the iron chain. Sweat prickled the pores along his hairline, bulging into beads that ran down his face and stung his eyes. *That's not even real sweat. Why must it sting so?* He felt like a bodybuilder attempting a deadlift two weight classes above his own. His flesh, imagined or real, quivered against the implacability of dumb iron. He released the chain with a final gasp and collapsed next to Harvey, staring in wonder at the chafe marks that marred his palms. *The chains are not real,* he insisted. *Just as the walls and floors and bodies are not real. I can pass through concrete, so why not iron?* He would never know exactly, but it was clear at least that the rules in this place were more complicated than he'd realized. There were limits to what he could accomplish with willpower alone. He wondered what this meant for his mission.

Harvey seemed to know through intuition what Roland had just learned through sweat and struggle. "You can't free me from this, friend. Can't you see I'm damned? Ain't no salvation from the pit. I weren't never the most church-going man, but I read me enough scripture to know that."

"But you are not damned, Harvey. Only God can make such a judgement, and God did not send you here."

Harvey raised an eyebrow. "So you're knowin' the will of God now, huh? Pretty high and mighty for a fella locked up in a loony bin last time I knew him."

Roland opened his mouth to argue and realized he had nothing to say. He hung his head between his knees and sighed. Harvey placed a comforting hand on his shoulder. Roland welcomed it with appreciation and shame, glad he had a friend in a place like this, but ashamed that it was him with his flight and his freedom who needed comforting, and Harvey emaciated in chains who gave it. Surely it should have been otherwise.

"You know something, friend?" asked Harvey. "I can't for the life of me decide if you're a spirit or a hallucination or what, but whatever you are, it's good to see your face."

Roland looked over at the older man. Whatever injustice Erasmus had done to him by imprisoning him here, it hadn't broken him. Roland doubted the same could be said of the true hell. This comparison comforted him. He put a hand on Harvey's shoulder to mirror the one on his own.

"And it is good to see yours, though I wish it were elsewhere that I saw it." He let his hand drop and looked to the blurred expanse of the horizon. "Perhaps these chains are beyond me for now, but I will stay true to my word. I *will* see to it that you leave this place."

"T'ain't for you or me to say, friend," said Harvey. "But I thank you all the same."

Roland left on foot. He could fly, but the joy of it was gone, and he knew in his heart that distance followed its own rules in this place, and he would reach his destination no faster any other way. He kept to the side of the tracks, mirroring their wends left and right but never treading on them directly. Occasionally he passed other souls bound to the earth as Harvey had been. Some looked at him with curiosity while others ignored him, but whatever their reaction he noticed in them a resignation unsullied by despair. They seemed to accept their lot, if not happily, then at least with a sort of tired fatalism. Roland felt like a cad each time he walked by one of them without trying to help, but his experience with Harvey showed him how useless he was against their plight. The captives seemed to understand this as well, for none called out to him as the old woman had. Indeed, none spoke at all, until a girl of twelve or so looked up at him as he passed.

"It was noble of you to help your friend," she said.

Roland stopped. He turned and looked at her, a waifish child in rags, her ringlets of black hair clinging with sweat to hollow cheeks. She twiddled a chain link idly between thumb and forefinger.

"I beg your pardon?"

"Your friend. Back there." She pointed the way Roland had come, though Harvey had long since disappeared with distance, and from her vantage nothing could be seen that way save dust and sky at the twin tracks converging on the horizon. "You stopped to help him. That was good of you."

"I thank you for your kind words," said Roland. "But I am sorry to say I could do nothing for him. His chains could not be broken."

"But you tried. An attempt is itself an action, isn't it? And in any case, you've done more than you think, coming this far."

Roland studied the girl closely. He didn't recognize her at all, and yet something about her struck an echo in the backmost corner of his mind. The girl, smiling, answered the questions he'd been posing himself.

"You've no cause for embarrassment in not recognizing me. We've never met, though I've long seen you, and you've heard tell of me in a small way. My name is Constance."

The name triggered the inner workings of his memory, and recognition trundled into place. "You're the girl Mr. Owens spoke of. In his confession."

The girl nodded. "We're of a kind, you and I. Did you sense it, when you read of me? I wouldn't blame you if you didn't. You'd much on your mind. And my imprisonment has given me much time to reflect."

Roland thought back on Owens' letter. "You had visions too, correct?"

"I suppose, though the term does it no justice. We are seers, Roland, blessed with the second sight. Or maybe cursed."

Roland shook his head. "I am no psychic. Had I such abilities, I would never have allowed myself to wind up in *Walpole* in the first place."

"You are awfully quick to discount your own observations. Did you not confess much the same to Nurse Donnelly?"

"How do you know that?" Roland asked.

"It is as I've said. I am a seer. Oh, I was blind to it too, at first, quick to dismiss my 'visions' as madness. After all, was I not an inmate at an asylum for lunatics? A cruel irony, then, to find that the asylum itself was what caused them."

"I saw my visions before I arrived in Walpole," countered Roland.

"But not before you arrived in Queenstown, correct?"

Roland opened his mouth to speak, paused, closed it.

"'It is as if there is a door in my mind that was long left shut. In the past few months, it has opened a crack, but the fever cabinet threw it open all the way.' Your own words. I could not have described it better. The force that Erasmus unleashed resonates in us, pries open doors that fear and reason had long sealed. The very source of his power becomes his gravest weakness, for we can see through and cross the threshold he alone wants to control. This is no meager feat, which explains why some trauma is needed to enact it.

For me, it was my fits. For you, the fever cabinet. But the more we could see this place from the worldly realm, the more Erasmus could see us. He fears our knowledge, and what we can do with it. You have proven his fears are valid."

"Have I?" asked Roland. "All that we've learned, all we've seen, what has it gotten us? I have saved no one. And you, you cannot even save yourself."

Roland winced at the harshness of his own words, but Constance appeared unstung by them. She merely nodded, as if in agreement with a simple statement of fact. "My strength has dwindled, it's true. After Owens gave me in offering, I no longer had a foot in the worldly realm. With great concentration, I can communicate, but only in symbols. A pale green glow around a book, for instance."

"That was you?"

The girl nodded. "Such is the extent of my strength. But your body still anchors you to the worldly realm, gives you a reservoir of will to draw from. Without it, I am merely a ghost, and ghosts in this place are his thralls. My sight remains, but the rest is lost to me."

"You speak of strength, but you saw as well as I did how I fared against my friend's chains."

"Would you call an unconquered army powerless because it couldn't bring back the dead? You are right that we will never return with you, but you may still free us. Not from death, but from damnation. Is this not the greater gift?"

"But how?" Roland cried.

"You have found the path. Follow it."

Roland looked at the tracks. His eyes followed them to where they disappeared in the distance. "Where do they lead?"

Constance glanced towards her feet, bound in shackles of sky-black iron. "That is one thing I can't see. They go to him, but between his throne and us lies a darkness my eyes can't penetrate. You must do so alone."

Roland pressed his fingers to his eyes, sending sparks across the firmament of his eyelids.

"I am afraid."

He expected the admission to shame him, but on speaking it he felt only relief. It was a small comfort, dwarfed by the fear that remained, but he relished it all the same.

Constance took his hand in hers. "That is because you are wise."

13

MARTHA DIPPED THE cloth in cold water, wrung the excess back into the basin, and smoothed it across Roland's forehead. His reaction was minimal, but in the loosening of muscles along his jaw and the exhalation of his breath she saw minute signs of relief, and felt a momentary pleasure of purpose. The sensation never lasted long, but she savored it when it came, for it was too easy to convince herself she was torturing this man needlessly. Could his illness really be baked from his brain, smoked out like bandits in a cheesy crime picture? It seemed improbable, even reckless, akin to burning the house down to rid oneself of an infestation of mice.

He asked for this treatment, if you remember. Insisted on it, in fact. The voice in her head was prim and self-assured, and though its goal was to assuage her guilt, she found she didn't much like it. There was something unpleasantly familiar in its clipped, forceful tones. It reminded her of the woman who'd interviewed her at Prince George Hospital, back what felt like a hundred lifetimes ago, all pristine arrogance and certainty about the world and its workings. *He may well have asked for it,* she wanted to counter. *But you'll recall that his decision stems from the belief that he has obtained psychic powers, and must now use them to combat an evil ghost intent on privatizing hell.* But, of course, there was no one to counter *to,* since she was talking to herself. She couldn't argue the point forcefully without seeming a touch mad herself, and so expressed her concerns in softer tones to Eloise.

"Are you sure this is the right thing to do?"

Eloise removed a thermometer from under Roland's tongue and studied the reading in its mercury band. "This is medicine, *ma choupette*. Only the worst of us are ever sure of anything. Good nurses doubt themselves always."

"I just feel like we should have insisted the treatment go on hold pending reassessment. How can we follow a protocol when the man who wrote it is dead?"

"He was not dead when he wrote it. What does his death change?"

Martha wasn't sure how to respond. She dipped her cloth back in the water, wrung it out, and continued tracing soft lines across Roland's face.

"He's done better this time anyway," said Martha. "Almost two hours, and no fits." She rapped her knuckles on the cabinet's wooden frame to ward off jinxes from her words.

Voices rattled up the hall. The solid door and echoey acoustics made it impossible to make out what they were saying, but by timbre alone Martha had no trouble discerning their source. It was the orderly Fox, and those two Neanderthals that always slouched about with him. MacCruiskeen and Pluck. Martha shuddered at the recollection, as if she'd come across something dead and rotting in the basement of her mind. She scraped the names from her thoughts and resumed tending to Roland, ignoring the voices and the jagged shards of their laughter as they came closer. *They'll pass in a moment,* she thought, but instead of passing, they culminated in a bang as one of them threw open the door and Fox stepped into the fever room, Pluck and MacCruiskeen's faces perched like imps over either shoulder.

"Afternoon, ladies," Fox crooned. "Don't stop chitchatting on my account."

"We are in the middle of a medical treatment, Mr. Fox," Eloise said. Martha felt the frost from it sting her cheek. "It is most essential that we are not disturbed."

"Sorry to interrupt you in your important business, but the boss man gave us our instructions, and I'm here to carry them out."

"I do not know these instructions you speak of, but it seems that you have missed the news. Dr. Verloc is dead."

Fox laughed. "Oh, I know all about that. Scuttlebutt has it the fat fucker's heart went and crapped out on him. Takes a lot of muscle to move that much meat around, and the ticker weren't up to the task. But no, Verloc ain't the boss man. Not now and not ever. I get my marching orders from the real head honcho around here, and he's got a bone to pick with Mr. Bratwurst over there." He pointed to Roland with a silver object in his right hand, and it was only at that moment that Martha noticed it and realized what it was.

It was a knife. And not a small-bladed tool of the sort used in surgery, but a hunting knife, with a ten-inch blade and serrations on its inward-curving edge. Such a weapon wasn't even legal to own, let alone carry around in a hospital.

Eloise, too, seemed newly aware of the blade, for her voice, though no friendlier, took on a cautious note. "Best to put the knife away, Mr. Fox. A hospital is no place for such a thing."

Fox barked a single dry laugh. "Please, this ain't a hospital. You guys've never cured a single person of anything. This is a warehouse for damaged goods, is all it is. You nurses are too proud to admit it, but it's true. Christ, even *Verloc* knew that, and that fat fucker could barely see the nose on his fat fucking face."

"Your opinions of this place are your own, but I would thank you to keep them to yourself. And I will ask you only one more time to rid yourself of your weapon. If you do not do this, I will report you. Possession of such things is a crime."

Fox's smile widened without curling upward, an ugly gesture that stretched his eyes into condescending slits. "You gotta leave the room first to report me, sweetheart. And the three of us are in the way."

Martha's stomach clenched at these words as if doused with a bucket of ice water, but Eloise appeared unfazed, even amused by them. "And I suppose you will cut me up with your little tool if I try to pass? The police would catch you before nightfall, and you do not wish to go to prison. You fear it almost as much as you fear the front. This is why you took this job, *n'est-ce pas*? Because those were your only two other options?"

Fox's smile sagged. His eyes, still slitted, hardened into clefts of stone. He cleared the three steps between him and Eloise in an instant, and without warning plunged the knife into her belly. The blade sank in to the hilt, twisted, and withdrew. Eloise doubled over, her breath expelled in a gasp. She clutched her stomach. Blood seeped through the gaps between her fingers. Her eyes met Fox's, glittering with defiance and contempt. She tried to straighten, but the pain undid her and she collapsed with a groan. Fox looked at her prostrate body. He scratched the back of his neck.

"She didn't get it," he said. Martha couldn't tell if he was speaking to her, or to the other men, or to the entire asylum. "None of you get it. You think the *cops* scare us? We work for the devil. We're his avenging angels. No death, no fear, no weakness. Only power."

Eloise rolled onto her side. Her body curled into a ball, legs bent double and pulled to her chest. With the last of her strength she raised her head and fixed Fox with a glare. Her words came out raspy and ragged, but whole.

"Il n'a pas d'anges, le Diable. Seulement des démons. Et ça c'est vous, vous espèce des bâtards. Petits et sans valeur et maudites pour toujours."

Having spoken these words, her neck went limp, and she lay on the tile in a widening pool of blood, her firm stare softening into sightlessness, her bronze skin bleached pale. Martha let out a single choked sob. She crouched before Eloise, forgetting for the moment Fox and the others, her vision clenched down into pinhole precision by convulsions of grief. Her trained hands detected no pulse, no breath, no heartbeat. She looked up at Fox, and the disdain that radiated from Eloise in her final moments seemed to pour into her, filling her with righteous heat.

"So," said Fox. "Now that we got the pleasantries out of the way, whaddaya say we get down to business?"

***

The plains seemed to go on forever. Roland trudged along, his shoulders hunched, an ache sinking into the spaces between his vertebrae like a dozen burning needles.

He wasn't sure when exactly he'd started walking, or where he was walking from, though the importance of his journey was beyond question. When he tried thinking back on it, the only flashes of memory he could pull from the muck of his recollections were tarnished and obviously phony. He somehow saw himself flying, but that was crazy of course. Probably a shard of an old dream that had poked through a consciousness worn thin from exhaustion after so many long marches.

His memory perked up at the word "marches" like a dog at the sound of his master's footsteps. Of course. He was in the *Deutsches Heer*. A glance down at his uniform confirmed it. He held a rifle in both hands, and grenades dangled from a strap over one shoulder, but the familiar weight of his pack was absent. Why was he so unencumbered? *Dummkopf! This is the front. You're on maneuvers. There's no room for packs.* As if in confirmation of this thought, a voice hissed in his ear from somewhere behind him.

"Bauch auf dem Boden, Jäger Hellmich, sonst geben dir die Tommys ein neues Kopfloch."

Roland's body responded to the command as if it had come from his brain directly. *"Ja, Oberleutnant,"* he said, his voice a whisper. *"Es tut mir leid, Oberleutnant."*

"Du weißt, was du musst. Sei ruhig, und blase das Maschinengewehrnest zur Hölle."

"Ja, Oberleutnant."

Roland started crawling. As he went, the flat, featureless hardpan on which he'd walked grew soft and heaving, pocked with clefts and craters from years of bombardment. Stagnant water pooled in valleys churned to knee-deep mud, while the peaks baked hard and jagged from the summer sun. Roland waded through muck and scraped across stone. The earth half-swallowed him in places where the ground was softest, his every movement disgorging bubbles of rot that burped to the surface and filled his nose with the vile-sweet smell of decaying flesh. Hands seeking purchase happened upon eyeless skulls and severed limbs, skin sloughing from bones at a touch. Along the peaks the smell was subtler but no less pungent in its way, a spice trader stink of mummified flesh and bones cured into pikes breaking through the earth like the relics of a war that ended centuries prior. Life here existed only in its ugliest forms, in rats gnawing thigh meat and flies buzzing atop burst bellies and mosquitos nesting in crater ponds scummy with discharged fluids.

Coils of barbed wire stretched between sawhorses, half of which had been long since blown to kindling. The sagging fence lay underground in places, but if anything, this made crossing more treacherous, for the ground was loose and damp and could easily yield enough for a passing limb to snag on a sharpened steel tooth. Better to cross where the fence remained standing. At least the wires could be seen, and the damaged sawhorses usually allowed enough give for even a large soldier to slip under. The real danger here was not the wires themselves, but the oscillation of their disturbance, which could signal to keen riflemen the approach of an enemy soldier. Roland dampened their motion with a palm as he snaked along a mortar-hewn trough, clearing the fence with an inch to spare.

The sky was dark and starless. Gashes of bone-hued moonlight seeped through cracks in the clouds, but these momentary bursts were thin as prison oatmeal and served only to deepen the shadows that stretched like tattered black ribbons across the battlefield. In the distance, Roland spotted the blocky silhouette of buttresses peeking above an otherwise flat horizon, subtle signals of the entrenched enemy line. It was much as the scouts had reported it: a single line, poorly reinforced and ripe for invasion. He saw no sentries or obvious defenses, and while gauging the number of enemy soldiers at this distance was impossible, the scout's report that they were undermanned seemed credible.

The sole impediment to their charge was a single machine gun nest. It crouched on the lip of the trench, dug into a natural hillock in an effort to provide some semblance of camouflage, though a soldier with any experience on the front could spot it for what it was at two hundred yards. A cleft curtained by shadows sank into its center, through which Roland could see the dim outline of a Vickers machine gun.

Roland's pace, cautious from the outset, slowed to an almost imperceptible creep. He oozed over the ground like spilled honey, filling cracks and wending along channels in a sluggish but inexorable slide. Inch by inch, foot by foot, yard by yard, the distance closed, until he found himself pooled at the base of the machine gun nest. Until that moment, he'd moved without impatience or fear. The action had been almost automatic, as if outside forces had drawn him unconscious in their currents to this place. But with his first goal attained, the second presented itself, and it was here that his courage, heretofore untried, met its first real challenge.

Rolling onto his side, he unclipped a grenade from his bandolier and held it cocked in his right hand, thumb clasped over the lever. He eyed the height of the nest and gauged the most effective throwing position. It was possible to do while lying prone, but risky, as too acute an angle would bounce the grenade off the ramparts and back into his lap, while one too obtuse would send it straight up in the air, where it would rain shrapnel down on him. He was more confident in a kneeling throw, but to rise above the muck outside the nest would put him clear in the gunner's sightline. He settled on a compromise approach, rising onto his left elbow while staying low enough to remain out of sight. When he found the right position, he brought the grenade toward his left hand and looped his finger through the pin.

A shrill, whistling screech cut the air, followed by a concussive thud that sounded in his ribs an instant before it reached his ears. It grew in volume like a door opened on the apocalypse. The force of it knocked Roland sideways and slammed him into the dirt, stamping an imprint of his body deep enough that a single sweep of wayward mud could have buried him.

The wet earth sucked at his eyes, invaded his nostrils, filled his mouth with its dead leaf funk. He tried to raise his head, but the earth held fast, mud lips pressed to his in a graveyard kiss. He pushed with both arms, reared back, and the ground gave way with a slurp. He spat out a mouthful of mud and wiped the residue from his eyes with his forearm, aware as he did that the hand that followed the motion still gripped the grenade. He fumbled frantically for the pin and found it still in place, leaving the grenade unprimed.

A voice sounded over the strip of no-man's land at Roland's back. It was *Oberleutnant* von Schoben—even at a distance, the sound of it was unmistakable.

"Jetzt, Männer! Aufladen! Töte die Schweinehunde!"

"Nein, Oberleutnant, nein," said Roland. *"Wir sind nicht bereit. Ich habe es nicht noch getan. Mehre Zeit, bitte, ich brauche mehre Zeit."* His words, spoken little above a mumble, had no chance of reaching the *Oberleutnant*. Even a scream wouldn't have done it. His blood was up, and the *Zug* charging at his heels would drown out a chorus of shouts from across the battlefield. He would hear nothing but the glory of his charge until the enemy machine gun spoke the final rattling word. Roland could see the smile on the gunman as he awaited the approach of his prey. Despite the darkness that rendered such a sight impossible, he could see it, a lupine grin glowing sickle-sharp and bone-bright in the cavern of its crenellation.

Machen Sie es nicht, cried a voice in his head. *Es ist nicht sicher.*

Ich muss! he yelled back. *Sonst werden sie alle sterben!*

Aber Sie können nicht deine Granate werfen! Um es zu versuchen, würden Sie aufstehen müssen! Und wenn Sie aufstehen, wird das Maschinengewehr Sie zu Fetzen scheiben!

Roland gritted his teeth in fury at his own weakness. His entire *Zug* would be shredded by machine gun fire in a few moments, and he was cowering in a hole, arguing with himself.

Are you sure that's what you're doing? Are you certain both those voices really belong to you?

Roland's eyes flew open. The voices seemed to come from inside him, but there was something alien about one of them. They'd been in German, for one thing, and his thoughts had increasingly adopted the tongue of his new country. But stranger still, one of them had called him by the formal *"Sie,"* not the intimate *"du."* And if ever a relationship merited the informal pronoun, it was the one that you held with your own mind.

Moving without thought, without prior volition, Roland slipped his index finger into the ring and pulled the pin from the grenade. The safety bar pressed with sudden pressure against Roland's thumb. He sprung from the crater and with a cry of manic fury lobbed the grenade over the wall of the machine gun nest. He closed his eyes, awaiting the rattle of gunfire that would end him, content to greet it on his own terms, having doomed his own doom's author in turn.

The force of his overhand throw carried him forward and down. He landed in the mud, fingers searching his chest for entry wounds. His fingers found no blood, no pain, no sign of injury at all. He looked down, assuming blood loss had numbed him, and saw a standard issue uniform—hopelessly rumpled and stained with mud, but free of bullet holes. His surprise was such that he almost failed to notice the *whoof* of his grenade detonating, an uncharacteristically muted and concussive sound. A blade of light jabbed through the crenellated gunner's perch, its colour not the orange-red of an explosion, but a pure and brilliant white. The machine gun crumbled to powder, followed by the machine gun nest, which toppled inward like a tent with its support rods kicked free. The entire bunker sluiced and melted with the precarity of a sandcastle before a rising tide. None of the earthworks seemed to have any substance at all.

Over his shoulder, the men in Roland's *Zug* turned to mist, the sound of their furious charge dissolving into the soft hiss of rainfall. A few moments later, Roland stood alone in an empty field, his hands still clutching a rifle. Of the visions that had ensnared him, it alone remained.

Memories of the intervening years flowed back into his mind, as if the phantasmal scenario he'd been acting out had been a dike holding them at bay. He recalled the warning from Eugene Owens: *the heart of his empire is guarded by a powerful hex, a conjuration of one's greatest fear.* Well, he supposed if he had a greatest fear, his memories of his last day of combat were probably it. And he'd conquered them. So why did he feel so unresolved?

Because you're not done yet, answered a voice, the same one that had warned him about the false thoughts whispering cowardice in his ear. It was a strange voice, not at all like his own. He decided that it sounded a little like Nurse Donnelly.

"Well, whoever you are," he said, "I thank you. And you are right. I am not done here yet."

This announcement made, he shouldered the rifle still hanging from its strap and scanned the plains. After a moment's search, he found what he was looking for: two ribbons of iron cutting across the earth. He walked over and stood in the middle of the tracks, staring down the point in the distance where they conjoined. There was no waystation in sight, no sign of a destination. It would be a long walk. But that was okay; time was one thing he had to spare.

14

MARTHA EXPECTED THE knife to be cold, but the wedge of metal that pressed flat against her cheek felt warm. Its tip dimpled the thin curtain of flesh beneath her lower eyelid, and a gentle prod would serve to blind her forever, but her mind turned with stubborn determination to the source of the blade's heat. Her fixation came to her as odd thoughts often did at times of great stress. She reasoned that Fox probably snuck the knife into the asylum under his clothes, and the warmth emanating from the blade had been stored there by prolonged and intimate exposure to his body heat. At this thought, a wave of revulsion splashed cold and slimy across the thorny ridges of her fear.

"Get that thing out of my face," she growled, surprised at the force her voice contained. "What do you even want from me?"

"We'll get to that," crooned Fox. "But first, I think I'll tend to your Hun buddy." He gave the knife a final press into her skin, wringing from her a twitch and a flush of shame, and withdrew it. The skin it had touched glowed pale from the pressure, but was unbroken. He sauntered over to the fever cabinet and lowered the blade to Roland's throat.

"Hey, Fox!" called MacCruiskeen. "Hold on a sec!"

Fox looked over at his friend. "Yeah?"

MacCruiskeen's eyes bulged, and his body trembled with the effort of containing an uprush of emotion. Martha felt a moment's hope, thinking the man's conscience might actually get the better of him, but his mouth curled up at the edges and burst with a childish giggle, and she realized the emotion he was suppressing wasn't guilt. It was excitement.

"Let's cook him!" he cried.

Fox's eyebrows sloped into a puzzled V-shape. "Huh?"

"This doohickey he's in, it's a steam box, right? Supposed to get his temperature up? Well, let's crank it and see what happens."

A grin dawned on Fox's face like a red-skied sunrise. He looked down at Roland, lips splitting to bare teeth.

"You're one sick puppy, Mac," Fox said.

MacCruiskeen shivered with pleasure at this pronouncement.

Fox turned back to Martha. "So, sweetheart, how exactly do we crank this bad boy to the max?" He gestured with the knife as he spoke. The motion wasn't overtly threatening, but there was no doubt in Martha's mind that she was intended to bear the blade in mind when responding.

"Why on earth should I tell you that?"

"Because I asked you real nice like?" Fox suggested.

"You're intending to murder one of my patients."

"Look, honey, we've got a long evening in store for you. We're three young bucks, and we can have a whole lotta fun before we tire out. But if you be a good girl and cooperate, we can finish our business and go on our merry way."

She nearly asked why she should believe him, but there was no point, as she knew the answer already: she shouldn't. But what else was there to do? She looked over at the boiler room. The shut door held her gaze for several seconds. Thoughts passed inscrutable behind her eyes. She nodded.

"The main valve is there. In the boiler room."

"That a girl. Now come on and show me which one."

She crossed the room, the three men following close behind her. Pluck thrust his hand against the door as she passed the doorway, preventing her from slamming it on them and barricading herself inside. She allowed herself to show a moment's dismay at this, as if such a move had been her plan all along. The men exchanged knowing smirks.

A cramped pathway ran through a forest of pipes and stocky heaters. Martha passed along it easily, but the men, particularly the bulky Pluck, had to duck and weave to avoid banging heads or barking elbows on the crisscrossing copper tubes. She walked with brisk strides, not running, but allowing her easier passage to gain her a few extra feet of distance from her pursuers. When she reached the main intake valve, she grabbed the monkey wrench off the maintenance tray, turned, and brandished it at them two-handed. Her legs hunkered in a batman's crouch, as if she were readying herself for a pitch.

"Stay back," she warned.

Fox looked at his friends out of the corner of his eye, a smirk smeared across his face. He offered an indulgent chuckle.

"Honey, there's three of us and only one of you. A wrench ain't gonna make much difference to your odds."

"Come here and try your luck, then."

Fox sighed. He shook his head, lips pinched in a restrained smile. It was the sort of look an indulgent parent might give a child who'd tried to bake pancakes and wound up covered head to toe in flour for the effort. Martha didn't think her hatred for Fox could deepen, but the patronizing sheen on that look managed it.

"You'll get one swing, sweetheart," he said, stepping forward. "You better make it a good one."

"Thank you," she said. "I believe I shall." With a grunt of exertion, she raised the wrench and brought it down on the thin juncture where the stem met the bonnet. There was a squeal of shorn metal as the handwheel came free from the pipe, followed by a roar of pressurized steam squirting from the break like blood from a nicked artery. A jet of it lanced straight into Fox's face, boiling through his eyelids in an instant and turning his eyes to blistered goo. He screamed, hands flying to his face. The knife slipped from his fingers and clattered to the floor.

Martha let the momentum of her swing carry her to the ground, and she felt no more than a gust of humid heat as the steam arced over her. MacCruiskeen and Pluck stared dumbfounded at their friend clawing divots of agony into his own face. Their shock lasted no more than half a second, but it was long enough for the bolt of steam to widen into a plume and swallow them from the chest up. It was less concentrated, but still hot enough to blind them and set them to howling. They ran for the exit, misjudging the direction in their panic and banging into pipes filled with superheated steam. Bands of lead as hot as blacksmith tongs peeled strips of scorched flesh from their arms, while jutting tubes of cooler metal bashed heads and tripped panic-blind legs. The three of them soon collapsed one onto the other and lay in a heap of limbs and misery.

Above them the steam kept coming, filling the room from top to bottom with a searing opaque mist. Martha grabbed the knife before the ground ahead of her disappeared in a summery mist and began crawling in the direction of the door. The steam had diffused enough to keep from burning her, but the heat was oppressive and growing. She pulled herself along with cocked elbows, face pressed to the floor, whose tiles offered a cooling balm against sweat-stung cheeks. A wedge of light signaled the door to the fever room, and Martha wriggled towards it.

A hand closed around her ankle. Its grip was desperate, crushing. She kicked out with her free leg, ramming the heel of her shoe into clenched knuckles, but the hand only tightened. She waited for it to pull her back, or drag its owner forward for vengeance, but it seemed to have no further goal behind seizing her in its death grip. Whoever controlled it—Pluck, she guessed by its girth—may not have even realized he was holding the woman who'd blinded him. She sat up, wincing at each inrush of steam-sour breath, and rammed the knife into her captor's wrist. The hand went limp, fingers twitching on the blood-slick tile. Martha tried to withdraw the knife, but the blade snagged on bone and she left it where it stood, crawling the rest of the way to the door.

She burst through the doorway like a surfacing freediver, grateful lungs snatching armfuls of air after endless minutes submerged in aquatic darkness, and kicked the door shut behind her. Staggering to her feet, she grabbed the padlock from the latch loop, shut the hasp, and hammered the locking to the housing with the heel of her hand. The tumblers clicked home, sealing the three men inside. The steel door muffled their cries, but there was no ignoring the sounds of their fruitless, tortured struggle.

Martha returned to the stool next to Roland and sat down. She took a cloth from the basin and wiped cool water across his forehead. It was clear to her that under the circumstances there was something else she should be doing—a hundred or so other things, in fact—but her mind seemed as incapable of picturing them as her body was of carrying them out. It was as if every ounce of initiative she had remained in the boiler room with the three dying men, and what had escaped was merely a golem of flesh and bone, mindlessly performing the tasks assigned to it by some forgotten and long-dead master.

**

The plains grew darker with every step, and Roland soon found himself ensconced in darkness. It was a strange sort of darkness, for in it he could see his own body as if illuminated by some ambient, featureless light, a light with no clear source, which gave no warmth and cast no shadows. Its glow extended to the tips of Roland's fingers and no farther. Beyond it was only an utter, silent blackness that he'd stumbled into so gradually, he couldn't rightly say when or from where it had come. There was no telling the ground from the sky, nor seeing any impediments he might walk into or attackers that might beset him. Even the tracks he followed vanished from sight, leaving him wandering through a void.

But the ground beneath his feet, unseen though it was, remained solid, and so he walked, a steady tread without hesitation or hope, anticipation or fear, keeping along the tracks by the feel of the wooden ties against his heels. There was nothing to say he wouldn't walk this blind path for eternity, stuck in some insidious loop meant to snare those who threatened Erasmus' realm. He knew this, and yet he couldn't bring himself to care. He was here, and there was nothing left to do but walk, so he walked.

The darkness parted and left Roland standing in a circle of stones. Beyond its border lay the same improbable darkness he'd walked through, a lusterless blackness of infinite depth. The line between darkness and light was so sharp it seemed painted on, yet a toe stretched beyond the shape circumscribed by the stones disappeared as if behind a curtain. Roland withdrew his foot and turned his attention back to the world within the ring of stones.

The ground in the circle was ashen and coated in a flaky grey-white gravel. Chips of it crunched beneath Roland's feet, crumbling into a fine dust that rose in plumes up to his heels. The rails he'd followed emerged from the darkness and ran to the center of the ring, where they stopped before a large stone altar. The altar was unadorned and plain in structure, a hard-edged rectangle seven feet long and maybe four feet wide, but it still gave an appearance of strength and value through the utter blackness of its stone. Roland would have guessed it to be obsidian, but even that famously black mineral gave off a sheen when light struck it, whereas the substance before him gave back nothing; it simply *took*, a block of negative space cut from the belly of the universe.

"Es ist schön, oder?" spoke a voice. It came not so much from outside the stone ring as above it, its casual comment at odds with its thunder-rumble timbre. Roland searched for its source, and as he looked, he noticed the darkness beyond the ring of stones condensing into five pillars. The space between them was still black, but a black of a lusterless, faded sort, while the obelisks bore a darkness so deep it

lacked dimension, and against the muted gloom beyond them they stood out as if haloed in a blinding white light.

The pillars lengthened and curled, their straight edges gaining a slight taper that terminated in a vicious point. Curves bound one to the next, and in the swoop of their conjoining they resembled an enormous hand, the ring of spotlit stones resting like a coin in its palm. An enormous head formed from the same onyx darkness, featureless in silhouette but unmistakable. Jagged protuberances grew from its brow, jutting first out then up, the stark geometry of their angles suggesting not horns but a crown. Though it had no eyes—or at least none that were visible—Roland could feel its gaze upon him. It fixed him with the curious but dispassionate look of a child observing an insect found in the garden.

"Willkommen in meinem Gefilde, Herr Hellmich," the figure said. *"Ich habe Sie gern erwartet."*

Roland resisted the urge to drop his gaze from the figure's immense face. *"Sie sprechen Deutsch, Herr Walpole? Das hab' ich nicht gewusst."*

"Ich spreche mit viele Stimmen. Das ist nur die Mindeste meiner Kräfte. Und sie konnten auch Ihnen gehören, wenn Sie nur ihnen wollen."

As Erasmus spoke, Roland felt his words draw closer even as his body remained still. They slinked soft as a whisper in his ear, tendrils of sound curling around the tender juncture of impulses where spine met brain. Roland felt his muscles softening, his mind dimming, lulled by a subaural buzz carried beneath the words. Roland closed his eyes and spoke his next statement through gritted teeth.

"We will speak English, please."

Erasmus tilted his head in a theatrical gesture of confusion. *"Sprechen Sie nicht gern Ihnen Geburtssprach?"*

"I will speak it where I choose to. But here is foreign soil, and I choose my second tongue."

"As you wish," Erasmus said. His tone broadcast indifference, but his voice came once again from outside of Roland's head. He watched the colossus from his perch on its palm, awaiting its fury, but if it had any concern about its lost advantage, it gave no sign.

Maybe it doesn't know.

Perhaps. Or maybe it considered its battle already won, and simply didn't care.

"I thank you," said Roland. "And while you are granting requests, could you speak to me down here, where I stand? I do not wish to hold a conversation with a giant."

"But of course," Erasmus said, standing across the altar from Roland. He remained the taller of the two—an impressive stature, since Roland was not small—but his size had shrunk to well within the conceivable range of the human form. His face remained as inscrutable as ever, every inch of him shrouded in that world-eating blackness. Yet somehow his expression came through as clear as if he were unmasked, broadcast to some ancillary receiver deep in Roland's subconscious. At the moment, he put forth the polite smile of a host greeting a guest who had arrived fifteen minutes early. "You have come far, my dear Roland. None before you has ever managed to crest my barricade. Impressive."

"How many before me have tried?"

"Enough," answered Erasmus, his tone curt. He resumed his unseen smile. "But we have more important matters to discuss."

Erasmus rounded the altar and grabbed Roland around the shoulder in a gesture of camaraderie. His skin was cold and rigid as iron, yet inside pulsed something soft and liquid and queasily alive.

"Have you ever tasted a man's soul, Roland? Of course you haven't. It is an experience unlike any other, a delicacy far surpassing the finest earthly cuisine, a sensation unrivalled by the most powerful drugs, and a source of strength unmatched by the most potent elixirs ever mentioned in myth. It is ownership in its purest form, and ownership is power. Slavery was the palest of substitutes, an imperfect and inefficient harnessing of man's most primal force. I have taken it and distilled it a hundredfold."

"But why?" asked Roland. "You speak of power, but power to what end? If you wanted so much to be a god, you could have made at least a heaven, not a hell."

"Contented souls are boring. And more than boring, they're bland. Much finer are those that have been cured by suffering, smashed tender by a private eternity at your mercy, scrubbed free of the grit of hope."

"There is a price to be paid for taking pleasure at the expense of another," said Roland.

Erasmus laughed. "And who precisely shall present me with the bill? I am the emperor of this place. No power, legal or divine, stands above me. And that power could be yours too. Stand by me, and all that you've ever wanted shall be yours for the taking."

Roland smiled. "You have made such offers before, have you not?"

"I have worked with imperfect vessels in the past, yes. Weak men, chosen not for their intelligence or vitality, but for the positions they held in a corporeal realm, and the convenience those positions afforded me. But you, Roland, you have a strength I have yet to witness, a rare and natural ability to bridge the corporeal realm with my own, unaided. Such a skill would be of great value to me."

"Are you asking me to be your apostle?"

Erasmus laughed. Unlike his voice, which came out polished and poised as a radio newscaster, his laugh had the buzzing, discordant sound of radio static.

"Dear Roland, you would be no mere apostle. You would be an envoy. Perhaps even a successor."

He drew his hand in a slow arc across the firmament. In its wake danced images of desire. Roland saw himself ensconced in wealth, money piled to his waist, fingers scaly with gold and jewels. He saw a three-story house in Queenstown's plumiest neighborhood. He saw bare-breasted women spread on sheets of silk.

"All of this, these vistas of promise, uncontested dominion over an entire universe—all this could one day be yours. To get it, you need only express your fealty to me."

Roland gazed at the promises painted across the sky. A small, petty part of him ached for each in turn. But it was a passing twinge, one securely moored to the knowledge that such things did not come through a single handshake, and behind the taut flimsy canvas of Erasmus' bargain lay a pit whose fetid depths Roland knew all too well.

"I thank you for the offer," Roland said. "But I decline." He plucked Erasmus' arm from his shoulder and tossed it aside.

Erasmus glowered at this affront. Anger roiled the midnight oval of his face. "Don't be a fool! Who are you to reject me? A common laborer, a detested alien, an inmate in a lunatic asylum. You have nothing. I am offering you the chance to rule an empire. It is not an offer I give lightly, nor one that I will proffer for long. If you cannot grasp that, I suggest you try harder."

"I understand precisely what you are offering me," said Roland. "It is much the same you offered Owens, and Verloc, and who knows how many others."

"Your impertinence may yet cost you dearly," Erasmus growled. His body grew like a shadow at dusk, legs stretching to obscene lengths, shoulders broadening to the span of a bridge. Black thunder crackled across the firmament of his chest. "You may count yourself fortunate that I am forgiving. But my forgiveness will not extend forever. I will put things simply, in a way even a man such as you can understand. Swear your fealty to me, or you shall be destroyed."

"Very well. Then destroy me."

Erasmus continued to grow, his body swelling until it comprised the world. Roland watched, arms folded across his chest. A roar of deafening rage battered at his ears like a horde at the gates. But it was a horde with no weapons, no leader, a rabble unequipped for invasion and too poorly provisioned for siege. Gradually the rumble faded, leaving an embarrassed silence over which Roland spoke.

"Curiously, I remain undestroyed. And I believe I know why. It is much the same reason you offer me a place at your side. After all, you had no interest in my fealty when you ordered my death from your apostles. Why should it interest you now? I have watched your realm for weeks, and while I feared it for a time, I have begun to see the false fronts and makeup. This place is just a stage play. Your thralls enslave themselves through their guilt or resignation, your servants delude themselves with their desires, and your attackers destroy themselves through their fear. But the knife that kills them is never yours, because you can hold no weapon. Your only tools are guile and fear. But I will not join you, and I do not fear you. So what is left?"

Roland turned to the altar and placed his hand on it. Its sense of fathomless depth belied the sensation of bare stone against his fingers. It was smooth as glass and cool to the touch, a bit like marble. A fine piece of masonry, but nothing at all unworldly.

"This is where you feed? It is no surprise. As in one realm, so in another. It looks strong, yes? Like it could outlast mountains. But looks mean little in this place."

Roland snapped to attention. The intervening years fell away, and he was a soldier again, youthful muscles thrumming with the limber strength of post-adolescence. His body performed the actions as if he'd drilled them that very morning. The barrel of his rifle slapped firm against his shoulder. He swept the stock into his right hand, cocked his elbows, and raised the weapon. He held it poised, butt ready to strike the altar.

"Stop!" Erasmus shrieked. He returned to his former stature and staggered towards Roland, shrinking with every step until he fell to his knees, a wizened gnome. The shroud of darkness melted from beneath his helm, revealing the face of an old man ravaged by time and illness beyond any hope of recovery. Wrinkles dug furrows thumbnail-deep across pale, flabby flesh, its pallor spotted with warts and half-healed sores. It clung taut only across the outsized bulge of his bald skull, where the skin stretched so thin that each blood vessel spread like an ink stain on ancient parchment. A sour-milk stink of age wafted from him

"Please," Erasmus begged. "You cannot." His divine arrogance was gone. What was left was nothing but a shriveled old man in robes of moth-eaten satin. A great figure once, perhaps, but reduced by time and avarice to a clumsy marionette held aloft by fraying strings. "Your soul is here with me. If you destroy this place, you shall die too!"

Roland shrugged. "There are worse things than death. I know that more than most men. Thanks to you."

And adjusting his grip on the rifle, he brought the stock down on the altar as hard as he could.

***

As the building began to rumble, Martha assumed the damage she'd done to the boiler room was more severe than she'd originally thought. Could a burst pipe damage the foundation of an entire building? She didn't see how, but she was no architect. Perhaps the force of the steam was resonating through the floorboards, or undermining some key bit of masonry.

Thoughts of such damage worried her until she remembered poor Eloise, still lying on the floor where she'd fallen, and any concern about bricks and mortar felt utterly trivial. Her memory jolted her free of the endless loop of ritual motion with which she'd presided over Roland—dunk the cloth, wring it out, draw it across his forehead—and she judged him sufficiently stable to tend to Eloise. She knelt over the body, smoothed a stray hair from her forehead, and used a cloth to clean a streak of dried blood from her face. The wound was too deep, and her clothes too sodden with blood, for Martha to tend to them with the items on hand, so she settled for covering her from neck to knees with a towel. This she folded under her body, taking care to smooth out creases with her thumb.

"I need to get out of here, don't I?" she asked, performing a few final tucks around Eloise's shoulders. Her friend was far beyond any response, but none was needed as the answer was obvious. She had just witnessed a murder, prevented another, and cooked the assailants to death in a locked boiler room. She needed to reach the authorities and tell them what had happened, even though doing so could land her in prison. She believed her actions were justified, but there was no denying that she'd killed three men, and killed them brutally. Who could say whether a jury would sympathize with her? She might even wind up taking the blame for Eloise's death too—after all, the knife was locked away in the boiler room, its handle doubtless covered with her fingerprints. The veneer of tenderness peeled away from her work tending to Roland and Eloise, revealing a rough and rotting substratum of fear. How could she make them see? How could she convey the vulpine hunger in Fox's eyes, the ugly, sinister camaraderie the three men tossed between them like a smaller boy's stolen bookbag?

The shaking stopped, leaving behind a silence that whistled in the upper limits of Martha's hearing. She pressed her ear to the floor, straining to hear if the sound had vanished altogether or simply diminished, and served only to smack her head against the tile as the ground buckled with an immense tectonic groan. The shaking returned, but this time it was no mere tremble. Walls warbled like sheets of rubber struck with mallets. The hallway resounded with thuds and crashes as fixtures fell from walls and windows shattered in their frames. A chorus of panicked inmates poured through fresh-rent fissures. Martha threw herself against the fever cabinet, legs curled to her belly, arms draped over her head to protect herself from falling bits of ceiling.

Dear Lord, she thought. *What have I done?*

But this wasn't the boiler. It couldn't be. Her damage to the steam pipe had brought the pressure down, not up. And even if it had caused some kind of chain reaction explosion in the basement, surely it wouldn't be powerful enough to tear a multi-story building in half. Something else was going on, something far beyond a broken valve. She looked at Roland, his head laying slack against the double-folded towel serving as a pillow, his face relaxed, even tranquil.

Dear Lord. What has he *done?*

This thought was even more ridiculous than the first. The man was unconscious and undergoing a medical procedure. How could he possibly have triggered the collapse of an entire hospital? And yet, the idea didn't vanish under scrutiny the way the first one had, however mad it might have seemed.

Martha gave her head a shake. Psychic or not, her patient was unlikely to survive a blow from a two-hundred-pound support beam plummeting onto him from ten feet overhead. She needed to get him out of here.

The damaged pipe in the boiler room had drained nearly all the pressure from the radiator, and the cabinet had cooled enough for her to unfasten the clasps barehanded without burning her skin—the metal was still uncomfortably warm, but not scalding—and the door opened without the geysering hiss of steam that had greeted her the first time she'd interrupted his treatment.

She called his name, prodded him, even slapped him across the face in desperation, yet nothing she did could awaken him from his comatose state. She upended the basin of cold water over his head, but this too proved ineffective, and he lay as he had for the last hour, still as a corpse. Fear crept across Martha's belly at this thought, and she pressed an ear to his chest, praying for a heartbeat. The answer was slow—perhaps forty beats a minute—but unmistakable. She felt a gush of relief cut short by a sickening lurch as the back-left corner of the room collapsed into a yawping black chasm. The force of the destruction spilled Martha from the cabinet, and she watched sprawled on the floor as a third of the room crumbled in on itself.

Chunks of floor cantilevered over the precipice, their great weight bending them down until fault lines rippled through the tile, sharp folds beyond which planks slanted steeply into darkness. The fever cabinet balanced on the edge of one such line. The bolts on its back two legs tore free of the collapsing tile, shifting its entire bulk onto the front two, which buckled under their burden. Metal squealed, wood rasped with the pincer-quick withdrawal of tortured screws, and the cabinet's undercarriage struck ground. It teetered on the brink of a fresh-formed canyon of stone and wood and steel, its top half rising a half-inch above the tile while its bottom jutted two feet beyond the point where the floor had given way. Between them rested its fulcrum: a pair of bolts drilled centrally in the housing along its length, which caught on a fragment of shattered tile and prevented, however tenuously, the cabinet's further slide over the edge.

Martha gathered herself off of the floor and rounded the cabinet until she'd positioned herself at its head. Roland remained unconscious, a fact that instantly discarded any hope she had of waking him. If the sudden collapse of half a room couldn't rouse him, nothing would. She had to get him out of there herself.

The only question was how. He outweighed her by nearly a hundred pounds, and the hospital was short on wheelchairs at the best of times—no doubt the few that remained were already being used to evacuate immobile patients. She hooked her arms beneath his armpits and pulled, but his inert body scarcely budged. The interior of the cabinet was recessed, which meant a patient couldn't be shifted out horizontally; they needed to move up and over the lip of the frame, and such a maneuver was simply beyond her strength.

Cracks spread along the remaining floorboards, which groaned beneath the weight of a dangling vestigial fringe of wood and masonry. The cabinet skidded along the broken tile an inch before catching on another snag of tile. A few more such moves and the preponderance of its weight would hang over the precipice. From there, even fresh bolts dug into concrete would struggle to hold the cabinet aloft for long. A wooden lip dug into her armpits, sending spines of tingling numbness from shoulder to wrist. She wriggled, hoping to find a better grip, and found herself pinned in place by Roland's upper body.

Tamping down the panic that rose in her belly, she planted her feet and leaned from side to side, using her weight to shift the cabinet on its teetering axis. This move would be either her salvation or her undoing, and she couldn't say for sure which was more likely.

The cabinet was immensely heavy, but balanced as it was along a narrow strip of its undercarriage, it moved with relative ease. Bolts scraped against tile with the ugly sound of a knife rasping on bone. After a few motions, the bolts came free of their crevices and the cabinet began to slide towards the cliff. Martha's legs dragged over the floor. She planted her feet and leaned back, throwing every ounce of herself backward. Her heels dug into the tile, and Roland's body, snagged by her arms locked around his armpits, lifted up and out of the cabinet.

Once his shoulders cleared the lip, the rest of him came in a rush. The cabinet, free of its final encumbrance, sledded along the sloping floor and vaulted into darkness. Even amidst the steady roar of the building's protracted collapse, Martha heard the immense crash as it struck bedrock somewhere far below. She managed two staggering steps before Roland's weight overtook her, and the two of them tumbled to the ground. His head, limp with unconsciousness, struck her in the bridge of the nose. A bit of blood dribbled out of her left nostril. She wiped it on her shoulder and squirmed out from beneath him, cupping his forehead and lowering it to the floor to avoid him cracking his skull on the tile. Exhaustion pulled like a riptide at her heels, but she paddled against it until the grey pall lifted from her vision. She grabbed Roland by the wrists and, with a grunt of effort, dragged him into the hallway.

The hall was even more chaotic than the fever room, but at least there were no fissures in the floor to contend with. Patients wheeled and shuffled and hobbled to the exits, wrangled by harried nurses speaking over-enunciated orders in voices that toed the sharp edge of panic but managed through some deft feat of acrobatics not to fall over it. Those who lacked the physical or cognitive ability to flee on their own rolled along on whatever wheeled device could be press-ganged into service—wheelchairs were common, but also gurneys, food trolleys, instrument carts, and even file cabinets, all stacked to capacity with inert bodies secured with straps and knotted bedsheets.

Martha flagged down a nurse whose gurney, with only two elderly patients astride it, was relatively under-burdened. The nurse seemed reluctant to slow, and Martha had to step into her path in order to keep her in place.

"I have an unconscious patient here," she said. "Quick, help me load him up."

"Can't do it," the nurse replied. "I'm over regulation as is."

"Look around you! There's nary a cart in this hall that isn't over regulation. The bloody building is coming down around our ears. If I don't get him out of here, he's done for."

"Just look at the size of him," the nurse countered. "You load him up on top of the other two I've already got, I won't be able to budge this thing an inch."

"There's two of us, isn't there? I can help push."

The nurse bit her lower lip. "All right. Make it quick."

"Great. Grab his arms. I'll take the legs." Martha took up her position without waiting for the other nurse to respond. Together they hoisted Roland off the ground and onto the gurney, where he settled into the gap between the two older patients. There was no way to strap him in, but his weight alone held him in place. Martha joined the other nurse at the back of the gurney and pushed. The wheels barely turned at first, but the two women kept pushing, and soon built enough momentum to keep the gurney rolling forward.

They burst out the front door and onto the forecourt before the foyer crumbled as if cleaved in two with a gigantic invisible axe. The roofs of the outer wings followed, and soon it seemed like the entire building was being sucked inward, drawn by a vacuum into a point of impossible density. The roar of destruction filled her ears to bursting.

The whole thing was over in a few minutes. It seemed to Martha both impossible and inevitable that such a venerable building, an edifice so gargantuan in stature and lifespan, could disappear in less time than a single gut-shot soldier took to die. A great pillar rose from the rubble, a phantom tower with bricks of dust and mortar of updrafting air. It reached the heavens, bent beneath the prevailing winds, and fell in silent pantomime of the dead building that had spawned it.

In the pillar's wake, there was nothing but naked space, revealing a great black crater that spanned the asylum's floorplan. Those nurses not tending to injured patients wandered towards the edge, drawn by the otherworldly grandeur of the wound. Many of the patients followed, and soon a crowd formed a living fence around a portion of the pit's circumference. A few muttered oaths or inane observations about the pit's size, but the majority stood silent. Much of the terror they'd felt only moments earlier was gone, swallowed along with the building by the vast and gaping pit.

Martha heard a groan behind her. She turned to see Roland stirring atop the gurney, his head rocking slowly. His eyes blinked open and peered through narrow slits at the overcast sky.

"I am...outside?" he said, pulling the statement into a question. He looked at Martha, then past her to the crowd. "What is going on?"

"I think it may be easier just to show you. Can you walk?"

Roland climbed off the gurney, moving gingerly to avoid hurting his elderly travel companions, and followed Martha to the edge of the pit. They stood side by side, peering over shoulders at the place where a hospital had, however impossible it currently seemed, stood only ten minutes before.

"It has collapsed?"

"A collapse would be alarming enough, but it looks as though a bomb levelled it. Where are the foundations? That pit must be a hundred feet deep, maybe more. How could a building even *stand* on ground like that?"

"By human means?" Roland asked. "It could not. Clearly, as we have seen."

"What are you saying, not by human means? What other means are there?"

Roland looked at her and said nothing. Martha rubbed her face with both hands.

"It's madness. It's just all complete madness." She looked up over the tips of her fingers. "Did you get him, at least?"

Roland smiled. "Yes. I got him."

"Well, that's good then."

They stood together for a while longer, contemplating the vast pit before them, but neither spoke another word. There seemed to be nothing left to say.

15

FOR ROLAND, THE following weeks passed in a haze of appointments, inspections, and interrogations. Men in uniforms shuttled him back and forth, as if he were the queen of spades in a citywide game of Old Maid. He was treated with a mixture of courtesy, hesitance, and derision, with the exact ratios varying based on the setting and the speaker. He spent nights in a range of accommodations that, through altruism or insistence, volunteered to house patients dispossessed by the asylum's sudden collapse: hotels, hospitals, rec centers hastily converted into shelters. He and a few of the other more fit patients even spent a night in a disused prison cell, before a civil liberties lawyer caught wind of their plight and charged to their rescue, brandishing a briefcase and lobbing threats of lawsuits for the violation of constitutional norms. He was a small man in a rumpled suit and a hat with a permanent crease in its brim, but he cut an impressive figure despite these limitations, inflated by his righteousness into a sufficiently impressive presence to secure their release to more comfortable accommodations.

During this period, he was neither incarcerated, nor precisely free, but existed in a sort of fluctuating liberty, the parameters of which he dared not test, lest too vigorous a prodding cause them to contract. Eventually he would need to clarify his position, but for the time being he found the change enjoyable. It was not as if there was much awaiting him on the outside.

The authorities tried to keep him as insulated as possible from the outside world, but news filtered through regardless, much of it gilded with rumor. They said that the pits beneath the asylum were pocked with tunnels wending miles through the earth, that they led to caverns filled with strange artifacts and macabre statues, that a brass chest buried in a stone sarcophagus held a collection of leather-bound texts scribed in undecipherable alien tongues, the only hint to their meaning the drawings depicting monsters and atrocities of every sort, and marginalia scrawled in High German and Latin. But most of all, they spoke of the bodies: thousands of them, many dating back to shortly after the hospital's founding, but some as recent as the turn of the century. None appeared less than thirty or forty years old, from which the authorities assumed no criminal liability among recent administrators. Roland knew better, of course. The killings never stopped; they simply became better hidden.

His final appointment arrived with little fanfare. It was no different than the dozens that came before it: men in medical garb sitting across a desk, eyeing him occasionally while reading summaries in his chart left by other doctors. Occasionally they would scrawl a few notes of their own, or amend additional pages with paperclips.

The latest configuration comprised two doctors in their early forties. One had the crew cut hair of a drill sergeant and wore a pencil-thin moustache over a pair of thick and perpetually pursed lips. The other was bald and likewise mustachioed, though his tended to bushiness and hung low enough to cover his mouth, which only appeared when he spoke or when he smiled, at which point its curled edges would peek shyly from behind a curtain of hair like nervous actors sizing up the crowd on opening night.

"Well, Mr. Hellmich," said the crew-cut doctor. "My name is Dr. Rutherford Hedges. My associate here is Dr. William Waters." He motioned to the bald doctor, who nodded. "We've been assigned by the state to review your case and reach a final decision on subsequent treatment."

"I see," said Roland. Dr. Waters spoke next, scratching his chin and flipping through the papers sheathed in a manilla folder.

"Now, in your admission chart, it says that you were ordered by the courts to undergo a physical and psychiatric examination, is that correct?"

Roland nodded. Dr. Waters continued.

"You received said inspection by one Dr. Arnold Verloc, director of the Erasmus Walpole Institution for Mental Hygiene, where you were diagnosed with tertiary-stage syphilis. Is that also correct?"

"I do not recall the exact stage, but otherwise, yes."

Waters glanced over at Hedges, who sighed and nodded for Waters to proceed. "Mr. Hellmich," Waters asked. "Do you recall exactly what Dr. Verloc's examination entailed? Did he ask where he could requisition any records of yours? Did he do a blood test? Did he conduct a full body examination, including genitals?"

At each of these questions, Roland shook his head. "I cannot say whether he sought outside records, but in terms of our meeting, he did none of these things."

With each negative response, Hedges' frown deepened. Waters remained impassive, though Roland sensed the glimmer of a smile in his eyes, and glimpsed further proof at the edges of his bushy moustache.

"Mr. Hellmich," blurted Hedges. "Do you recall approximately how long Dr. Verloc spent examining you?"

Roland thought back. "Five minutes?" he ventured. "It may have been less."

The gaze that passed between the doctors was charged enough to bear a high voltage warning. Waters jotted something on his form.

"The reason we ask this, Mr. Hellmich," said Dr. Waters, "is that in the examinations you've taken since the incident at Walpole, none of the doctors who've treated you have found any evidence whatsoever of a syphilis infection. Nor did they find any symptoms that would suggest even a superficial diagnosis of syphilis."

Roland blinked. "So, forgive me. You are saying that I do not have syphilis?"

"Correct. Diagnosis doesn't seem to have been Dr. Verloc's strong suit, to put it lightly. We've found a number of patients who should have undergone hours of admission interviews being processed in minutes. It seems his primary interest was in gathering as large a patient roster as possible, rather than treating those who were in actual need of care."

"An unacceptable practice," interjected Hedges. "And one not in any way sanctioned by the Ministry of Health."

Waters rolled his eyes at this. "In any case, your hallucinatory episode seems not to have any physical cause, and likely stems from your past experiences as a soldier."

"Shell shock," Roland ventured.

"They call it battle fatigue these days," said Waters. "But essentially, yes. Our experts prescribe thrice weekly psychotherapy to address the root issues of your lapses. This is entirely voluntary, of course, but if you accept, the Province is willing to pay the full cost of your sessions from a private practitioner."

"Though note that this in no way suggests liability on behalf of the Province or the Ministry," added Hedges.

"I see," said Roland. "You say this is voluntary, but what should happen to me if I refuse?"

Waters shrugged. "You go about your life, I suppose."

"You mean, I am no longer incarcerated?"

Waters nodded. "Your initial diagnosis has been invalidated, and in light of the observations by outside physicians, there is no further cause for you to be housed against your will. You can walk out that door right now if you want."

Roland thanked the doctors for their candor and agreed to treatment. They gave him a few options for referral, directed him to the temporary housing where he would stay while he reestablished financial independence, and wished him well.

"I have only one more question," said Roland. "Since I did not have syphilis, my treatments in the fever cabinet, did they have any purpose at all?"

"I'm afraid not," said Waters. "Frankly, there's two schools of thought for whether they even work for syphilis patients, so beyond them, there's no therapeutic purpose whatsoever."

"Though I would add," said Dr. Hedges, shooting a dark glance at his colleague. "That the decision to instigate this treatment was Dr. Verloc's alone, and neither the Province nor the Ministry can be held liable for..."

The doctor trailed off, but Roland didn't notice, for he was clutching his belly and had doubled over with laughter.

***

Most mornings, the first thing Martha noticed about the room was its brightness.

Light streamed through a dozen windows set floor to ceiling along the hospital's southern wall, behind which stood a slope of pasture leading to a wend of old growth forest. Birds twittered among the trees planted along the hill's crest, their recently bare branches stippled with buds. Thin crescents of snow still clung to the shadowy folds between their roots, but for the most part the city had shed winter and donned its first flashes of spring plumage. The air was still cool enough to show breath once the sun set, but in the hours just past its zenith it held sway over the fields and valleys and filled the room with such warmth that the caretaker could let the boiler fires dwindle to embers until nightfall.

When she'd first arrived, Martha found the windows pretty but ostentatious, an extravagance whose cost could have been put to better use in items more directly tailored to the patients' care. But after a few days at her duties, she grew to appreciate the green-gold cast they spread over the room as something beyond a decorative flourish. She saw the way the wounded soldiers would gaze at the landscape, whether propped up in their beds or sitting in wheelchairs or leaning, crutches momentarily set aside, against the railing that divided the floor from the glass, and watch the pall of the battlefield melt away like frost from sunlit grass. She found herself taking in the view on a short break between duties, when a familiar voice called her back.

"This place suits you."

Martha turned. Roland stood before her in a pair of faded dungarees and a woolen sweater. She had never seen him dressed in anything but hospital garb, and the sight of him in street clothes reminded her of the disorienting sensations she'd felt as a child whenever she spotted her priest out of his cassock. The feeling soon faded, for however unexpected, there was no arguing that he looked much better than he had the last time she'd seen him. Color had returned to his cheeks, which were smooth shaven and unmottled by exhaustion, and his hair had been trimmed by someone with more talent than an intake orderly.

"Roland!" she said, hugging him. Part of her wondered whether this intimacy was a breech of decorum, but the strangest part about it was how normal, even proper, it felt. Holding him felt like embracing a brother after a long separation. "It's good to see you. How are you?"

"I am well," he replied. "Dr. Palmer has been a great help to me. Together we have explored every inch of my...visions, and his perspective has been most enlightening."

"And have there been any since?"

He shook his head. "Not a glimpse since the asylum."

"I'm glad to hear it. So, what are you doing with yourself now?"

"I am catching a train for Toronto this evening, then overnight to Montreal. Another to Halifax, and from there, I sail."

"Sail? For where?"

Roland raised an eyebrow. "For Germany, of course."

Martha bit the inside of her cheek. "Roland, do you think it wise to return? It's nothing but war, from the coast to the steppes. And however well your country has fared so far—"

Roland raised a hand to interject. "You misunderstand me, Martha. I am not returning there to live. I am returning there to fight."

Martha's eyes widened. "You enlisted?"

Roland gave a proud nod. He reached into his bag and showed her a stack of papers he kept in a manila envelope. "Yes, you are looking at Private First Class Roland Hellmich, of Her Majesty's Royal Canadian Armed Forces."

"Why, that's wonderful," Martha said. "And I'm sure you will do your country proud. But, if I may ask, was there not some reticence due to your..."

"Condition?" Roland asked. "Or background?"

Martha gave a sheepish smile. "Both, frankly."

Roland raised his hand and made a seesaw motion. "I suspect there was some chatter among the recruiting officers. My application took nearly a week to be approved. But in the end, it seems they decided that they fear Herr Hitler more than they fear me. Also, I am not an armed combatant—my history made such a role a poor fit in the eyes of the recruiters. But there are many ways to fight a war of this size. The army needs men who can repair their tanks and vehicles and keep the lights running. And also those who speak the enemy tongue."

Martha smiled. "Well, for what it's worth, I think they made the right decision. I hope you stay safe over there."

"If I do not, then perhaps I will see you again."

"I do hope we see each other again, but let's do ourselves both a favor and wait until the war is over, shall we?"

It was Roland's turn to smile. "As you wish."

He said his goodbyes and turned to leave, when his name rose unbidden to her lips and she called him back.

"Oh, Roland."

She wanted to ask him about the final day in the asylum, what he'd seen while he lay unconscious in the fever cabinet. How a thousand tons of stone can stand upon a pit of ash and bone for three hundred years, only to topple in a single hour, and how a man in a steam-stoked coffin could bring about such cataclysmic change. All of these questions and a hundred others of their ilk poised on the edge of her tongue, ready to dive like paratroopers one after the other, an overwhelming force. But was it her place to ask? Whatever he'd seen, he'd worked hard these past months to overcome it, to make peace with it. If speaking about it would help him, it was for him to decide, not her.

Besides, if he did choose to tell her, would she even believe him?

Roland turned at her call, eyebrows arched expectantly.

"I just wanted to say thank you," she said. "For serving our country."

"And I you, Nurse Donnelly."

And with that, he left.

ACKNOWLEDGMENTS

PEOPLE OFTEN ASK authors where they get their ideas, and while I can only speak for myself, I'd say that there isn't any one answer. Most of my books start as brief images that gestate over months or years into plots or characters—discrete particles large enough to form a foothold from which a story can be climbed and surveyed. Others land as raw materials all at once, not birthed so much as quarried. There's a big lump of granite with a story inside, and it's up to me to chip away the dross and free the gem without doing too much damage in the process.

The Fever Cabinet was the second type, and the vast slab that contained it dropped onto my desk in 2016, when a professor I'd worked with gave my name to a PhD student looking for help editing her thesis. It was an interesting piece of medical history, comprising case studies of patients treated by an esoteric and largely forgotten medical apparatus called a fever cabinet. As soon as heard the name, I knew there had to be a story there.

Fever cabinets built on the existing understanding that, by raising body temperature, a fever serves to kill invasive microbes and rid the body of disease. Doctors had already been using controlled infection with malaria to induce fevers in patients for years, and the fever cabinet was seen as a safer, more easily controlled alternative. Rather than contracting an illness that could wreak havoc in its own right, patients could simply rest in an artificially heated environment for a prolonged period, their internal temperature carefully monitored by a nurse. As a procedure, it was unpleasant but largely safe. And since its principal use was for treating neurosyphilis—arguably the nastiest manifestation of a truly nasty disease—such discomfort was seen as trivial against the benefits of a cure.

As a medical treatment, fever cabinets didn't last long. By the time they became widely available, advances in antibiotics demonstrated penicillin to be a far easier and more effective treatment, and so fever cabinets disappeared. It's possible they never worked in the first place. Evidence is scant, and the spirochete that causes syphilis may survive in temperatures higher than humans can tolerate, making the whole thing fairly pointless.

But I wasn't interested in treating syphilis; I was interested in a good story. And that paper gave me one, which is a long-winded (but hopefully interesting) way to get around to the actual business of this acknowledgements section.

Thanks, then, to Mary Connell, whose thesis formed the germ of this story, and to Nicole Letourneau, who gave Mary my contact information and was the co-author on my very first published book (which, a popular science book for parents, is very different from this one but still worth reading).

Thanks also to Scarlett R. Algee and the good folks at JournalStone, who liked the story enough to roll the dice on it, and to Alec Shane, whose skill as an agent is eclipsed only by his editorial eye.

And, most of all, thanks as always to my loving wife Chantal, and our three wonderful children, Lavender, Hannela, and Leo.

ABOUT THE AUTHOR

Justin Joschko is an author from Niagara Falls, Ontario. He has written several novels, including WHITETOOTH FALLS, winner of a Gold Medal in Horror Fiction from the Independent Book Publisher's Association 2020 Ben Franklin Awards. His writing has appeared in newspapers and literary journals across Canada. He currently lives in Ottawa with his wife and three children.

www.ingramcontent.com/pod-product-compliance
Lightning Source LLC
Chambersburg PA
CBHW030122260626
47156CB00008B/2750